Magpies and Sunsets

Neil Alexander Marr

BeWrite Books, UK
www.bewrite.net

Published internationally by BeWrite Books, UK.
32 Bryn Road South, Wigan, Lancashire, WN4 8QR.

British Library Cataloguing in Publication Data.

A catalogue record for this book is available from the British Library

ISBN 1-904492-29-0

Also available in eBook and cd-rom formats from www.bewrite.net

Digitally produced by BeWrite Books

Cover design by
© Adam Freeman 2003

One deep breath wasn't enough to dissuade James' heart from its increased tempo, as the inevitability of his destination became apparent. Here he was, some twenty-two years since his departure, about to return to the land of his birth. A glance out the window revealed only that the captain's forecast was accurate, in an understated sort of way, yet he was reluctant to withdraw and continued to attempt to catch a glimpse of land through the clouds. Nothing could be seen until suddenly the runway was visible and almost immediately the plane had touched down.

"Business or pleasure?" enquired a rather disinterested official without looking up.

"Aah … pleasure, I suppose."

This less than convincing response was enough to cause the retirement-nearing official to glance at James, but he seemed satisfied that there was no threat to national security and waved James through with a well practised gesture of the arm that made James feel like an annoying child pestering his elder.

The car rental went relatively smoothly. A red Mondeo was the result. Standard transmission. This was the only drawback as James would have preferred automatic, in deference to the challenge of driving on the left. Upon entering the car, the prudent thing to do prior to embarking on a journey in rainy, misty, conditions in an unfamiliar land where vehicles drove on the opposite side of the road, would have been to familiarise oneself with the car's controls and perhaps peruse a map. However, James possessed a Y chromosome which by design prevented him from doing any of the above. New gene therapy held future hope, but for the time being, James was off and cruising, attempting to become accustomed to the clutch as he headed in a vaguely eastward direction.

For my wife, Priscilla

Neil A. Marr was born in Edinburgh, Scotland and lived there until the age of fourteen. Since 1974 he has lived in Southern Ontario, Canada. After a career in the business world, he is now employed as a high school English teacher. Neil is married and has two teenage daughters. *Magpies and Sunsets* is his first novel.

Magpies and Sunsets

Chapter 1

There is a direct correlation between a man's age and the warmth with which he greets the light of each new day. Having slept and dreamt well, a young man has contempt for the rays that signal the commencement of a day's hard labour, of hours of study, of uncertainty, of the need to secure the rent that's due. Better to slumber on, resuming the tack of the fantasy left in extended REM. With the passage of time, mornings come to mean the absence of darkness, relief, a respite from the demons that hover in the blackness.

Alarm clocks become allies in the effort to prematurely curtail the frustrations of middle age dream patterns. Not that anyone used alarm clocks anymore. Clock radios were the agents entrusted with the task of snatching one from dreamland.

James McPherson awoke to the measured tones of CFRB radio, that final buffer before reconciling oneself to the tedious prattle of CBC radio; its endless interviews spanning the continuum of Canadian culture: From the host of a tea party for octogenarian widows in Victoria, to the dilemma of being a native, disabled lesbian in Frozen Gonad, Saskatchewan, periodically punctuated by classical music and commercials for pre-arranged funerals, and the advantages of wearing a device that allowed one to piss one's pants with dignity. James reasoned to himself that CFRB gave the best news and weather reports, but it was another indication that youth had long since been relegated to the past, along with his seldom played LPs of The Who, Supertramp, and The Moody Blues. James McPherson was by now a well-established member of the society that embraced the light.

Women are not privy to this affliction, or at least so thought James as he fumbled for the pack of cigarettes he was sure he had left on the table next to the bed. Karen never had a problem with sleep. James was jealous of that talent. How he would love to be able to sleep soundly, and dream well.

When she remembered her dreams she would readily share them with her husband. James was no longer curious about her dreams, for they were too mundane and healthy to be of interest. For a while he had been interested, if only to compare what his distorted mind was nocturnally concocting, but he would never share his secrets. Fortunately she was not overtly inquisitive, and he could dismiss her infrequent enquiries with a terse, "not much," or a confident quip: "You tend to dream what you fear, and I don't really have anything to fear."

It was stupid really because James had a lot to fear on a daily basis, both real and imagined: finances at home and at work, the children's social direction, that mole on his back that required him to contort his body in order to monitor its progress in the bathroom mirror, crabgrass in the lawn, the disturbing rate at which his forehead was expanding, the threat of a giant meteor hitting the earth, the ever present possibility of a visit from his mother in law, and there was that phone message he received the other day, well, Tuesday evening at seven forty-five to be precise. But Karen allowed him to play the role of mighty protector, even though her independence rendered that role redundant.

Sitting up, he slipped the cigarette between his lips, but decided against lighting, as it would be sure to arouse Karen's olfactory alarm system. It amazed him that she could go on sleeping with the radio on, or the television, or both, but light a cigarette and she would promptly awake and deliver a firm, but well-intentioned harangue on the perils of tobacco. She was right of course, as she almost always was.

So he sat and watched her sleep, the light from the morning sun penetrating the blinds and soaking into her blonde hair. Even after seventeen years of marriage, and in the unforgiving light of day, she appeared very beautiful to her husband, with her lithe body and nymph like features. Her blonde hair, recently shorn, added to this impression and even gave her a boyish look, which James found very fetching. This was further fuel for concern. Did this mean he had latent homosexual tendencies?

In the absence of any major challenges in his life, James felt it necessary to manufacture an abundance of petty woes. James loved his wife and he was sure she loved him. Sometimes he wondered why she loved him, but this was not one of the details he worried about too much. Occasionally, James would let his mind wander and consider the possibility that Karen would find another. She must have had plenty of opportunity, after all James was a man who lived in a man's world and was quite aware all men were lecherous pigs, ready, willing and able to jump at any chance of a liaison with one such as his Karen. But no, not his Karen.

Many of James' friends were at the stage of life where complaining about one's spouse was a full-fledged recreational activity. It was the period immediately preceding taking offence on a full-time basis that tends to afflict those couples whose children have left home, married and curtail their visits to Easter, Thanksgiving, and/or Christmas. James and Karen did not participate in this ritual, nor were they likely to move into the next phase, as they looked forward to the years ahead, when the girls would leave the well-feathered nest, while they themselves were still young enough to enjoy the rewards of life.

James often thought of the television commercial that usually aired on the U.S. network news, piped in from Buffalo, New York, where a very benign looking couple of fifty-year-olds glided along a gently undulating country road in their brand new Cadillac Seville. They looked so perfectly comfortable, beaming their absolute contentedness with their lot in life. The blonde wife adoringly glancing over to her middle-aged stud of a husband, as if she'd just had a multi-orgasmic experience. He cradling the wheel as a new father wraps his hands around his first born child, all the while with a look that says my balls are sitting precisely where I want them to sit, and the temperature down there could not be more accommodating. Surely that day would come.

Of course there was always the threat that something insidious would creep into their lives to spoil things. They were at the age when an acquaintance's diagnosis with some frightful disease was no longer shocking, merely tragic. Enough to cause James to banish cigarettes from his lips for a month, or a couple of days, depending on how much he liked the victim.

There was that woman from the accounting department at Karen's work who he met at last year's Christmas party, forty-one years old, dropped dead from an aneurysm. Chatting away at lunch one minute, face down in her French onion soup the next. Burnt her face so badly her husband elected to have a closed casket funeral despite the protestations of her family.

That was in March, and even now James still thought about the sudden nature of her demise. An aneurysm. It was just like at the Victoria Day fireworks display on Monday, the rocket shot up high in the cool, night sky, as if it would continue on to the stars, then suddenly exploded with a deafening bang, falling back, landing in the outfield grass, where it was quickly forgotten.

In some ways James thought a quick death would be much more preferable to a long drawn out affair that would force one to evaluate and re-evaluate both the life led, and the finality of it all, not to mention the contempt it would engender from the family as they lost patience with the time it took you to die. Just like Ivan

Ilyitch. Tolstoy was right about that. Better to die like Beckett's Malone than die piece-by-piece in front of your loved ones. Sudden death had its drawbacks though, in that it would be terrible to check out having just had a quarrel with your daughter, for instance, over some trivial thing that would end up haunting her for the rest of her life, ultimately condemning her to a life of prostitution, attempting in some warped way to please men. James often let his mind run away like this. Perhaps he did exhibit obsessive-compulsive tendencies, he thought. This was something else to worry about. On the other hand, a slow tortuous demise would not be to James' taste, as he did not want to take stock of his life, at least not the ante-Karenian period, as he liked to refer to it.

In spite of the disproportionate time James allotted to worrying, life was, on the whole, progressing as it should. If only he could sleep with more proficiency, and dream something akin to normal. Why couldn't he awake refreshed, or at least as refreshed as could be expected, having just sexually fulfilled a harem full of nubile young Swedish nymphos? As much as he liked to consider himself a modern man, a feminist in the Alan Alda tradition, this still had huge appeal. Like Sting though, he would even have settled for a dream about the adventures of a blue turtle, as it would have superseded last night's bizarre effort; some ridiculous encounter with a couple of business acquaintances in an elevator that turned out to be a refrigerator, all cramped and stuffy, with no exit. The precise details were always hard to recall. Perhaps he would open a window tonight.

Karen was beginning to stir. James opened the curtains to allow the morning sun to stream in, supplying everything it reached with a golden glow. This enticement was enough to nudge Karen into consciousness, and her eyelids lifted to reveal those bright blue eyes. She smiled with feeling and expressed her approval: "Hey babe, it looks like a great day."

"Yeah, a nice warm one."

James smiled at her, because to Karen it was always a great day. If it had been raining she would have commented on the romantic sound the raindrops made on the windows and she would remind James of when they got caught in the rain in Muskoka, many years ago. On a bad day she might just take up the cause of the flowers, or the lawn, and remind him they needed a good soaking. She could wake to two feet of snow and marvel at its glistening beauty, while James would be busy worrying about how he would get to work and the impact it would have on sales. A tornado would be a challenge, but James was confident she would have something positive to say in its defence.

"Are you going to the office today?"

"All day," said Karen. "You?"

"I'll go in for ten," James replied.

"I'm going in the shower then. Care to join me?" Karen asked with that flirtish tilt of the head. She could do it because she always had a look that signalled sexual intent, no matter what time of day.

"I think I'll wait. Maybe go for a jog."

Karen smiled, hopped over and kissed him wetly on the lips, breath be damned, and disappeared into the bathroom.

James often signalled his intent to go for a morning jog, but he rarely followed through, preferring to slip onto the veranda for a morning cigarette. Not that he was against exercise; it was just that running was so boring. Much better to get exercise while playing squash, or tennis, or soccer, or anything other than jogging. This morning it was just an excuse that was the least likely to hurt Karen's feelings, but James never liked sharing a morning shower, which due to time constraints offered the prospect of emerging with nothing more than a clean, unrequited erection.

As James re-emerged from the deck, having only smoked half his cigarette – this was a good step toward quitting – he could hear the girls downstairs completing their final preparations before leaving for school. As much as he liked to spend time with his daughters, it was always best to stay clear of three teenage girls in the morning. If he timed it right he would be half way descended the stairs as they were exiting, just in time to bid them his best for the day. They would tell him that they loved him, and he would respond in kind. That was never a problem.

With Karen though, James always had trouble verbalising his love for her, but she never relented. From time to time James would acquiesce and manage to force out something akin to: "I uff you," quickly moving away to some task requiring his immediate attention. Karen didn't take offence though, she was confident that eventually she could cure James of this affliction which she was convinced was left over baggage from growing up in an orphanage. James was always handy with a line to deflect her concerns, and he was sure that eventually he could persuade her that it was entirely consistent with his Scots-Presbyterian heritage. In fact, he would tell her, the last record of any Scotsman expressing love for another adult had something to do with the emergence of beer in carryout cans, and to this day there were lingering questions as to their sobriety.

As soon as Karen left, James decided to forego the morning paper in favour of the internet. He liked to sample the world's newspapers over a coffee prior to starting the workday, despite his impression they were becoming remarkably homogenised. First, he checked his email. James was a firm believer that no mail was always best as it limited surprises, but there was always mail. Today though, there was only a reminder from Alan that he had secured a one o'clock tee-off time for Friday. A quick response from James would confirm his intent to be there.

Unfortunately there was no such thing as a quick response from James when it involved typing, who, having just turned forty the previous year, was from the generation who were too young to ignore computers and hang on till retirement, but were too old to have received anything remotely like preparation for a computer world whilst at school. Women of his age were often far better off, having learned to type in high school, but with the odd exception there was a whole segment of the male population hammering away at keyboards with two fingers.

Karen had bought a Learn to Type programme for him. He did attempt to learn how to type properly, but his efforts were too often interrupted and would be abandoned. After a while he would return to the programme and assign himself a new entry name since the last one was still poised to re-commence at a level that was too advanced after the hiatus. After this cycle had exhausted itself many times, James had finally given up, his last entry name being thickhead, concluding it was daft that the "n" came before the "m" anyway. He resigned himself to typing with two fingers till the day he died, or till the emergence of voice activated computers. Eventually, he was convinced, it would be just like on Star Trek. After all they were right about cell phones.

Having bashed his way through a response, James clicked onto the Scotsman web-site. After a cursory glance at the headlines he went into the obituary section, as he often did. Sometimes he would read item by item, and sometimes he would go directly to "M" to see if his uncle had worn out his welcome of God's creation. Not today, but then it was unlikely anyone would spring for a newspaper notice. Once, James had noticed the name of a childhood school friend who had died "suddenly," it said. That usually meant a heart attack. "Tragically," tended to refer to a traffic accident. So and so died tragically, was a euphemism for mowed down by some irresponsible bastard. Ewan had died suddenly, it said, at the age of forty. When you turn forty that could happen, especially if you subjected yourself to a traditional Scottish diet.

He was having difficulty concentrating on reading anything this morning, as his mind repeatedly wandered to Tuesday night's message on the answering machine. Terse as it was, it had the potential to disrupt the comfortable life James was creating for himself and his family. All it said was: "Jimmy, if this is ye ... yer no there. Ah'll huftae call back ... Ah'm at a call box." No name, but James, still, after all these years, never allowed himself to believe he had freed himself from his past.

When they had returned from the restaurant on Tuesday it was Valerie, at thirteen, his youngest daughter, who had played back the answering machine. Whenever they returned from anywhere, Valerie dutifully headed straight for the machine. Justifiably so, as more often than not, the majority of the messages were for her or to a lesser degree her sisters. Evidently thirteen was the age when girls felt the need to communicate extensively. James rarely bothered with the machine and regarded it as one more nuisance he would rather not have to deal with. Anything important would go to his office anyway, but Valerie said: "There was a message for Jimmy, whoever he is," rolling her eyes, and offering her palms in bewilderment as she emphasised the Jimmy. It struck her as amusing as her father was always James, never Jimmy.

"Did they say who it was?"

"Nope."

That was all. It was clear James would have to replay the messages and subject himself to any number of hormonally inspired thirteen-year-old offerings, alternating with the quaking voices of hopeful adolescent boys, just to satisfy his curiosity as to the identity of the caller who would refer to him as Jimmy.

It was probably one of his team mates from the football club he played for on a weekly basis. Occasionally, he would be referred to as Jimmy on the field, but he was always quick to correct the error off the field. Adding a "y" on to a team-mate's name clearly was a universal malaise afflicting anyone blessed with athletic talent. Watch any interview on television involving an athlete and it was obvious that the gene for athleticism was also associated with a speech impediment rendering the individual unable to verbalise a team-mate's name without adding a "y" as a suffix. This trait seemed to persist even on James' team of has-beens and wannabees. So James tended to be forgiving. But outside the sporting realm he was insistent that his name was James, not Jimmy, not Jim, nor any other contraction. As he listened to the tape however, he had some doubts as to the identity of the caller. He didn't recognise it as the voice of anyone from his team. There were three other Scots on the team, but their brogue had been tempered by many years in Canada. Besides they were not likely to call from a phone booth, let alone refer to it as a call box. James strongly suspected that the call originated in Scotland and was from Ronnie.

Now, on Thursday morning trying to read the paper, he was convinced it was Ronnie who had called. Seven forty-five would be twelve forty-five a.m. in Scotland. The late hour would account for the incoherent nature of the caller. Failing to leave his name was probably directly related to the quantity of alcohol consumed. On the up side it also probably meant that Ronnie, if it was him, was not calling from within the confines of Saughton Prison, or any other of Her Majesty's fine establishments.

There had been no call back as promised. For the first time James lamented terminating all the extra services the phone company had proffered. Caller ID probably would have been useless anyway, but at least it would have ruled out a few possibilities. On second thought, James was glad he had ended the array of options they had acquired over the last few years. Enticed by offers of first month free, they had accumulated about eighty-six features that did anything from alter the ring of a long distance call, to have the phone operate as an answering machine. James was sure that next month there would be a new feature that would allow your telephone to operate as a vacuum cleaner, for an additional $4.95 per month, of course. One thing was clear: it was time for another cigarette.

Spring had long since wrested Toronto from winter's harness and the city was on the brink of easing into another glorious summer as James made his way into work. After growing up in the banality of the Scottish climate where it was often difficult to differentiate summer from winter, James never ceased to be impressed with the transformation that the city underwent annually.

Toronto and its suburbanites paid dearly for the right to have a white Christmas more often than not though. The charm of a pristine December snowfall quickly gave way to the monotony of dirty grey piles of snow and ice, and the longing for the luxuriously warm days of summer. Just when it seemed winter would never leave, spring would arrive and with the fury of an amateur boxer delivering his effort in three frenzied rounds, spring would work its magic and the city would burst into life. The appearance of leaves on the trees that embraced the city was accompanied by the re-emergence of outdoor cafes, populated with citizens who had readily forsaken their winter garb, recklessly displaying hopelessly white flesh, making an offering to the sun in an annual act of homage.

As James wound his way into the restaurant, he had decided he needed to deal with Ronnie's unfortunate effort to contact him. For twenty years he had hoped this day would never come, but it had come, and it had supplanted the more tedious concerns that James made a habit of worrying about.

James liked to go into the office before the staff arrived for the lunch shift. He liked to engender the belief amongst his staff that he was a workaholic, and for all they knew he had been there since seven a.m., busily working on some new way to improve the restaurant's menu, or shrewdly re-shuffling his stock portfolio to take advantage of the latest economic conditions. The truth was that while he had at one time worked very hard for what he had, he was now more inclined to work on his back-swing and leave the mundane day-to-day operations to the people he had hired for that purpose. It was not that he had become lazy. Boredom might more aptly describe his demeanour, as the business had become a successful formula that just needed to be repeated on a daily basis.

The name Pentland Gardens was something of a misnomer as restaurant names often are. There was a well kept lawn area at the front that was accentuated with skyrocket junipers and variegated leafed euonymus. In the summer the company that looked after the property planted red geraniums and white petunias, and it was quite neat and attractive. But the name suggested more than there was. No matter. This was commonplace in the business, and was less out of place than many of the trendy English style pubs that were sprouting up around the city. With names like the Hen and the Hound, located in the labyrinth of shopping concourses snaking their way underneath the city's downtown core, they were as far from the image of a village pub in rural Somerset as one could imagine.

The overwhelming majority of land that the restaurant was located on was devoted to parking. Adequate parking and spotless washroom facilities were of paramount importance in this business as far as James was concerned. They did not substitute the necessity for good food and service, but without the former two facilities the good food and service were a wasted effort. James parked at the rear of the property, under the shade afforded by the large maple tree. When he had first opened the restaurant in 1985, he would park prominently near the door and would encourage the staff to do the same in an effort to show the public that the establishment was open for lunch. When this failed to achieve the desired results, he allowed the car dealership next door to park some of their cars on the property. This did the trick and soon James had to withdraw the offer. A complimentary dinner for the sales manager and his wife helped to allay any bad feelings, and James and Alan became friends and golf partners. Alan was probably James' best friend, but like the name of the restaurant this was slightly misleading, for as best friends go they were not that close. They played golf, they went to the occasional hockey or baseball game, but there was no baring one's souls to one another. Discussions over a beer were largely restricted to the state of each other's golf game or expressing mutual bewilderment at why the Leafs continued to play this winger with that centre. There was an understanding they were there for each other, whatever that meant. James did attend the funeral for Alan's father three years ago, which entailed a lot of nodding and wan smiles. Karen was relied upon to say the right things at the right times, but he did his duty as a friend.

The menu leaned heavily on seafood, but there was no tank of live lobsters to greet the guests. James believed this practice actually detracted from sales, and, if he were to be totally honest, was rather cruel, though he would never admit that to anyone. In its place was a waterfall set against a mural of autumnal Muskoka. Again it was far from the Pentlands, but it was warming and the water passing over the rocks was a melodious complement to the soothing quality of the classical music that was piped through the restaurant. There were, in deference to the garden theme, a good number of large plants, strategically placed throughout the restaurant, that required constant nurturing since the light was kept low, particularly in the evening. The restaurant was an open concept with a series of different levels, which meant there were enough little clusters of stairs as to require the waiters to be alert at all times. The exception was the bar area at the western side of the building that was separate and was favoured by the businessmen for lunch when in fact they were not having a business lunch. It was tacitly understood that the bar area was the domain of the hardened smoker, and with the resurgence of the cigar aficionados, it could get quite thick in there. In the restaurant proper there was a section reserved for non-smokers. A rather futile gesture really, as it was tantamount to having a swimming pool with a peeing and non-peeing section. However, there were two large devices affixed to the ceiling constantly vacuuming the offending smoke, made by a company well-placed to benefit from the growing militancy of non-smokers.

James' office was not an ostentatious affair, as it was not large and had a small window that did not afford much of a view. It was however tastefully decorated and furnished with oak cabinets, the shelves of which were dotted with photographs and ornaments that served to remind him of his family and the places they had been. The oldest item was a simple mug James had brought with him from Scotland. His father had bought it for him when he was a young boy and it bore the emblem of his favourite football team. As a boy he loved to drink from the mug, but ever since he had been on his own he had retired it from use, and it stayed on the shelf having the distinction of being the only memento of his homeland.

It was time to call Ronnie. Better to call him than risk him calling at the house. James did not relish his options but some things were best dealt with head on.

Chapter 2

"Yer startin yer life fir real the day son."

"Aye, Mah."

She wis lookin doon at me an smilin.

"Now wave tae yer Granny."

Ma Granny wis wavin fi the windie, so wis ma wee sister, but ma wee brother didnae ken what wis goin oan, an Ah could see him greetin fir Mah. Ah liked ma Granny. She used tae come doon oan the bus an take me back tae her flat fir the day tae gie Mah a wee break cos she hud her hands full wi ma wee brother an sister. Granda wid come hame fir his dinner an the three i us wid sit there an they wid ask me stuff, an there wis aye puddin. Efter dinner Granda wid get oot the moothie an play a few tunes, make me laugh.

"Almost there."

"Mah, what are thae big gates fir?"

"Och dinnae be daft, they're jist fir show."

Ah wis startin tae huv second thoughts aboot this school thing. Didnae like the looks i thae big irin gates. As soon as the bell went they'd probably shut the gates an that wid be ye. Ma Mah could tell Ah wis startin tae shite it, an she held ontae me tight in case Ah tried tae make a run fir it.

"Onywye yer goin tae like the school. Ah'm sure i it," she said. Bit how did she ken if Ah'd like it or no. She said that Ah wid like marzipan an Ah didnae. Ah'd jist is soon huv a bath as eat that shite again. Ah didnae say nowt though, cos Ah didnae want tae get a clout roon the ear. Ah wis sure the big yins were goanni kick the crap oot i me at playtime so Ah didnae need a heid start. Jist keep ma mooth shut an play the wee hard man. Best plan.

In we went an sat doon oan one i the seats ootside the heidmaister's room. There wis loads i other bairns there wi their mahs awready. One cadger wis there wi an old wifie that hud tae be his Granny. Mibbee no, but she wis awfie old. Wee Stevie fi up by the roonaboot wis there wi his mah tae. Ah dinnae ken why he wis kent as Wee Stevie. It's no as if there wis a Big Stevie oan the street. Mind, he wis awfie wee fir his age. Aw the other bairns waitin there wir bigger than him. Even his mah wis a wee woman. Aye well, Ah suppose that's it, Ah thought; he's Wee Stevie cos he's awfie wee. Ah'd only been at school five minutes an Ah'd learnt somethin awready.

It wis aboot then that George Cruickshank started tae greet. Mibbee he'd heard somethin the rest i us hudnae. He did huv a big sister that went tae the school. Ah wis jist startin tae feel better aboot the place when he hud tae start. Ma Mah bent doon an whispered in ma ear an said: "Dinnae ye worry, some bairns greet fir nae good reason … if he wis mine Ah'd gie him somethin tae greet aboot," noddin her heid the whole time she wis tellin me, jist like one i thae wee dogs ye'd see oan the back windie i cars. That didnae make me feel ony better an Ah think she kent it. Then she pointed tae a picture oan the wa.

"That's Mr Sanderson, the headmaster. He has a masters degree from Edinburgh University. A very good man, I hear," she said in her best accent so's ivryone could hear her.

Mibbee he wis an mibbee he wisnae, but could he stoat a ba oan his heid fir twenty minutes like ma old man? Ah dooted it by the looks i him.

George Cruickshank shut up again. Jist as well cos it wis startin tae get oan ma nerves. That's what ma dad said when we were too noisy: "Yer startin tae get oan ma nerves!"

The bell went at nine oan the dot, an as Ah sat there Ah could hear the older ones scufflin intae their classes. Right then a wifie comes oot i the heidmaister's oaffice an says: "Sylvia Anderson please," like she wis orderin a scone at Crawford's. A wee red-haired lassie wi mair freckles than Ah'd iver seen oan one pan jumps up wi her mah an walks intae the oaffice. Ma Mah says they must be dain it by alphabetical order cos we wir certainly there before thame. That wid be awfie, Ah thought, tae huv yer name at the beginnin i the alphabet, aye first tae be takin, no kennin what wis up. They wirnae in but a couple i minutes an oot they come again. Walked right past us, an doon the hall. "Stuart Chalmers," says the wifie, an in went Stewie wi his mah. This went oan fir a while an Ah wis fair startin tae get bored. Ma Mah telt me tae stoap fidgetin, an sit nice like the other bairns. But Ah wisnae fidgetin cos Ah wis bored. It wis the chair Ah wis oan. It wis awfie hard, an Ah wis thinkin how Ah'd like tae be settin oan the couch at hame watchin the telly.

Efter they called oot Fiona McLeod ma Mah pulled oot a hanky fi her handbag. Aw naw, Ah thought, cos Ah kent what wis comin next. Right enough she spits intae the hanky and gies ma face a wee wipe, like Ah wis a cat or somethin. Ah really think it hud jist goat tae be a habit wi her. She didnae really ken that she wis dain it like. It's no as if Ah wis clarty cos Ah'd hud a bath oan Saturday. So much fir the hard man act, Ah thought. Ah mean lets face it, ye cannae play the hard man when yer Mah wis dain that.

Sure enough it wis oor turn next.

"Good morning Mr Sanderson," said ma Mah, ivry one i her teeth showin.

"Good morning Mrs McPherson," said this wee, baldy, fat man, wi these awfie big eyebrows, like some joker hud glued oan a couple i wire brushes jist fir a laugh.

"Welcome to primary school, James."

"Mr Sanderson's talking to you," said ma Mah as she smacked me oan the back i ma heid.

"Aw aye, hullo," wis aw Ah could manage. Ah felt a bit stewpit, it's jist that naebdy iver called me James, jist Jimmy. Besides Ah couldnae stoap starin at thae eyebrows. Ah mean it seemed a bit daft tae huv aw that hair there an none oan toap i his heid. Onywye he jist wanted tae ken if Ah hud hud aw ma jags, which Ah hud. It would be a long time before Ah forgot that day. It wisnae that Ah minded gettin the jag, cos it wisnae bad really, but efter, this wifie makes us take doon ma troosers an cops a feel i ma baws. Wee Stevie fi up by the roonaboot says she did the same tae him. Didnae ken what that wis aboot though an we wirnae askin neither. Ah wis wonderin if Mr Sanderson wis goanni ask us if the nurse copped a feel i ma baws, but he didnae. Jist seemed tae want tae ken if Ah hud ma jags. Jist as well wi ma Mah there an aw. Mibbee he wid ask me later.

Ma Mah walked me doon tae ma class. When we goat tae the door she telt me tae be good an no tae make ony trouble.

"I'll see ye at dinner time. Mind and come right hame an ye kin watch Bill an Ben oan the telly before ye go back fir the efternoon."

"Aye awright," Ah said an in Ah went. Ah kent Ah hud the right classroom cos Ah could hear George Cruickshank greetin fir his mah.

"You must be James. I'm Miss Winterbottom," said this lanky woman. Well, Ah couldnae help it. Ah jist laughed right oot. The rest i the class wir pritty quiet though.

"I might as well tell you now, James, just as I've told the others, I will not countenance any ridicule of the good name I was born to."

Ah wisnae exactly sure what she meant, but Ah goat the general idea.

"I trust this matter has been put to rest, but if it has not, you will be sent down to discuss it with the headmaster."

Oh aye, what's he goanni dae? Scratch me tae death wi his eyebrows, Ah wis thinkin, but no sayin, cos like Ah says, Ah goat the general idea where she stood. Ah went an sat doon at ma seat which wisnae too bad cos it wis near the back an no too near George Cruickshank.

The other bairns eventually aw came in one by one an took their seats. Billy Strachan fair hud a good laugh at the teacher's name, an he goat the same tellin oaf that Ah'd goat. He wis still snickerin when he sat doon next tae me, which impressed me nae end. Nane i the lassies seemed tae find the teacher's name aw that funny though, which made me wonder what wis wrong wi thame. Still Ah wis awfie glad that this Billy Strachan goat sat doon next tae me, cos Ah mean tae keep oan snickerin efter he'd bein telt tae shut it wis a good sign.

"Now children. We're going to have a story, and I want you to listen closely because there will be questions after," said Miss Winterbottom. Billy Strachan leaned over an said: "Ye hear that, we're gawn tae get telt a story fi Miss Cauld Erse."

We both hud a good laugh, but as soon as Ah looked up there she wis stahnin right in front i ma desk.

"These boys seem to think that school is very amusing, class. Do you think school is very amusing young man? Hmm."

"No … no really miss," Ah said.

"What about you Mr Strachan?"

"No miss, Ah don't," said Billy wi a big smile oan his face. Ah turned away fi him cos Ah thought Ah wid burst oot laughin again an that wouldnae be good.

"Well, there'll be no more need for any more unfortunate outbursts, thank you very much."

At that she did a perfect half turn an went back tae her desk at the front. Ah wis thinkin how sometimes things didnae turn oot like ye hud imagined. Ah mean Ah thought the school wis goanni be hard, but Ah didnae think the hardest part wid be tae keep masel fi laughin. Billy kept elboin me tae get ma attention, but Ah wouldnae look at him cos Ah kent Ah wid burst oot again. So Ah jist listened as hard as Ah could tae the story, but every now an then Ah'd catch ma mind wanderin back tae Billy sayin Miss Cauld Erse an Ah'd feel masel wantin tae laugh again in spite i masel.

She telt us a story aboot this lassie that sent a letter tae another lassie in Canada. Efter, she asked us questions tae see if we'd been listenin. Ye hud tae put up yer hand if ye kent the answer. The questions were easy but, an most i the class pit up their hand tae try an answer. Ah wis pittin up ma hand, but she wouldnae ask us tae answer. Then she asked what wis the name i the girl's dug, but Ah couldnae remember so Ah didnae pit ma hand up fir that one. Well, disnae she decide tae ask me what wis the dug's name.

"Ah didnae huv ma hand up Miss," Ah said. Ah didnae ken why she didnae ask the lassie two desks up fi me. Ah mean she musta hud her hand up fir ivry question.

"Perhaps you should pay more attention in future Mr McPherson."

Ah nivir pit ma hand up fir ony mair questions.

The lassie two desks in front i me didnae gie up though, an efter a while she jist kept her hand up the whole time, but the teacher didnae ask her once. Ah thought aboot tellin her tae pit her hand doon an then the teacher would ask her. Efter a while she started tae wave her hand, but the teacher still wouldnae ask her nowt, cos she probably thought she wis bein a smartarse by keepin her hand up. Naebdy likes a smartarse, that's what ma Dad always said. But then we aw found oot why her hand wis up wavin aboot, cos right then her hand quickly went doon an she slumped doon at her desk. Ah thought she'd jist gied up, but then Ah heard that sound like ye hud a leak in yer bike. Sure enough there wis soon a big puddle under her desk cos she'd pished hersel.

Billy gied me the elbow again an he wis laughin his erse oaf, but Ah didnae laugh cos the lassie hud started tae greet an Ah wis feelin sorry fir her. Besides, the puddle hud started tae flow ma wye an Ah hud tae get oot i there. What a wye tae start school Ah wis thinkin. Ah mean if ye wir tae live tae be a hunderd ye'd nivir live that doon.

Right then the bell rang fir playtime which wis lucky cos Ah wis in real danger i floatin in pish.

"Don't worry my dear," said the teacher tae the lassie who wis still bawlin an she pit her airm aroon her. Ah hud thought the teacher wid huv yelled at her, but she didnae. It wis goanni take a wee while tae sus what wis what wi this Miss Cauld Erse. Mibbee it wis some deal the lassies hud wi her where they promised no tae laugh at her name an then it wid be awright if they pished their pants in class. Ah'd huftae wait an see. If a boy wir tae pish his pants then Ah'd huv a better idea. George Cruickshank wis liable tae pish himsel, but mibbee no cos efter aw his greetin there couldnae be much left in him tae pish oot.

Most i ma class jist hung aboot ootside the door at playtime. Billy Strachan seemed awfie interested in chasin the lassies so's he could lift up their skirts, but they wir huvin nane i it an Helen Hamilton smacked him one in the mooth. Billy wis dain his best tae laugh it oaf, but Ah could tell he'd felt that awright. Helen wis awfie big fir her age an she wis bigger than ony the laddies in the class.

Chasin lassies didnae appeal tae me. What Ah really wanted wis tae play a wee bit fitba. There wir some older boys playin a game oan the gress so Ah went over an jist hung aboot at the side. Efter a while Ah goat ma bottle up.

"Ony chance i a game?"

"Go git shagged ye wee bugger," said this big yin. Ah didnae ken what it meant, but Ah did ken Ah wouldnae be playin fitba this playtime or any time soon. Ah wandered back over tae the door an Billy wis still tryin tae annoy the lassies, but he wis keepin his distance fi Helen Hamilton. That wis fir sure.

Ah met up wi Billy when the bell rang and he asked us if Ah'd been playin fitba. Ah jist said that Ah didnae feel like it the day.

Miss Cauld Erse telt us we wir supposed tae line up in single file when the bell rang and wait at the door fir her tae let us in. Efter we goat back intae class the teacher said that we wir goin tae get oor milk. Right enough, someone hud delivered a crate i wee milk bottles and they wir sittin right next tae the teacher's desk.

"You will come row by row and take one, repeat *one* bottle, and one, repeat, *one* straw back to your desk, and you will drink your milk quietly and without spilling it."

Now Ah must say that Ah've nivir really hud much taste fir milk. No that Ah'm really a fussy bairn when it comes tae food. Marzipan, honey, and porridge Ah cannae eat, cos they taste like shite. Milk Ah kin take or leave it taste-wise. Ah mean, Ah kin drink it without wantin tae boke, unlike marzipan an honey. Porridge Ah could eat at a push, fir money like, or if Ah wis starvin. The trouble wi milk though is it hurts yer belly an gies ye the shites somethin terrible. So as far as Ah'm concerned there's nae point in drinkin it if its goanni dae that tae ye.

Everybody went up fir their milk so Ah jist went up an goat mine anaw. Ah pealed the wee foil cap oaf the toap an stuck ma straw in slowly an watched it sink through the yelli cream intae the rest i the milk. Ah took a quick look roon the class an aw the other bairns seemed tae be drinkin theirs. Billy Strachan hud awready finished his an wis flickin the dregs fi his straw at the lassie that hud pished hersel before playtime.

Ah took a wee sip an goat nuthin but cream, an Ah huftae say it felt like a seagull hud jist shat in ma mooth. Ah decided tae pit ma hand up tae see if it wis a school rule that ye hud tae drink aw yer milk or no.

"Yes, James, what is it?"

"Miss Ah dinnae really like milk so dae Ah huftae drink it or can Ah leave it?"

Ah couldnae bring masel tae callin her by her name cos Ah wis likely tae laugh again an she'd be sure tae make me drink it aw. She looked at me kinda funny, like she wis an owl strainin tae see fi the toap i a tree, an said: "Of course you have to drink it all … it's very good for you."

"But miss," Ah said, "it gies me the shh… a sair belly."

"Don't be silly boy; drink it up. There are children in Africa starving who would be glad of a little sip of that milk."

Ah kent Ah wis done fir now cos ma Mah aye said that when Ah wouldnae eat ma porridge. Ah mean, what could ye say tae that. One time Ah telt ma Mah that they starvin bairns in Africa were welcome tae eat aw ma porridge, but that didnae go over too well an she belted me one right there at the table. It wisnae sae bad though cos she knocked me right intae ma gless i milk an sent it flyin so's at least Ah didnae huftae drink it that day. Ah wished someone hud knocked over this bottle i milk fir me, but that wisnae likely tae happen. So Ah jist sipped it through the straw, but Ah left aboot an inch in the bottom i the bottle an pit it back in the crate. Ah really jist wanted tae see if Miss Cauld Erse would make me drink it aw or if Ah could get away wi leavin some. Sure enough she nivir said nowt, so Ah thought Ah could leave mair the morn, an a wee bit mair the next day, till eventually Ah wouldnae be drinkin hardly any.

Mind you, the whole milk thing wis a good skive, cos the teacher didnae make ye dae ony work while ye wir drinkin. Besides, someone wis sure tae knock over their milk an slow things doon. Sure enough; big Helen Hamilton sent her's fir a burton aw doon the side i her desk and ontae the flair. Miss Cauld Erse wisnae too pleased anaw. Clearly, makin a mess wi yer milk wis much worse in her book than pishin oan the flair wis. That

31

seemed strange tae me cos if Ah hud tae clean it up Ah wid much prefer tae clean up milk than pish. Onywye, Billy wis fair pleased that it wis Helen that hud done it an he said tae me: "The big clumsy galoot, serves her right." Ah think he wis still smartin fi the belt she'd gied him at playtime. Tae her credit Helen nivir started tae greet, or nuthin like that. Ah think she wis used tae dain that kind i thing and bein telt she wis clumsy. Helen kindae dottered aboot as if she wis tryin tae help clean up the mess, but she wis jist gettin in the wye i the teacher, who wis gettin a bit impatient wi her.

When Miss Cauld Erse finally goat situated at the front, she telt us tae pull oot oor jotters fi the drawer, cos we wir goanni practise oor writin. As she went tae the big blackboard at the front Ah could feel that milk hit ma belly. It wis like someone hud pit a cat in there an telt it tae find its own wye oot. Ah looked at the clock oan the wa an Ah wisnae sure what time it wis but it wis naewhere near twelve a'clock. It wis goanni be a struggle tae hud ontae this milk till the bell fir dinner.

The teacher drew the letter "a" oan the board, an turns tae us an tells us tae copy it doon in oor jotters ten times. Ah awready kent how tae read, but Ah hudnae really done any writin. Ah wis hopin we would be dain some readin, but Ah hudnae thought that we would huftae start writin letters oan oor first day. Ah took ma new yelli HB pencil an copied the "a" that wis oan the blackboard as best Ah could, but jist as Ah wis finishin up wi the tail Ah goat a right pain in ma belly an it made me make the tail way too long. Miss Cauld Erse, who'd by this time managed tae sneak up tae me an wis stahnin right next tae ma desk, leaned over an said: "That's a good attempt, James, but try and finish better next time."

"Miss," Ah said "could Ah go tae the toilet?" but Ah wisnae too hopeful.

"Come now, James, you had ample time to go at playtime. Try and wait until the dinner bell."

"Aye, right, Miss."

She moved oan tae inspect Billy's efforts.

"Try and keep within the lines, Billy."

Billy nivir said nowt. Ah'm no sure if it wis cos he wis mad he wisnae very good, or mibbee cos he wis gaspin fir air. Ah'd let one i ma specialty milk farts go an it wis fair mingin. Miss Cauld Erse wisnae sae daft, cos she hud cleared the area an wis workin her wye tae the front in a big hurry.

"Did you let oaf?" says Billy.

"Aye, SBD … silent but deadly," Ah said wi a chuckle, cos Ah wis quite proud i it, despite puttin ma mate's life in danger. At least it hud released some pressure fi within. But Ah kent fi past experience it wouldnae hud me fir long.

"Now class, on the next line I want you to copy down the letter "b" ten times. Be sure and keep in the lines."

Miss Cauld Erse wis certainly a neat printer, Ah hud tae gie her that, an Ah wis keen tae get the hang i this printin. Trouble wis that milk hud turned intae shite an wis lookin fir a new hame. Ah wid huv loved tae let go another SBD, even if it meant riskin Billy's life, no tae mention that poor lassie behind me. But that wisnae oan. It wis jist too risky.

Plan B. Ah wrapped ma airms tight aroon ma belly an pit ma heid doon oan ma desk. This usually could be counted oan tae buy some time. As Ah rocked forward Ah took a keek at the clock oan the wa an it wis still naewhere near dinner time. Ah thought tae masel again how school wisnae hard like Ah thought it wis goanni be, but it wis hard in other wyes. Tryin no tae laugh, or tryin tae keep fi shitin yersel. Ma mind wis wanderin. That wis a luxury Ah couldnae afford. Ah hud tae concentrate oan keepin this shite in till dinner. Jist then the pain goat worse. The shite wis bangin at the door an it wisnae takin, NO, fir an answer. Ah managed tae pit up ma hand but Ah couldnae bring masel tae liftin ma heid.

"Yeees Mr McPherson, what is it now?"

"Please Miss Ah really need tae go tae the toilet; Ah cannae wait."

"Aye, let him go. He's killin us wi his fartin," piped in Billy.

Quiet enough so's only Ah could hear.

"Alright go on, but don't make a habit of it," said Miss Cauld Erse.

Did she mean dinnae make a habit i shitin, or jist goin tae the bogs at school time, Ah wondered.

Now came the hard part; actually gettin masel tae the bogs. Trouble wis as soon as the teacher hud said, "Go on," it wis as if she hud been talkin directly tae ma erse, and as bad as the urge tae shite hud been it goat even worse when she said that. As Ah goat up fi ma seat, still unwillin tae risk the full upright position, Ah hud tae clear somethin up wi ma erse muscle, an that wis that it could take orders fi me an only me! Ma erse muscle seemed unconvinced as Ah slunk away tae the door, still huddin ma belly wi both airms.

"That's enough theatrics, James. Just hurry along. I think we have a budding Stanley Baxter on our hands, class."

Finally Ah wis oot the door. Jist a wee bit further tae the glorious bogs. As Ah goat in Ah saw the cubicle, which wis a better sight than the ice-cream van oan a Friday night. Ma erse musta seen it anaw, an bypassin earlier instructions hud started evacuation orders. In the door, troosers an keks doon aw in one motion an Ah heard a heavy splashin before ma cheeks felt the cauld i the seat. Scorin the winnin goal against England at Hampden couldnae be as good a feelin as this. Ah jist sat there an enjoyed the moment. Efter a few minutes Ah sussed it wis safe tae get up, but jist as Ah did the shites wir back. It wis jist like last year's Guy Fawkes night when we aw thought that Roman candle wis aw done, and didnae it shoot oot a pinky-red blast i fire. Best sit tight awhile, Ah thought. Make sure Ah get it aw oot, cos Miss

Cauld Erse wouldnae be too keen tae let us oot again before dinner time.

Back at the door i the class Ah didnae ken if Ah should knock oan the door or no, so Ah jist walked in, makin sure no tae make too much noise, an Ah made it back tae ma seat as quick as Ah could. It wis nice tae sit doon, an the sun wis beamin in the windie, makin it nice an warm.

As the teams line-up for the kick-off, in a surprise move Jimmy McPherson has been selected to play in the striker position. And as they get underway it's the youngster, McPherson looking to make an early impression. He's running straight at the heart of this formidable Celtic defence. He's past Billy McNeil, Kennedy misses with a desperate slide tackle, only the keeper to beat. He lets go a thundering drive past the outstretched hands of Ronnie Simpson into the back of the net! What a goal! A sensational start for Hearts, and for this young man from Edinburgh, being congratulated by his team-mates, waving to the fans in this cavernous stadium, and Hearts have served notice that the Scottish Cup might well be heading back to the capital.

"Yes or no, James?"

"Eh … Ah mean, pardon, Miss."

There she wis starin doon at me wi thae owl eyes again.

"Did you hear the question?"

"Yes, Miss."

"Then what is the answer: YES or NO?"

Jist then Billy whispered: "Yes."

"Yes, Miss," Ah said wi confidence.

Then the whole class burst oot laughin.

"So you think that pink elephants fly off the Scott Monument every hour, on the hour?"

Ah said nowt. Ah didnae ken if Ah wis mair mad at Cauld Erse or Billy, who Ah thought wis ma mate.

"Perhaps in future you will pay attention in class, when in fact you do grace us with your presence."

Ah wisnae sayin nowt.

Chapter 3

After a less than friendly experience with the operator, James managed to narrow down the possibilities to four Edinburgh telephone numbers. The first turned out to be an answering machine with a voice too refined and cultured to be the object of James' search. The second call reached an elderly woman, who, he learned, was a widow, and who told him she kept her listing under her long deceased husband's name in order to discourage would be robbers. James also learned that this Mrs McPherson served as a W.A.C. in the war, that she suffered from arthritis, and was fully expecting the Second Coming any day. After twenty minutes, which seemed more like an hour, James managed to cut her off before she got too involved in describing the surgery her cat recently underwent.

After a brief respite, which James allowed himself, he dialled the third number on his list. Just as he was about to concede a no answer, the ringing stopped, and he was greeted with a terse hullo.

"Ronnie?"

"Aye, who's this?"

"It's me, James."

"James who?"

"Jimmy."

"Jimmy, well Ah'd nivir huv recognised ye. A right American, eh?"

"Canadian, actually," said James, his apprehension now superseded by annoyance.

"How did ye get ma number?"

"A few enquiries, tracked you down. How did you get mine? It was you that called Tuesday night wasn't it?"

"It wis indeed. It wisnae easy. Ah thought ye wir in Toronto?"

"Well, its just outside Toronto really, not Toronto proper."

"Ah ken that now. The operator hud a sister that lived in Ajax or somethin, and she tried aw the toons roon aboot fir me. Where is it ye are?"

"Aurora township."

"Aye, that wis it. Ye goat a nice pad then?"

"No … not really," James lied. "So why the call on Tuesday?"

"Right, that, well it's ma Dah. He's no well, in a hame like, an he's askin fir ye, Jimmy."

There was a silence while James absorbed this piece of information.

"What's wrong with him?"

"Well, he's old maistlie, an his mind's, eh, startin tae wander like. Ah telt him Ah'd try and find ye."

"Well you've found me, but I really couldn't get away. Busy, you know how it is."

"So what dae ye dae, Jimmy?"

"This and that," replied James evasively. "You?"

"Ah've no goat onythin steady the now like," Ronnie stated without shame. "Aw these years, Jimmy, we thought ye'd come back fir a visit … no?"

"Time goes by. Kept meaning to come back and visit," James lied again. He was becoming more accomplished at spurning the truth. Although in truth there were some things he missed about his homeland. Mostly the Pentland hills that bordered the city to the south, and the highlands where he would retreat to as a youth as often as he could. Some day he would go back. When he was retired and successful, and not to visit his uncle and cousin Ronnie. Take Karen with him. Stay at that posh hotel at the west end of Princes Street.

"So could ye no come over fir a wee while? He keeps askin fir ye," persisted Ronnie.

"Sorry, Ronnie, I just don't see it happening. I should be going now."

"We'll keep in touch, eh Jimmy?"

"Best if I call you, Ronnie."

"Aye, whatever ye want, Jimmy. Call me then eh?"

"Sure, Ronnie, bye."

"Right, bye."

James was left with a very empty feeling as he placed the receiver in its cradle. He had hoped to snuff out this intrusion into his life with a pre-emptive strike, but that no longer seemed probable. Ronnie still had his phone number. He would set about changing that, but he still knew roughly where he lived. This was unforeseen. James had no plan on the shelf to deal with this. The passage of time had engendered a false sense of security. James generally had a plan for every contingency. That was the way he liked to deal with unexpected crises, but this was different.

James stayed at his desk and tried to review the numbers for May. They were much the same as the numbers for April, and the month before that. The lack of anything remarkable meant it was too easy for his mind to wander. Inevitably, he scrutinised every detail of the phone conversation with Ronnie. It was only a few minutes ago but already it had acquired a surreal quality.

James moved on to the financial section of the newspaper, which garnered more of his attention as it could always be counted on to do. He read about the potential for another bank merger, and tried to busy himself with how it would impact his portfolio, given that he held stock in both banks. It was no good however; there was nothing there to supplant thinking about Ronnie, his apparently dying uncle, and what he was supposed to do about it. He paced the floor of his office; he peered out his small window; he reorganised his desk drawer, which didn't need reorganising; he scrunched up pieces of paper, and with his best effort at a Michael Jordan jump shot, he fired at the wastepaper basket. Enough! He had to get out of the office.

As James emerged, he appeared tired.

"Morning, James. Busy day?" enquired the lunch manager, Aldo.

"I've got some things I need to take care of. Going to head out. Anything I need to know about?"

Aldo was in his early thirties. A large man, though not overweight, who took his job in stride. His biggest challenge in life appeared to be the need to avoid acquiring a five o'clock shadow. He even found it necessary to wear a white undershirt beneath his dress shirt in the event that a sudden lateral movement would result in weeds of jet black hair sprouting through the cracks between his buttons. Not quite the image that they were striving to achieve in the restaurant. He was single and usually worked the evening, but was filling in for Peter, the regular day manager. James had a great deal of confidence in Aldo. He had been with him for six years now; nothing could arise he couldn't handle, or that would even fluster him. That hadn't always been the case. Always competent, Aldo was given to rushing about the restaurant in the early days. After many attempts to dissuade him from this, James purchased a copy of George Orwell's *Down and Out in Paris and London* and told Aldo it was required reading. Some ten days later, Aldo appeared in James' office with the somewhat dog-eared book and a look of bewilderment on his face. Eventually, James managed to convince Aldo the vital lesson was it was of paramount importance that a waiter or maitre d' glided on the dining room floor, regardless of what mayhem was going on in the kitchen.

It was one of James' favourite books, written by the man he considered to be one of the great essayists of his time. James read it one day while his flight was delayed in Miami, and forgot, as he often did, that others, including Aldo, might not share his enthusiasm for written works, nor the ability to devour a book in a short period of time. Aldo left the office that day with two thoughts; the first, that James must be mad to make him read an entire book just for one small point; the second, that it must be extremely important to glide on the dining room floor. Regardless, the assignment bore fruit, as Aldo was cured from his affliction, and indeed conveyed the message to the staff with a missionary zeal. The exercise did not, however, make a reader out of Aldo, and this was always a mystery to James.

"Looks like a good number, full staff, everything's A-okay," said Aldo. Aldo always said A-okay. Thursday lunch was always busy, more so than Friday, which had traditionally been the busiest day in years gone by. Friday was evolving into the third day of the weekend for many, or at least a work-at-home day. Modems and computers were alleviating traffic congestion at the expense of city commerce. James nodded and made straight for the parking lot without reviewing the kitchen. If Aldo said everything was A-okay, then it was.

Outside the sun was beating down with purpose. With the push of a button the top was down on the Mercedes, and James was heading for the Don Valley Parkway, and north to the golf club. James spent the half-hour drive pushing the pre-set buttons on the car radio, searching in vain for some music he could listen to. Finally he found Van Morrison. But as was usually the case it signalled his arrival at his destination. He made a mental note to bring some CDs from the house and leave them in the car to avoid this frustration tomorrow.

A little lunch, well lubricated, was definitely in order. James was ushered to a seat overlooking the eighteenth green, which was surrounded by water with Austrian pines down both sides. The perfect finish to a long par-five. It was a hole that could make or break a round. James always viewed it with fondness as he recalled holing out from 105 yards for an eagle the previous year. Of course, he had also triple bogeyed, and one time thinned a six iron clean across the green, then the water, bouncing off the window of the club house on a Saturday afternoon no less. There had been howls of laughter from the members of his foursome, which was embarrassing enough, and then further razzing when he had entered the club house for the post game pint. Even now, the memory still brought a smile to his face.

James ordered the "heart choice" special of the day, which was a rice and tuna creation. After all, at forty you had to start thinking about your heart, he reasoned. James resisted the urge to smoke, but did wash down lunch with two pints of beer, which was enough to thwart any thoughts of sneaking in a quick eighteen. He had come here to think, and that was what he was going to attempt to do.

Chapter 4

"Okay kids, we're goin tae surprise yer Dad an meet him at his work when he gets oot at dinner."

It wis Saturday, an ma Dad only hud tae work tae twelve, an that wid be him done tae Monday mornin.

"Ah want to be oot that door at eleven oan the dot ye hear … oan the dot."

We hud oor orders.

"Can Ah play fitba till eleven then, Mah?"

"Ye can play till a quarter tae, then Ah want ye in and cleaned up, cos we're goin tae a restaurant fir dinner wi yer dad."

This wis brilliant. Ma wee sister Shona jist kept playin wi her doll, an ma wee brother wis still tryin tae get his heid through his jersey. They didnae ken what a restaurant wis, but Ah did. Ma Granny took me intae one once, jist oaf the Royal Mile. She ordered a tea an a scone then asked me what Ah wanted. Ah jist blurted oot "puddin," cos that wis aw Ah could think i, cos that wis a year ago an Ah wis only seven. It wis good though. The waitress brought me a big dish i orange blemanche an Ah ate ivry last bit i it. Ah sucked it in first quick, then efter a while Ah churned it aroon in ma mooth and squirted it through ma teeth till the gaps would clog up wi wee bits i orange. An we goat tae sit by the windie an watch aw the people walk by. Ah remember thinkin that in heaven ye probably get orange blemanche fir dinner ivry day, an

Ah wis lookin forward tae gettin some the day at the restaurant.

Ah went ootside where the game wis jist startin tae get goin. A few boys wir knockin the ba aboot. Naebdy ivir said what time the game wid start, but it aye seemed tae work oot jist right, an ivry one wid be there aboot the same time ivry day. Saturday wisnae si good but, cos there wir a few cars parked oan the street, but the owners kent tae keep them parked away fi where we usually played. No that many folk on oor street hud a car onywye, but sometimes there wid be visitors an they'd get in the wye. Mind, they wid only dae it once, cos we didnae care if we hoofed the ba oaf it. In fact, jist last week Jimmy Weir fi the tenement across the street broke a mirror oan a red-an-white Consul, but the man hud been watchin fi the windie an came runnin oot ontae the street. He grabbed Jimmy by the ear an twisted it till Jimmy telt him his name. The man, who didnae live oan the street, took a right hairy an wis yellin oot: "Where does this Jimmy live?" tae the other boys, like we wir goanni shop him or somethin. Ma Mah heard aw the commotion an came oot an asked why he wanted tae ken where Jimmy lived, an when the man telt her she belted me one oan the heid. When the man said it wisnae me an that it wis Jimmy Weir she telt him where he lived an Jimmy goat a right doin cos the man said he did it oan purpose, which he probably did, cos the car wis in the wye. Ma Mah said Ah probably deserved the belt onywye, an that Ah should watch ma step. She wis aye sayin that: "Jist ye watch yer step young man."

Tommy McFarlane brought his school tie wi him an tied it across the toap i the open gate that led tae the close next tae ma hoose. That wis aye the one goal, an we aw thought the tie wis brilliant cos finally someone hud found somethin useful tae dae wi a school tie. There wis nae gate tae the tenement across the road, so ye couldnae put a tie oan there. The goals wir jist the gap between the hedge where the path tae the door went. Tommy an Davey always picked the teams cos they were eleven an the oldest an they thought they wir the best players, an Davey always defended the goal oan ma side i the street. Ah wis hopin Tommy wid pick me the day cos Ah fair wanted tae shoot at the goal wi the crossbar.

Jist when the teams were divvied up George Black showed up lookin fir a game, so that messed ivrythin up an it took aboot ten minutes tae swap players so that Tommy an Davey were happy. Ah wis oan Tommy's team which wis good, cos Ah goat tae shoot at the goal wi the crossbar, but Tommy wis aye moanin if ye didnae pass tae him. We goat George Black oan oor team which wis good too, cos he always played goalie so ye didnae need tae take a turn in the goals. It wisnae that he wis a very good keeper, it's jist that George couldnae run very well cos he hud a bad limp ever since his accident. He wis comin hame wi his big brother oan the bus an instead i gettin oaf at the bus stoap, they waited till the bus wis passin the end i the street an jumped oaf there. Ivrybody did that, at least aw the men who wirnae too old. George's big brother went first, nae bother, cos the bus aye went slow aroon the roonaboot onywye, but it wis George's first time an he lost his nerve an waited too long, an when he finally panicked an jumped, he went right intae the lampost. Ma Dad said he wis too young tae be jumpin oaf a bus, an he made me promise that Ah wouldnae dae that.

Iain Dillon goat tae play centre forward cos it wis his ba, an it wis the only time onyone called him Iain, cos at school we aye called him Tubby. If onyone called him Tubby, he wid pick up his ba an say he wis goin hame. But he nivir did, cos we'd gie him some sweeties an he'd let us play wi his ba. It hud, "England, Champions 1966," an aw the players' names autographed oan it. Tubby wis aye gettin stuff. His dad didnae live at hame but he wid visit him an bring him stuff. Last week he goat a James Bond car that ejected the man fi the passenger seat an he let me play wi it fir a while cos Ah gied him ma biscuit – a chocolate digestive. There

wis usually someone hud a ba, especially efter Christmas, but if we
didnae, we jist used a tennis ba. Ma Dad said it wouldnae dae us
ony harm tae use a tennis ba an it would improve oor skills, an
that's what he used when he wis a laddie.

Ah liked tae make like Ah wis George Best cos he wis a
brilliant dribbler an he played fir Manchester United. Ah used tae
pretend Ah wis Jimmy Johnstone, cos he wis magic even though
he didnae play fir Hearts, but ma Dad said he played fir Celtic an
they wir a Fenian team, but when Celtic won the European Cup ma
Dad wis fair pleased.

"Best steals the ball, around one man, another …"

Ah wis runnin oot i room.

"Pass, pass it!" Tommy wis screamin fir it.

"Cuts it back to Charlton."

Ah passed it back tae Tommy an he blasted it in oaf the side i
the gate, an sticks both his airms up in the air an waits fir ivryone
tae tell him he's great. Disnae tell me nice pass or nowt. See if Ah
pass tae him again!

Mrs Cormack wis waddlin up the path fi the close yammerin
away at us aboot the tie across the gate, an how naebdy can get in
or oot, an that this street isnae a fitba field, an that we aw needed a
good hidin fi oor dads. That wis the end i the crossbar an Ah
didnae get a chance tae shoot yet. It turned oot tae be a decent
game. We were up 6 - 4 efter aboot an hour, because the goals wir
awfie wee an it wis hard tae score, an Ah hud one goal, Best
volley, a screamer, an Ah wis fair enjoyin masel cos this wis what
Ah lived fir. Tubby said he wis gettin tired but, an he wanted tae
pack it in, but Tommy said no tae be a spoilsport, but Tubby said
he wis goin hame an takin his ba wi him. Onywye, the grocery van
pulls up an parks right across the goals, an aw the wifies pour oot
their hooses, an the bairns runnin tae be first in line tae spend their
pocket money, if they hudnae spent it oan the ice cream van that
came oan Friday night. An that killed the game.

Ah wis tryin tae save ma pocket money, cos ma Grandad said he wid gie me five bob if Ah could save five bob by ma birthday. Besides, Ah hud ma heart set oan some orange blemanche at the restaurant, an Ah didnae need ony chocolate the day. The grocery van wis there fir aboot half an hour, an Tubby went hame wi his ba efter he bought himsel a Caramac. Hud it eaten before he goat hame. Me an Bobby Nicholson hung aboot in the grocery van an hid behind the empty crisp boxes. The driver shut the door an drove up tae the toap i the street tae his next stoap. We always did this whenever we could. Ah dinnae ken why, cos we jist hud tae walk back doon the street, but we always did it an hud a laugh, cos we thought the driver wis daft fir no noticin us.

"Bobby Ah've goat tae get hame cos Ah'm goin oot tae a restaurant fir dinner," Ah said beamin.

"That right, ya lucky bastard?" said Bobby. He wis ten an didnae go tae Sunday school an he said bastard aw the time, an ma Mah said he wis goanni get the burnin fire, an so wid Ah if Ah hung aboot wi him.

"Ah wis at a restaurant once, when ma big sister goat engaged, an it wis brammer."

"Aye, Ah aye get the orange blemanche whenever we go tae the restaurant. D'ye?" Ah said as if we went ivry month.

"Na Ah dinnae mind gettin that, but Ah'll tell ye what tae dae," said Bobby.

"What dae ye mean what ye dae, ye eat the grub," Ah said.

"Of course ye eat the grub, ye daft bastard, but efter that when ivryone's leavin, ye hing back at the table an there'll be some money there. That's the tip see." Ah wis interested.

"Jist pit it in yer pocket see."

"Aye, Ah could dae that, but it wid be sorta like stealin," Ah said, but wishin Ah hudnae cos Bobby wid think Ah wis a sissy.

"It's no stealin really cos the waitress gets paid an that's jist a wee extra fir thame."

"Ah suppose so," Ah said unconvinced.

"Aw aye," said Bobby, "nae bother, an ye can split it wi me since Ah gied ye the idea. D'ye want a crisp?"

Ah hudnae noticed, but Bobby hud lifted a packet i crisps, an wis searchin fir the wee pouch i salt wi his manky hands. Ah hud a few crisps an wis thinkin aboot the tip.

"Jimmy, did ye hear the one aboot the three men stuck oan an island wi a camel?"

Bobby wis aye tellin jokes.

"Naw, Ah didnae hear that one."

"These three men wir stuck oan this island fir weeks an wir starvin an they hud nae food. But there wis this old camel an the first man said we're goanni huftae eat this old camel or we'll starve tae death. So the other two men say: 'Aye that's right enough.' So they kill the camel an the first man disnae ken where tae start so finally he says: 'Well Ah'm a Manchester United fan so Ah'll eat the chest.' The second man says: 'Ah'm a Liverpool fan so Ah'll eat the liver.' An the third man says: 'Ah'm an Arsenal fan an Ah'm no that hungry.'"

"Ha ha."

Half eleven an we walk up tae the bus stop oan the other side i the roonaboot, an it starts tae spit rain, so ma Mah makes us aw stand in the shelter.

"When's the bus goanni come Mah?" said ma wee sister Shona.

"It'll be here when it gets here, and don't stand against that, an boys stop that, keep yer hands tae yersels, or so help me …"

Mah wis aye sayin that, but she never finished it.

"Where dae ye think yer goin Jimmy McPherson? Come back here this instant."

Ah wis two steps oot the shelter.

"Ah'm jist goanni walk roon the corner tae see if the bus is comin."

"Oh ye are, are ye? Get back in here before Ah belt ye one."

The bus arrives. Brakes screech as it comes tae a halt. Ah make tae go up the stairs.

"Get doon here, Jimmy, or so help me ..."

She nivir wants tae go up the stairs. Halfway in the bus there's some seats an jist as we go tae sit doon the bus takes oaf an we're aw seated quicker than we'd planned. Ma sister bangs her mooth oan the toap i the seat in front an starts tae greet. No much, jist a whimper.

"Let's see it," said ma Mah. "Och, yer fine."

We're in the toon an there's people ivrywhere, an cars an buses, an big black taxis, an restaurants. An the toon has its ain smell; jist like ivry hoose has its ain smell. This wis Edinburgh's smell. Old Reekie.

"Jimmy, ye watch yer wee brother an hold his hand."

Ah didnae want tae watch ma wee brother. Ah always hud tae watch ma wee brother.

"Ma, what are thae people sittin ootside that shop dain?" They hud sleepin bags, an blankets, an flasks i tea, an a man wis readin a book an a woman wis dain her knittin.

"Och it's some daft thing where the first in line tae the sale get tae buy a couch an armchairs fir a pound."

"Why does the shop sell aw that fir a pound, Mah?"

"Och, it's tae draw attention. Get in the paper, so's more folk will go intae the shop."

"Why did we no get first in line, Mah?"

"Cos we've got some self respect," she said.

Too bad, cos Ah would huv loved tae dae that. Stay oot aw night. Ah didnae care too much aboot the couch an chair fir a pound.

"We've goat a few minutes before yer dad gets here so lets nip intae this shoe shop."

In we went an the magic i the street wis gone an aw i a sudden it seemed awfie quiet.

"Now dinnae touch onythin, boys, ye hear me? Shona's needin a pair i shoes so we're goin tae huv a quick look."

Ma wee brother Davy broke that rule right away, cos he wanted tae measure his foot, an he hud his shoe oaf an intae the measurin thing. The man came over an telt us tae sit doon an wait fir oor Mah, or we'd huftae wait ootside. It wis aw Ah could dae tae keep him sittin still, an he started tae kick me cos Ah wis huddin him in the seat, so Ah punched him oan the airm.

"Ah'm tellin Mah."

He wis oaf.

"Mah, Jimmy hit me."

"Jimmy, can ye no watch him fir a minute?"

"But, Mah, he …"

"But Mah, nothin. I'll dae the hittin," she said, an she usually did. It wis nae use.

"What's Shona dain, Mah?"

Davy wis lookin at Shona who hud her foot in this big boxy machine.

"Ah'm lookin at ma foot in the shoe. Ah can see ma bones!" said Shona.

"Ah wanni try," said Davy.

"Gie him a turn," said ma Mah.

Efter Davy hud a go it wis ma turn. Ah stepped up an stuck ma foot in an looked through this wee binocular thing that wis attached tae the toap i the box. Sure enough Ah could see aw the bones in ma foot. Ah wiggled ma toes an Ah could see the bones movin in ma foot. Ah changed feet. Same thing.

"Ah want another go. Mah, tell Jimmy tae gie me another turn."

"Come oan, Jimmy, ye've hud it long enough. Gie yer brother another go," said ma Mah.

"How does it work, Mah?"

Ah wis curious.

"It's jist like at the hoaspital. They can take a picture i yer bones tae see if they're broken. It's jist tae see if yer foot's sittin properly in yer shoes."

"Come oan, Davy. Gies another go."

"There's Dad," said Shona, an Davy started runnin tae him, an Dad grabbed him an threw him up in the air an caught him, an Davy wis laughin.

"Who wants tae go tae a restaurant?" said ma Dad.

Mah wis smilin, an we wir aw excited.

It wisnae as nice a place as where Ah went wi ma Granny, an it wis a lot noisier, but it definitely smelled better. It wis a mixture i fish an chips, coffee, ice cream, an cigarettes. We aw goat sat at a booth an a waitress came up tae get oor order.

"Can Ah huv chicken an chips, Dad?" Ah asked.

"How about you three split a fish an chips?" said ma Mah.

"Ah can eat ma ain." Ah wis insulted.

She nivir looked up fi the menu an jist ignored me.

"Three fish suppers an five plates please, two teas, an what dae ye want tae drink?"

"Dae we get oor ain drink then?" Ah asked hopefully.

Ah got ma ain Irn Brew at least. Ah didnae like sharin wi Davy cos he put as much in as he drunk oot. Last time Ah hud tae share wi him, Ah found a half chewed mushy pea at the bottom i the tumbler.

Mah split the fish supper intae three an Ah wolfed it doon in nae time, an Ah wis hopin ma sister wouldnae want aw i hers, but she ate it aw efter a while. Spent half the day waitin on her eatin her dinner. Davy ate aw his anaw, but most i it ended up oan the flair. Nivir mind, ma Mah gied me some i her chips.

"Dae yis want ice cream?" said ma Dad.

"Ask a stupid question …" said ma Mah.

"So three ice creams is it?" said the waitress.

"Can Ah huv the orange blemanche instead?" Ah asked.

She tilted her heid tae the side, some lines appeared oan her forehead an she said: "We dinnae huv ice lollies, son."

"It's no an ice lolly," Ah said, "Ah've hud it before."

"No here ye've no, son."

"Gie him an ice cream," said ma Mah.

The waitress wrote it doon, said nowt an went back tae the counter.

Ah'd huftae ask ma Granny aboot orange blemanche, but the ice cream wis good onywye. It came in a wee, roon silver bowl, like a miniature Scottish Cup, an there wis a wafer stuck in it. Ah ate the wafer first. Save the best till last. Ma Mah put her teaspoon in an took a taste. If Ah'd done that tae her Ah would've lost a hand, but then she gied me some i her chips before. The waitress came back wi the bill an gied it tae ma Dad an then she picked up the dirty dishes. Before she went back tae the kitchen, ma Dad gied her some money an telt her tae keep the change. Ah wonder if Bobby Nicholson will believe me.

It wis a nice day an ma Mah said we should go tae Princes Street Gardens because it might be a while before we get a good day like this again. As we walked doon the Mound there wis a loud bang, an aw the pigeons took off.

"The pigeons never get used tae the one o'clock gun," said ma Dad.

"Ah dinnae blame them," said ma Mah. "A right racket, so it is."

The floral clock at the entrance tae the gardens wis goin, an there wir aw kinds i Americans, wi woollen jumpers an coats takin pictures an waitin fur the cuckoo tae stick oot its heid.

"Mah there's nothin tae dae in here," Ah said.

"We're goin tae have a nice walk, so dinnae spoil it fir ivryone else."

What she meant wis dinnae spoil it fir her, cos naebdy else thought it wis a nice walk. Shona wid rather be wi her friends playin wi their dolls, an Ah'd sooner be playin fitba, an ma Dad wid much rather be at Tynecastle. Who ever kent what ma daft wee brother wanted tae dae. Probably stick his foot in that machine in the shoe store. But it didnae matter, cos when ma Mah said that we should aw go fir a walk, then that's what we did.

We finally made oor way tae the bandstand, an there wis a pipe band playin fir free, so we aw went an hud a seat. They wirnae bad, but efter a few minutes Ah wis gettin bored, so ma Mah said Ah could go play if Ah took ma wee brother wi me. Ah always hud tae take ma wee brother wi me. There wisnae much tae dae but, so Ah wandered doon behind the bandstand, draggin Davy. He wis a right pain in the erse him. Whenever Ah hud tae watch him, he wouldnae come wi me, or he'd try tae run oaf. But when Ah didnae huftae watch him, he'd follow me tae ma pal's hoose, or want tae play fitba wi me. Ah usually tried tae get rid i him by tellin him that Mah hud chocolate fir him, but he wisnae fallin fir it so much lately. Onywye, we made oor wye tae a wee bridge that went over the railway tracks, an we hung aboot there waitin fir a train. There wis some other folk stahnin oan the bridge anaw. Efter a while a train starts comin roon the bend taewards us, an it's fair sendin up a lot i smoke, an aw the other folk run oaf the bridge, but now Davy disnae want tae come wi me, so Ah stay oan the bridge wi him. The puffin billy blasts its horn jist before it gets tae the bridge, an as it goes under there's so much white smoke Ah expect it tae blow the bridge up in the air. Davy thinks it's the best thing he's iver seen. Ah hud tae drag him doon here, an now he disnae want tae go back, so Ah huftae drag him back.

"Can Ah huv ma chocolate, Mah?" said Davy.

"There's nae chocolate son, an dinnae ask again. Ye've jist hud ice cream at the restaurant," said ma Mah.

"Jimmy said ye hud chocolate fir me."

"Jimmy's always tellin him that, Mah," said Shona.

Ma wee sister's main goal in life wis tae get me in trouble.

"So help me Jimmy …"

Chapter 5

"How was your day hon?"

Karen burst in the door. After all these years, and all these entrances, Karen hedged her dialogue so that it could be construed as rhetorical, in the event, as was often the case, that it was a struggle to engage her husband. How she managed to maintain a consistent love affair with life was a mystery to James. Their marriage was a testament to the aphorism that opposites attract. James made his mouth wider. To say he smiled would have been an exaggeration.

"Hi Dad."

"Hey darlin', how was school?"

Lisa followed her mother in the door. The eldest, at sixteen, Lisa was the complete package. School had always come easily to her, and she excelled in the sciences. Come the summer, she would have only one more year of high school before what both James and Karen anticipated would be a fruitful spell at university. Beyond that, who knew? She certainly had the ability to do whatever she wanted. James was by now convinced she would indeed go to university and had started dropping hints she should give first consideration to the University of Toronto. That way she could stay at home, where she would be safer.

There was no shortage of suitors already, and according to James, none of them could be trusted. Lisa had her mother's striking looks, and with her father's height, could be described as statuesque. There were lots of friends of both gender, but there was, as yet, no serious boyfriend. This pleased James, as it meant she could devote time to her studies and stay focussed.

Karen returned from upstairs and met James with a kiss in the kitchen, where James was pouring her a glass of white wine; a ritual performed whenever they were both at home in the late afternoon. Little acts of servitude were a substitute for James' verbal shortcomings.

"How was your day?"

"Fairly uneventful," said James, who had never been able to outwardly lie to Karen, though he had become adept at avoiding topics, and at worse could be convicted of prevarication on occasion.

"Fairly uneventful," said Karen with an over emphasis on fairly.

"No, really, in fact I cut out early and went to the club. Hit some balls. Had lunch."

"You should have called me, I could have met you there if I'd known," protested Karen.

"I thought you said that you'd be at the office all day."

"I planned to but I had a meeting in Richmond Hill this afternoon. Maybe next time."

James and Karen retreated through the French doors onto the deck, where they sipped their wine and enjoyed the warmth of the late afternoon. This was their time together; a chance to unwind after the workday. It was their goal to have this time every day, but in reality it only came to fruition once or twice a week, as schedules would not always permit, and James was often called upon to play taxi driver for his daughters.

"Where's Val and Sarah tonight?" enquired James.

"Val's at her friend's house for dinner, and Sarah's practising with her band," replied Karen.

Sarah, the middle child, was the musician of the family and along with four others from school had formed a band, which was commanding a great deal of their time and energy. James and Karen were experiencing a measure of ambivalence over this development. They were pleased that Sarah was pursuing her talent, yet it was not quite the career choice they had anticipated when, having noticed her interest in music at an early age, they enrolled her in piano lessons from an ageing spinster recommended by her grade three teacher.

Sarah's piano-lesson days, where the stuttering utterances of Bach and Beethoven once permeated the house, had now been supplanted by the louder, angrier, musical offerings of a teenager. Clad in clothes that were altogether too dark and confused, much like the mind of their owner, Sarah lived her music and musical culture. She was well on her way to Bohemia, James mused, although in some ways they must have shared the same fashion sense, as Sarah could often be found in one of her father's over sized sweaters. Being the only male in the house presented its challenges, but James had thought at least he would have been immune to the laundry return confusion that afflicted the female members of the household. But as the girls moved into the teen years, James would experience separation anxiety from pullovers and even some of his shirts on occasion. And yet, James was proud of Sarah's drive and determination to develop her talent and encouraged her especially when she wrote her own music. It's just that he wanted to protect her, both from potential disappointment, and from the situations an attractive fifteen-year-old member of a rock band might find herself in.

"What are we having for dinner tonight?" enquired Karen.

"That depends," said James.

"Depends on what?"

"It depends on who's making it."

"You are, aren't you?" There was that tilt of the head again.

"In that case we're having Kraft dinner."

Karen's proclivity for preparing meals had taken a serious decline since her foray into the business world some five years ago, and it was James rather than his daughters who had taken up the challenge. Though never a chef he did have his considerable restaurant experience to fall back on and for the last couple of years certainly had more disposable time. His culinary efforts, while not spectacular, were certainly far superior to Kraft dinner, and once underway James tackled the job with the same commitment and tenacity that he employed for any endeavour he decided to undertake. On the days he was very busy, or just didn't feel inclined to prepare the meal, Karen would usually acquiesce. Otherwise, they would eat out at a restaurant near by, with the exception of Tuesdays, when, if schedules permitted, the whole family would eat at the Pentland Gardens. As much as anything, this was a quality control exercise for James, but the girls liked to dine there, as they felt a certain ownership in the establishment. James was quite pleased at this and looked forward to the day when they would perhaps work alongside him. Lisa had already indicated her desire to do so in the soon to arrive summer holidays.

James was well into his cannelloni and Karen and Lisa had simultaneously finished their salads when Sarah sauntered in.

"What's for dinner?" she asked.

"Nice of you to join us, Sarah. There's dinner in the oven. Help yourself."

Returning to the table, Sarah plunged into her meal with the same enthusiasm with which she played her guitar, and was destined to catch up to her elder sibling. Lisa ate as if it was a task to complete, like homework, not something that she particularly enjoyed doing. She ate perfunctorily, and was much more interested in the social side of mealtime. In fact, she would often dominate the conversation. Had her younger sister, Valerie, been present, she would compete in this regard, but Sarah viewed dinner as something to be consumed as quickly as possible, then on to other things. So generally at family meal times, there were efforts by James and Karen to elicit Sarah's thoughts and concerns, at the expense of stifling the two more enthusiastic siblings.

"So I don't think I'll take French next year," proclaimed Lisa.

This was her apparently final decision on what courses she would take in her last year of high school.

"It would be a shame to drop it now, wouldn't it?" countered Karen.

"There's only so many courses I can take …"

"How's the band going, Sarah?"

James realised how lame this sounded as soon as it left his mouth, but it was too late. It would have to do. No answer from Sarah, but James, recovering from a poor opening, consoled himself with his thorough knowledge of leadership management. He reassured himself; at least he led with an open ended question that could not be answered by a simple yes or no. He hung onto the silence and pretended he was conducting an interview. Never be the first to break the silence.

"Goin' alright."

Success … she speaks.

"Writing anything new?"

Well done, James, he congratulated himself. Much better. If he could just get that ball to the top of the hill.

"You know," said Sarah.

"No, he doesn't know," said Lisa, "that's why he's asking."

So much for any progress. Sarah, still chewing, got up from the table, deposited her plate in the dishwasher, and was off to her room.

"What did I say?"

"Lisa, when your dad's talking to Sarah, just let them talk," chirped Karen, trying to help.

Alarms were now going off in James' head; abort, abort … retire immediately to the den and secure the hatch. Having finished, James excused himself, refilled his wine glass, and was off to the seclusion of his den.

"Don't forget the meeting at the high school tonight," implored Karen.

"I haven't." But he was hoping that she had.

This was the third and last, "introduction to high school," meeting that James would be forced to endure, as Valerie would embark on her high school education in September. After the previous two experiences, James and Karen knew not to arrive on time, even though the letter stated, in bold letters, the meeting would begin promptly at seven-thirty. Prompt arrival would just mean they would have to sit and wait for the meeting to begin fifteen minutes after the scheduled starting time. The substance of the form letter had not really altered since the first one they received four years ago when Lisa was the first in the family to go there. Days and dates had simply been inserted in the form that was on file. They ambled in at seven-forty, moved past the parents who were already there eagerly anticipating what awaited their firstborn, and waded to the back of the gymnasium which was giving olfactory evidence it had been well used this warm day in May.

Karen, ever the optimist, was assuring James it wouldn't take long as she waved intermittently at the other parents whom she knew. At the back there were only muffled utterances of parents who had been in previous years but were determined to demonstrate to their adolescent they were just as committed to them as they were to their older sibling. James shared this façade of dedication. It was important not to show any hint of favouritism, but he didn't have to enjoy being there.

As James attempted to wait patiently, something he had never quite mastered, he glanced through the pamphlet he had been given as he entered. It was much the same as it had been in years past, thanking the parents for sending their children to the school (as if there were any choice in the matter) as it set forth the objectives they were endeavouring to impart. James nudged Karen and pointed to item six under the heading *Codes of Conduct*: 'Students will demonstrate punctuality at all times'.

Karen rolled her eyes and smiled.

"I wonder how they could best impart this quality … Oh, I know, by starting their own meetings on time." James liked to hurl sarcasm at every opportunity.

"Check this out in the school news," said Karen as she pointed to the back of the pamphlet.

"Needed immediately, any parent that could help coach the soccer team."

"Yes, I can actually read myself," said James.

"You'd be good at that, and you have the time now, don't you?"

James was non-committal, as was his policy.

James tried his best to stay conscious during the principal's speech, which, like the pamphlet, was much the same as in years previous. The only real difference was a few shots, albeit in measured tones, at the provincial government's interference in the running of the education system. The speech was then concluded with the assurance that under no circumstances would the current political controversy enter the classroom. Even Karen, with all her positive energy, had difficulty with that.

Fortunately, the information session, as it was billed, finished in half an hour, and the parents were encouraged to visit with the teachers. Karen was always keen to do so and make an impression, whatever that meant, and James followed in tow like a snot nosed toddler hanging off his mother's overcoat.

"Why don't you talk to the English teacher while I see the art director?"

This wasn't desirable, but at least it would reduce the amount of time James would have to spend in the school. He felt like an adolescent himself again, as his prime directive was to get out of school.

"Okay, but don't be too long."

There were no other parents in the English teacher's classroom when James made his entry, and this didn't surprise him. The computer lab was probably crammed wall to wall.

"Hello."

A pretty young woman looked up from the book she was reading. James wasn't sure if she was a student or the teacher.

"Well, a visitor, how nice."

Too much confidence for a student. Had to be the English teacher. James felt decidedly middle-aged.

"Hi, I'm James McPherson."

"Sally Jenkins."

"Well I don't remember any of my English teachers looking like you." *Idiot.* "What I mean is they all seemed to be about one-hundred years old." *Keep digging you, complete idiot.*

"Maybe they just seemed that old to you then."

"Yes, I'm sure that's it."

"So is there something I could help you with?"

You could start by helping me remove my foot from my mouth.

"Well, I think my wife wanted to know if the curriculum had changed from previous years."

"Actually it's similar to last year, except that we'll be doing Romeo and Juliet instead of Hamlet."

"Seems a shame that they have to do Shakespeare at all."

"So you're not a fan, Mr McPherson?"

"On the contrary, Miss Jenkins."

"Sally."

"Okay, Sally. I like Shakespeare."

"Then why don't you think we should teach Shakespeare?"

"Because it's a waste of time on this computer generation. By-and-large they can barely read. If we expose them to Shakespeare now, it'll only turn them off and it's unlikely they'll ever go back to it."

"Hmmm. You may have a point. So what would you suggest?"

"Stephen King. The History of Wrestlemania. Whatever they're actually interested in. At least they might learn to read at some level of competence."

"It's not that dire a situation is it?"

"Trust me it is. I have to employ these people when you're done with them, and, as a rule, I would classify them as functionally illiterate. When we hire a busboy, the first application with the name of the restaurant spelled correctly is the one hired."

James was actually demonstrating passion about a cause.

"What's it called?"

"Sprazwinski's."

"Oh."

"I'm kidding. It's the Pentland Gardens."

James was questioning himself as to whether he had taken this too far.

"Nice place."

"You've been there then?"

"Last year, just before Christmas."

"Look, I didn't mean to come in and browbeat you about the state of literacy in the world."

"No, it's okay. It's all my fault."

She was smiling, but did she mean it? James wondered.

"Next time you and your husband feel like a meal, give me a call and I'll take care of you."

"I'm not married."

"Hi, I'm Karen McPherson."

In the car on the way home James was indignant.

"You don't actually believe I was coming on to her do you? I mean she's not much older than Lisa."

"That's exactly what I was thinking," said Karen finding it hard to contain laughter, never mind the grin that couldn't be stifled.

James felt insulted.

"Not that I was, mind you, but you don't think I would have a chance, do you?"

The grin broke into a snicker.

"You don't, do you?"

"I think you're the most handsome man I know."

"That's it, patronise me."

More laughter, accompanied by a there-there type pat on the head.

Fortunately for James and his bruised ego it was a short drive home. He should have seen the funny side, but he couldn't. He just felt old, well middle-aged, and tried to check his hairline in the rear view mirror. Was it really receding or was it just his imagination?

"Anyway, what's the English curriculum like for next year? Same stuff, or have they added *Lolita*, or *Love in The Time of Cholera*?"

It wasn't like Karen to crack jokes, but she seemed to find them funny. James did think it rather clever, but there was no way he would give her the satisfaction of knowing that.

"That's hilarious Karen. I'm splitting my sides here. Anyway, for your information I think I insulted her."

"How did you manage that? Don't tell me you launched into one of your state of education tirades, did you?"

"Not exactly. I merely pointed out …"

"Does it occur to you that Val has to suffer the consequences?"

"What consequences? She can read. That probably puts her in the top five in the class."

"All I'm saying is there's a time and place for that and that wasn't the time or the place."

Karen was right. Karen was always right.

"Hey Dad."

"Hi Val. How was dinner?"

"Gross. Like mega gross. But guess what? Cindy's dog had puppies and they're sooo cute, and could we get one, Dad, please? And oh, there was a call for you."

"No to the dog, and who was the call from?"

"Some guy, I wrote down the number."

"Progress. Welcome to the world of grown ups. It's just one big list of phone numbers and things to do. If you can write things down you're halfway there."

"Huh?"

"Never mind."

James drifted into the kitchen to retrieve the note, but Karen had beaten him to it.

"Someone called for you, James."

"I know. Who was it?"

"Gwynneth Paltrow." She just managed to get it out before the giggles caught up with her.

"Karen, just drop it, okay."

"Ronnie, no last name, but a long telephone number. Who's that?"

James just shrugged, picked up the note, and tried very hard to look as if it was a great mystery to him.

"Well, are you going to call him?"

"Not tonight. I'll call tomorrow."

"I don't recognise the area code, do you?"

"Yeah … yeah, I think so."

James headed for the den to contemplate his options.

The den, his den, was something that James cherished. It wasn't particularly ornate, but it was imbued with order and neatness, and most of all it was his undisputed territory, off limits to anyone else. The walls were painted a dark green, hunter green if you were to ask a woman, well Karen, but dark green to any man outside the interior decorating business. It didn't really matter much what colour the walls were though because most of the wall area was obscured by oak bookcases, which were filled with an eclectic collection of literature. James had organised the shelves thoroughly. Authors by country and era for the most part. It didn't make much sense to anyone else, but it made perfect sense to James. He did struggle with the varying sizes of books and how disorderly it appeared, and at one point he rearranged everything by segregating the hardbacks from the paperbacks, so that in reality he had a sort of double filing system, but it worked for him. At one end of the room was the computer, and at the other was a black leather reclining chair which was a gift from Karen, and a modern style lamp that curved directly overhead to provide the perfect light for reading. Sometimes James just liked to sit in the chair and look at the collection and imagine that the books could talk to their neighbours on the shelf. It would have made for some interesting conversations. Turgenev and Tolstoy. That would be animated, if, of course, Leo could convince Turgenev it was worth while to debate. Irvine Welsh and Oscar Wilde were even more problematic. Try as he might he just couldn't see those two discussing Hibs' chances in the league over a pint and a pie. No matter, soon the British collection would be divided. There were so many young Scottish writers on the scene as to make this necessary. He even had a cabinet with a little bar inside. Liqueurs mostly. Unfortunately the cabinet was right above Dylan Thomas, which seemed more tragic than ironic to James.

Even Karen felt it necessary to knock before entering, and while this seemed a bit much to James he didn't discourage the practice. He liked to think that Karen held great reverence for the time he spent reading, or working, or quietly sipping a cognac, but perhaps she just lived in mortal fear of walking in on her husband masturbating. Who could tell what women were thinking? It was something that all men must wonder, James thought. Women didn't have this problem. They know what men are thinking. The real mystery is why they tolerate it.

Strangely enough, as James sat in his little kingdom, this concession to him being the only owner of a Y chromosome in the house, he thought about Sally Jenkins. Actually he thought about shagging Sally Jenkins, right there on her desk, preferably with her reading glasses still on, perched precariously on her nose. This puzzled him as he should have been devoting his thoughts and energies into how to handle the Ronnie situation, and if truth were told, he had never considered having an extra-marital affair. Well, not really considered. Sure he had noticed other women and he'd thought about it, but not seriously considered. There was a big difference.

He'd have to tell Karen. He'd have to tell her everything.

Chapter 6

The car wis aw packed an ma Dad wis tellin ma Mah no tae be hard oan the clutch cos it wisnae too reliable at the moment, then he gied her a kiss oan the lips right there oan the street.

Dad stuck his heid in the side windie an said: "Be good fir yer Mah now, boys. Jimmy, Ah'm countin oan ye now."

Then he rubbed his big hand oan ma sister's heid who wis sittin in the front. Countin oan me fir what, Ah wondered.

"How far is it tae Oban, Mah?"

"It's one hundred and twenty-three miles, 1-2-3. Now dinnae ask again."

"When is it ma turn in the front?" said Davy.

"It's your turn when Ah say it's your turn. Why don't we play I spy?"

"Do we huftae," Ah said.

"Can Ah go first?" said Davy.

"Davy can go first, then Shona, then Jimmy."

"Ah spy wi ma little eye somethin that begins wi 'p'."

"A parked car," said Shona.

"Nut."

"A poodle," Shona again.

"Nut."

"A pansy," Shona kept on.

"Nut."

Davy's fair enjoyin himsel.

"Have ye goat a guess, Jimmy?" asks ma Mah.

"Ah dinnae want tae play."

"Cos ye dinnae ken what it is."

"It's a poof an Ah'm lookin at him," Ah said tae Davy, but no loud enough fir ma Mah tae hear.

"Mah, Jimmy called me a poof."

"Jimmy McPherson, is it a doin yer efter? Cos if it is, Ah'll stoap the car an gie ye one."

"What wis it Davy?" asks ma wee sister, as she brushes the hair i her doll.

"A pigeon."

"Ah cannae see ony pigeon," goes Shona.

"Ah saw one, Ah did!"

"Ye're a wee cheat. Boys always cheat."

"No Ah didnae."

"Did so."

"Did not."

"For the love i goodness would yous aw shut up an look oot yer windie."

As we left the lowlands behind it started tae cloud over an soon the toaps i the higher hills were hidden, an Ah wis thinkin how it wid be good tae walk through that tae the toap. But wid ye actually notice when ye were walkin through it, or wid it jist sortie gradually happen an then ye'd be at the toap? Mibbee it wid be aw clear at the toap or mibbee ye'd still be stuck in the mist. Mibbee it wid be so misty ye widnae even ken ye were at the toap, an then ye'd wish ye'd spent mair time at the brook or in the glen, or lookin at the heather. Mibbee even ye'd get half way up an then think it wisnae worth botherin aboot.

Ye could see train tracks now an then, as they wound their way aroon the mountains an hills. Sometimes they'd go through tunnels, but they'd nivir get tae the toap. They jist worked their way aboot one third i the wye up, back and forth, an aroon.

We were makin pritty good time. So said ma Mah, but then we came ontae some roadworks aroon Loch Awe an that slowed us doon.

"Look, Mah at thae flowers," said Shona.

"Aye, they're wild primroses."

Sure enough, clingin tae the side i the bank, against aw odds wir these wee yelli flowers sittin oan toap i a cushion i dark green leaves. Oan the other side i the road wis the loch an it wis dark grey, almost black, an ye could nivir imagine the water ever lookin blue.

The windscreen wipers were screechin, because we were stoaped an the mist wisnae heavy enough tae justify them bein oan. The light changed tae green up ahead an Ah calculated that if ivryone goat a move oan we'd make it through this time. Jist before we goat tae the mini traffic light, held in place by a couple i sand bags, it changed tae amber.

"Keep goin, Mah," Ah said.

"Stoap, Mah," said Shona.

Mah stoaped.

"Ye coulda easily huv made it, Mah," Ah said.

"Better safe than sorry," she said.

"Dad would've went."

"Read yer book."

We pulled intae the postcard that wis Oban. This wid be ma summer holidays. Butlins it wisnae. We drove along the waterfront, past the hotel an the other places that hud signs that said B&B, VACANCIES, NO VACANCIES, AA, RAC. Oan the sea side wir fishin boats an a big ferryboat.

"Now mind yer Aunt Morag is old an she's dain us a favour by lettin us stay in her flat, an she's no used tae children. So oan yer best behaviour. Eat what's put in front i ye, cos that'll be aw there is."

Ah'd nivir met Aunt Morag, but she must be nice tae let us aw stay in her wee flat. Mibbee she wis that lonely. It wis hard tae imagine. When Ah wis younger, Aunt Morag used tae make tablet, an once a year she'd post it doon tae us. It would arrive in an old shortbread tin that wis wrapped in aboot ten yards i brown paper an it tasted brilliant. She didnae send it onymair, an when she opened the door Ah could see why. She didnae look strong enough tae lift an empty shortbread tin, let alone a pot. The cracks oan her face moved tae the side an she smiled at us.

"C'moan in, c'moan in."

She waved us in wi her right arm an held ontae the door wi the other. Jist as well cos the draught might huv blown her over.

It wis a wee flat. No TV. Ah wisnae feelin sorry fir ma Dad huvin tae stay behind an work onymair. He wisnae sae daft. Aunt Morag hud a pot i tea oan the go an we aw sat aroon her table. Clearly this wis a big deal fir her. There wis this contraption in the middle i the table that wis a three-storey plate. Wee egg sandwiches oan the toap, scones that were awready buttered wi jam oan the middle level, an sticky buns oan the bottom. They were too big really an one hud half fallen oaf ontae the lace table cloth, that wis too big fir the table, cos it wis draped aroon ma knees where Ah sat, an it felt like what it must feel like tae wear a dress.

Aunt Morag toddles oot fi the scullery wi a bottle i Irn Bru. She hus tae hud it wi both hands, an her slippers make a shush-shush sound as she drags them across the wood flair.

"Are ye sure we cannae help ye," says ma Mah, who has her bum aboot four inches oaf her seat, ready tae catch the bottle i Irn Bru in case Aunt Morag cannae hoist it ontae the table. It's funny seein ma Mah like this, like she's the bairn tryin tae make sure she's dain the right thing, even though it's no clear what's quite expected i her.

"No, no we're aw set now."

This is like Christmas fir her.

"D'ye aw like Irn Bru?"

"Oh aye, Aunt Morag, grand."

"Now ye'll huftae stoap callin me Aunt Morag, that's what ye call an aunt ye dinnae like. D'ye think Ah'm a nice aunt?"

"Oh aye we do," Ah said oan behalf i ma brother an sister. Wisnae lyin either. Sticky buns an Irn Bru.

"Well then, ye'll huftae call me Auntie Morag; Aunt is only if ye dinnae like yer auntie. Is that no right Muriel?"

"Aye, it is."

Mah wis smilin at us. Auntie Morag goat tae the table, passed oaf the bottle tae ma Mah, who looked relieved tae take it, an then she jist sorta leaned back until the back i her knees pivoted oan the chair an she plunged intae the seat. Her legs slowly came doon fi the straight oot position, carryin the over-sized table cloth doon wi them, jist like a plane comin through the clouds fir a nice easy landin.

"Stick in till ye stick oot," she said, an we did.

Auntie Morag had plenty i stories aboot the olden days, an she kept oan long efter we'd finished the sticky buns. Ma Mah wis lookin anxious, but she couldnae get a word in edge wise. Finally Auntie Morag stoaped tae take a breath an ma Mah seized her chance before we were back oan Mull, in nineteen twenty-four.

"Let me help ye clean-up, then Ah'll nip over tae the hoaspital."

"Och dinnae ye worry hen. Away ye go. Ah'll clean it up nae bother wi ma three helpers."

"Are ye sure now?"

"Och aye. Ye should go the now, before it gets late."

"Right then. Make sure ye aw help yer Auntie Morag, an Ah'll be back later."

Mah leaned over tae Auntie Morag's ear an said: "Shona's a good help." Like Ah wis useless or somethin.

Shona an Davy were fair taken by Auntie Morag an her stories, an so wis Ah, but Ah wanted tae go tae the hoaspital tae see ma Granny. Ah went over tae ask ma Mah quietly if Ah could go wi her, cos Ah didnae want tae hurt ma Auntie's feelins, an tae ma surprise she said yes. Course, as soon as Davy heard that, he wanted tae come tae. Shona wis quite happy tae stay wi Auntie Morag though. Mah said Davy hud tae stay, cos she didnae think bairns wid be allowed in. Fortunately he didnae put up much i a fight, especially efter Auntie Morag asked him if he wanted mair Irn Bru.

"Now are ye sure i the directions?"

"Aye, Ah've goat them written doon in the car," said ma Mah.

Auntie Morag then proceeded tae give Mah the directions onywye in scunnerin detail. It wis a good five minutes before she wis done an we were oot the door.

"Is Auntie Morag's husband deid, Mah?"

"She nivir married son. There wis a shortage i men when she wis marryin age because i the First World War."

It seemed like a strange thing tae huv a shortage i. Ye always heard aboot shortages i things like electricity, or turkeys at Christmas time, but a shortage i men seemed strange. We were oot in the country again, an the roads were gettin awfie narrow. At one point we went over a section i metal rollers that were there tae keep the sheep oot. It seemed like a strange place fir a hoaspital. If ye didnae die oan yer way tae the hoaspital, then ye probably wirnae goanni die at aw.

It wis a wee cottage hoaspital that didnae seem tae be near onythin except sheep. There wis nae shortage i sheep.

"Jist come in wi me Jimmy. If yer no allowed, then yer no

allowed, ye'll jist huftae come back ootside."

There wis nae need tae ask where tae find ma Granny. There wis only one women's ward, an one fir the men. The place hud a right ming tae it. That combination i disinfectant, medicines, food, an flowers. Ah'd only been in a few hoaspitals, but it wis amazin how they aw managed tae smell the same. Mibbee the National Health approved a certain smell fir hoaspitals that they hud tae stick tae. Ah could jist picture a wee bald heided man wi a brief case an a raincoat that didnae quite fit him, drivin aroon the country inspectin the hoaspitals tae make sure they aw smelled jist right.

It wis ma Granda that Ah saw first. He wis stahnin at the foot i ma Granny's bed wi his hands restin oan the frame. We were in an naebdy wis objectin tae ma bein there. In fact the nurse at the desk smiled at us as we came in. It wisnae a city smile either. It wis like she meant it. Mah gied ma Granny a kiss oan her hair, which seemed like a strange place tae kiss someone; like kissin candy floss. Either way, Mah had kissed twice in one day; both times in front i awbody. Grandad wis showin me the wee TV screen that monitored ma Granny's heart. As long as the line wis squiggly, then she wis okay.

It's a funny thing. Ye hear that yer Granny took a heart attack oan holiday an it wis touch an go fir a while. Ye go tae yer room cos ye feel a lump comin up in yer throat, an the eyes start tae get a bit watery, an ye dinnae want onyone tae see ye. Then ye sit in yer room hopin an prayin that she'll be awright, an ye think aboot aw the things ye've done together, an then when ye finally get tae see her in the hoaspital ye dinnae huv much tae say, save fir the usual hullo and how ye dain kinda stuff . Efter a while Granny suggested Ah go across the ward an sit wi an old woman, cos she didnae get many visitors. As Ah wis crossin the ward she says: "Mind, she jist speaks the Gaelic, but Ah've taught her tae say good mornin."

Brilliant Gran, what am Ah goanni talk tae her aboot? Ah went over an wi ma hands stuck in ma pocket, Ah half smiled, no wantin tae scare her, nodded ma heid up an doon a few times, thrust ma jaw oot an in, feelin like an eejit.

"That's oor oldest grandson … Jimmy," ma Granda's shoutin altogether too loud fir a hoaspital, thinkin as a lot i people dae, that ye can make them understand jist by speakin louder. The poor old wifie, who looked old enough tae huv hud a brother fight at Culloden, jist smiled back, probably wishin she could jist die in peace. Even if Ah could talk tae her, what would we talk aboot? "Some highland dancin at the Mod last year, eh?"

Granda's bed and breakfast place wis an old hoose that wis filled wi too many antiques an wooden bookcases. It wis too dark tae spend yer summer holiday in, but the folk there, from what Ah saw i them, were aw old an didnae seem tae mind. Ah goat a good lookin over as Ah made ma wye up the creaky stairs fi the other inmates. Onythin that came efter the Second World War wis viewed upon wi great suspicion. Aw by masel Ah'd be bringin the average age i the guests doon by a good thirty years. Still it wis better than sharin a pull oot bed wi ma wee brother.

We went fir a walk along the waterfront, an shared a poke i chips. Extra brown sauce. Brammer. The smell i the chips wis competin wi the salt water and fish. The tide wis in an there wis a good size dead fish, Ah didnae ken what kind, lappin up against the wa among the seaweed. The weather hud cleared up fi the efternoon rain an the sun wis startin tae go doon over the islands tae the west.

"Gran's goanni be okay now, eh, Granda?"

"Och aye, son. Jist a wee scare; that's aw."

"When does she get tae come hame?"

"A week or two. They're no jist sure. They'll huftae see."

"Bad luck it hud tae happen oan yer holidays."

"Aye it is that, but it jist goes tae show ye there's nothin fir sure in life. Jist when ye think everythin's set up jist right, somethin like this comes along. Coulda been me jist as easy as yer Gran. Go oan, finish those up."

The last few chips were the best. Swimmin in grease they jist floated doon ma throat. Ah hardly needed tae chew them.

"Aye, ye want tae live yer life like ye're eatin those chips son. Go efter them, grab them an enjoy ivry second."

"What d'ye mean?" Ah kent he didnae expect me tae spend the rest i ma days chasin doon chip vans, gettin fat, but Ah wisnae sure what he wis tryin tae tell me either.

"Ah'm jist sayin that … well … what Ah mean is Ah'm no complainin. Ah've hud a good life, made it through the war, married well, always hud steady work. But Ah've nivir really pushed masel either. Nivir taken a chance, like emigratin tae Canada, or startin ma ain business."

"Did ye want tae move tae Canada?"

"Aye, well that's jist an example like, ye ken, a fir instance, but aye, Ah did think aboot it once efter the war, jist like Ah thought aboot startin ma ain shop once but Ah nivir did."

"What if ye could go back in time?"

"Well, Ah'd definitely huv taken mair chances, mair risks. Ye'll huftae promise me that when ye grow up, Jimmy, that ye'll take some chances. Ah'm no sayin throw yer money aroon an be daft. Jist if ye've goat a good feelin aboot somethin, an it makes sense, then gie it yer best shot. Usually that'll mean dain the opposite i ivryone else mind."

"Ah will."

"That's ma boy."

Back at the bed an breakfast, there were still some old biddies hingin aboot the sittin room, readin the paper or a book. One old man wis jist sittin in the big brown armchair starin intae space, his elbow restin oan the arm so that his hand looked as if it wis hingin in mid air, cos his cardigan wis the same colour as the chair, an in the murky light i the sittin room that wis how it looked. Dusk came late at this time i year, but when it did it made the place look right gloomy. This hoose wis destined tae huv a Sunday feel tae it ivry day i the year. Ye ken that grey, dull, nothin tae dae but read the bible an sit an wait fir a visit fi yer aunt that smelled i mothballs kinda feel.

Granda could fair snore, an it kept me awake fir quite a while. This wis the worst part aboot goin oan holidays. If ye could jist transport yer ain bed, an even yer bedroom then it wid be perfect. Ah tried tae count sheep. It seemed tae work fir Oor Wuillie, but it wisnae workin fir me. Instead Ah jist thought aboot what ma granda said, an Ah decided right there an then that Ah wid follow his advice. Granda wis good that wye. He talked tae ye like ye were a real person.

"Wake up son. There'll be bacon an eggs oan fir us."

Where am Ah? Oh aye, right.

"Mornin, Granda."

"Time tae get up, Jimmy."

Ah wis dreamin aboot aw the sheep oan the hills. Thousands i them, jist hingin aboot oan the hills, below the mist.

Right enough, ye could smell the bacon cookin. We sat doon together. The other guests were filin in an takin their seats. They aw said good mornin like they hud been practisin fir an hour an wanted tae make it sound jist right. Granda hud tae gie an update oan Gran's condition tae ivryone as they arrived. He should've jist waited till they aw arrived an done it the once, but he didnae seem tae mind. The old chap came in last, an wi the slightly better light i the mornin ye could see that his hand wis actually attached, an he used it tae half wave like the queen does, cos speakin would probably huv been too tirin fir him.

"Mister Buchan stays here year roon," said Granda.

Ah wisnae sure what the proper response tae that wis. Not

congratulations. So Ah didnae say onythin, jist nodded as if sayin: "Aye that's the wye it should be." At least that explained somethin, cos Ah didnae think that aw these old folk looked like they were oan holiday. Ah mean, why bother? Ye could plant yersel in an armchair in a dimly lit room at hame as well as ye could here.

There wir two other couples aboot the same age as ma Granda who wir jist there fir the bed an breakfast, but certainly nae one near ma age. Even the dug looked old, cos it didnae move much. It's a wonder it wisnae wearin a tie. The grub wis good though, once Ah cleared up the fact that Ah wisnae goanni eat the porridge that goat sent oot first. Ah think ma Granda wis embarrassed that Ah didnae like porridge, an there were a few tuts an tsk tsks from the other guests. It wis like Ah wis unpatriotic or somethin. What wid William Wallace think? The ony good thing aboot it wis the lassie that brought it oot fi the kitchen wis right pritty tae look at, an she smiled at me, an Ah felt a different feelin than Ah'd iver felt before. At the school if ye talked tae a girl like she wis a real person, ivryone said that ye were gettin oaf wi her, an sometimes it seemed like it wisnae worth aw the trouble. Sometimes though, like when Ah saw Angela Lumsden in Woolworths wi her mah, we talked an smiled an it wis nice, but when Ah saw her at the school oan the Monday it wis like it nivir happened. It wis the same at the school dance we hud fir finishin primary school, jist last week. Ah asked Fiona Black tae go wi me an she said yes. Ah went by her hoose an we goat the bus doon tae the school together. Sat upstairs at the very front, even although it wisnae very far tae go. We danced a few times an Ah felt a bit daft, but it wis nice bein next tae her an she smelled brilliant, an at the end i the night Ah wanted tae gie her a wee kiss, but her mah wis there tae pick her up an Ah didnae. Onywye, by the Monday it wis like it wis aw a dream an ivrythin wis back tae normal, but there wir rumours goin roon that me an Fiona were gettin oaf, which probably jist meant that somebody hud seen us sittin together oan the bus. Fiona probably jist couldnae be bothered. Or mibbee she didnae really fancy me. Couple i weeks an it would be summer holidays onywye.

Mah picked us up efter breakfast, an we were goanni go fir a wee drive before goin tae the hoaspital tae see Gran.

"How d'ye like stayin at a hotel, ye wee toff?"

"Grand, Mah. Bacon an eggs fir breakfast."

"There's no much fir him really. Naebdy his ain age," said Granda.

We drove oot i the toon, cos Granda wanted us tae see the bridge over the Atlantic Ocean. He kept talkin aboot this bridge that went over the ocean, but nane i us were buyin it; even Davy wis too old no tae suspect somethin. But oan we drove oan the narrow, windy road, up an doon over the hills, ivry now an then catchin a glimpse i the sea. At one point we came aroon a bend, an there wis a wee van parked oaf oan the gress wi a family aw aroon. They hud a washin line set up an a fire goin wi a big pot oan it.

"Gypsies," said ma Granda.

It wis a far cry fi the picture i gypsies Ah'd seen in a book Ah read when Ah wis younger. *Famous Five,* or somethin like it. Gypsies were supposed tae huv big decorated caravans, pulled along by a horse, an the whole family wid be smilin an mibbee singin. This bunch jist looked miserable. Nane i them looked happy at aw. The old man wis puffin oan his pipe, but that wis it as far as resemblin what the picture looked like.

We goat tae the bridge over the Atlantic, much tae ma Granda's great pleasure.

"Ye see how the ocean comes in an the bridge crosses it."

It wis a wee estuary, no an ocean, an the three i us in the back seat could barely muster a smile when Granda turned his heid roon tae look at us. Mah stoaped the car an told us tae stand oan the bridge tae get oor photie taken, an that wis that, save fir throwin a few stanes in the water, which me an Davy felt obliged tae dae whenever the occasion presented itsel.

The car trundled over the sheep stop, which meant the hoaspital wis very close. That wis a relief cos it wis kinda cramped in the back i the Anglia, an Shona kept elboin me. But Ah didnae complain cos at least Ah'd goat a windie seat. There wis a sheep oan the road that didnae seem too interested in gettin oot the wye, an Mah hud tae slow doon.

"Mind yer bum, chum," said ma Granda an the three i us laughed. It wisnae that funny, but it wis, comin fi ma Granda. Bum wis one i the words that Mah wisnae too keen oan ye usin. It wis right oan the border. No as bad as shite, or bugger, or bastard, but no proper, if ye were tae ask her. When dad let oot a word that mibbee wisnae proper then that wid complicate things. She hud a whole list somewhere in her heid aboot what words ye could and couldnae use, an they'd change a bit dependin oan her mood. There wir a few obvious ones which wid probably get ye executed, but there wir others that ye hud tae be careful wi. If she wis in a bad mood ye would nivir refer tae her as *she.* Fir that ye'd get a look i utter contempt, followed by: "Who's she? The cat's mother?" That would often be delivered simultaneously wi a slap tae the face. Sticks and stones can break yer bones, but personal pronouns could get ye killed.

The sheep needed a toot i the horn tae get him goin.

Davy said: "Mind yer bum, chum," an that goat us aw laughin again, except fir Mah, who pretended she didnae hear. The trouble wi bein nine is that ye still think that if somethin is funny once, it'll always be funny, an Davy wis nine. Efter a few minutes Mah gave up pretendin she wisnae listenin an told Davy tae shut it. Ah dinnae think she wis too pleased wi Granda who did get the whole thing started but what could she dae? She couldnae tell her ain Dad oaf. That's the best part aboot bein old; ye can dae an say what ye want tae without somebody tellin ye that ye're a smart erse.

Ah hud tae watch Davy while Mah, Granda an Shona went in tae see ma Granny, but we wandered aroon tae the windie an waved at her. She looked aboot the same as she did when Ah went in the day before, but Mah said she wis dain much better, an soon they'd let her get oot i bed fir a wee walk. That wis the last time a saw ma Granny, cos the next day Ah stayed at Auntie Morag's, an the day efter that Ah met up wi some boys who played fitba ivryday, at their lunch hour, an break times an that's what Ah did except fir the Thursday when ma Mah dragged us aw along tae a gless shop. It wisnae so bad really cos the man made the stuff right in front i ye. Blew intae this big pipe thing that shaped the hot gless. Onywye, it wis pourin an no a good day fir fitba. Oan the Saturday it wis time tae come hame again, an that wis ma summer holidays. Worst part wis Ah hud tae go back tae school oan Monday cos it wisnae school holidays yet. Still it wis a good skive, an aw the others would be jealous cos Ah goat a week oaf.

Granda came hame wi us, cos he hud tae get back tae work. He wis goanni go up the next weekend wi a friend who hud a car. Mah hud promised Gran that she would go back up oan the Wednesday fir one night tae bridge the gap, an then we were aw goanni go back up in two weeks if she wis still in the hoaspital. When we dropped Granda oaf at his flat he wis tryin no tae show it, but ye could tell he wis sad tae be goin hame by himsel. Ah helped him wi the luggage up the stairs that wir always dark. Ye hud tae be careful at the best i times oan thae stairs, because they were aboot a hundred years old an the stane hud worn away in the middle i each step, but we managed tae get the bags up. Granda gied me thirty pence, an told me tae gie ten each tae Shona an Davy. Ah hated tae take it fi him.

Chapter 7

Friday turned into another glorious day and this helped lift James' spirits. There was almost a feeling of relief that fell over him, now that he had committed himself to educating Karen as to the identity of the mystery caller. Still, he felt compelled to mentally rehearse his speech over and over as he made his way round the golf course. He was even playing well. This he took as a good omen. Although golf was the great game of concentration, James' mental rehearsals served to halt his tendency to over-analyse his game, and the positive results that were a consequence were what he always suspected might happen.

After the round, James accompanied his partners into the clubhouse for the obligatory pint. A quick check in the restaurant revealed that Karen was not early for their dinner engagement, which didn't surprise James. Karen, for all she was extremely capable, was regularly guilty of under-estimating the passage of time. She tended to offer overly optimistic predictions of when she would be able to rendezvous, but over the years James had learned to take this shortcoming into consideration, rather than expect her to change. The first pint was accompanied by a chaser of scotch, as was the second. James thought about another, but feeling sufficiently braced he settled the bets and bade farewell a little richer than when he'd arrived. Nothing serious, just enough to keep the round interesting. It was five after the appointed hour when he checked the dining room for the second time and true to form Karen had not yet arrived, so he needn't rush his ablution.

James re-appeared in the dining room looking and smelling considerably better at six twenty-five. Karen was seated at the table beside the window that he had reserved, and waved discreetly across the dining room as if James would not have been able to spot her amongst the thorns.

"You haven't been waiting too long have you?" said James as he seated himself, neglecting to offer a kiss in greeting. His first mistake. Not that Karen would have expected a public display of affection, but on this occasion it would have scored valuable points that might come in handy.

"No, no, five minutes, that's all. How was your game?"

"Fine, great."

Just then the waiter appeared at the table and James ordered a bloody Caesar, Karen having already ordered a chardonnay upon her arrival. He would have liked another boilermaker, but a Caesar would give the impression it was his first drink, and it would suffice to bolster the waning courage the earlier drinks had manufactured.

"So how was your day?"

"Okay. Having a few problems trying to free up some time next month. So I'm not sure if it's going to work as far as that weekend in New York."

Karen tilted her head and scrunched her nose in apologetic punctuation.

"Don't worry about it. We'll just go another time that's all."

James was pleased at this unexpected opportunity to demonstrate how magnanimous he could be and his willingness to adapt to his wife's schedule.

"I feel so bad because you've made some arrangements."

"Please, Karen, it's no problem, really."

In fact, James was rather pleased as he had only suggested the trip because Karen enjoyed such excursions, but if he had his choice he would prefer to stay home near the golf course and the pool. But Karen did feel a little disappointed and there followed an awkward silence. James turned to catch the waiter's eye and waved his empty glass. A controlled nod signified that he would promptly bring another.

"Who sings that song?" asked James attempting to move on.

"Oh, I can't remember. Definitely seventies though. At least."

"Seventies, for sure."

James had mentioned this only as a diversion, but now it was starting to annoy him that he couldn't put a name to the artist, whose voice was discreetly imbuing the restaurant.

Karen sang along quietly ... "killing me softly with his song ..."

The drink arrived along with an enquiry as to whether they were ready to order. They were not, and, in fact, they hadn't even perused the menu, so the waiter perfunctorily recited the specials and left the table.

"Actually Karen, there's something I need to discuss with you."

There, he'd done it. No turning back now. Even displayed the furrowed brow with some élan. Karen's head twitched as she leaned forward, genuinely surprised at the uncharacteristic gravity with which James was attempting to initiate a dialogue. Cancer, another woman? No, that couldn't be it. Financial, maybe.

"I've always tried to be very honest with you, and in fact I think I can say that I've never really lied to you." James reached over the table, deftly avoiding the narrow vase that housed a single yellow rose, and held onto Karen's hand that had instinctively moved into place.

"But the truth is, I've left a few details out about the past, and ... well ... yes ... I guess I have lied to you, but I never did ... this is starting to sound clichéd."

Karen had a tear in her eye.

"No, no, it's nothing like that. It's just all that stuff about the orphanage, and no relatives, well … it's not really accurate, well … not true actually. See … I just wanted to make a clean break from the past."

"So, why now after all this time?"

"Well, as I said, I've always meant to tell you anyway, but there's been a couple of calls from my cousin."

"Your cousin?"

"Yes, he's been calling because his father's apparently dying."

"You don't sound too upset about it."

"Yeah, well, it's not like he's young."

Karen was struggling to try and put it all together and didn't quite know what to ask.

"See, my dad had an older brother, and they took me in."

"I just don't understand why you couldn't tell me this before. It's not like you did anything wrong."

"I know … like I said I always meant to …" James didn't know what the right answer to that was.

"I had no idea."

"Well, anyway, it seems the old man is hell-bent on seeing me again."

"So when are you going?"

"I haven't decided *if* I am going yet."

"So it's safe to assume that you're not close."

"No."

"I'm wondering how close we are right now."

"Karen, I … I don't really know what to say, except that I never meant to hurt your feelings."

James couldn't believe how weak that sounded. Karen would think he had been studying the soaps for lines.

"I'm trying to understand here, James."

"I know and I appreciate it, I really do."

"Well what about … oh never mind."

"What …"

"Let's just leave this for now."

"Okay, whatever you want darling."

James nearly choked on the "darling." Try as he might it was destined to sound contrived.

"Let's just order dinner for now. We can talk about this later," said Karen.

Karen ordered a Greek salad, her appetite having deserted her. James thought about feigning a loss of appetite in sympathy, but the truth was he was starving and decided to risk the appearance of insensitivity in favour of a T-bone steak. Karen ate methodically and looked through James. James ploughed through his food and tried to think of a subject to initiate a conversation.

"Roberta Flack."

"Pardon," said Karen.

"Roberta Flack. That's who sang that song."

"Hmm."

James reached over and switched the car radio on in an effort to ward off the over-bearing silence. Karen turned it off.

"What are you going to do, James?"

"Well, I was thinking I could change the phone number and get an unlisted one."

"What?"

"You know, so Ronnie can't call again."

"That's hardly any solution is it? You should go back. You need to go back."

Karen was right. Karen was always right.

Chapter 8

It wis oan the news. It wis aw over the front page i the Evening News, an The Scotsman. That made it seem mair real. Final in a wye. It must be true then. The minister had said that it must be like a bad dream, but it wisnae quite like that. Ah kent Ah wisnae in a dream; mair like a trance. When Ah saw the papers Ah kent it wis true. There wis no chance they'd made a mistake. Up till then Ah'd held oot hope. Ah'd still thought that it could aw be a big mistake an Ah'd go hame an they'd aw be there sittin aroon the table huvin tea.

The dreams wir strange really. Ah mean, ye'd think that ye would dream aboot yer Mah an Dad, an brother an sister, but it wis the cold blackness i the loch mostly. Then Ah'd wake up an Ah'd think aboot them. Think aboot what they were thinkin aboot as the car slid intae the loch. Mah would be screamin, cos she would huv been in the front an seen it aw. Dad, foot so hard oan the brake it would almost be through the floor, desperate tae try an stoap the unthinkable fi happenin. Davy widnae have kent what wis happenin. Shona wis found clutchin her doll. Ah nivir kent what Granda would be dain. Probably tellin Davy an Shona that ivrythin would be okay. Mibbee no, but Ah liked tae think that. Then Ah'd feel aw alone. Ye see films oan the TV aboot tragedies an ye wonder why the survivors dinnae go an kick the crap ootta the bus driver, or whoever caused the accident, but when it happens tae ye that's no what ye want tae dae. In fact, if truth be telt Ah felt a little bit sorry fir him. Ah mean he should huv been mair careful, but ye could tell he felt like shite. Me takin a run at him nivir really entered ma mind.

Ah nivir hud ony say in the funeral. Ah didnae pay much attention tae what the minister hud tae say, but it entered ma heid onywye. He said a bunch i nice things aboot ma Mah an Dad. Talked aboot ma Granda bein in the war. Didnae say much aboot Davy an Shona except that it wis a tragedy that their lives were snuffed oot so early. Ah remember that because i the wye he said snuffed. He leaned forward an hung oantae the "s" like a snake an shook his heid as he finished oaf wi the rest i the word. He wis nice enough though an before the funeral started he told me that people would probably say some things that didnae make sense, an no tae worry aboot it because they were jist tryin tae be sympathetic. Ah didnae think much aboot it until this stewpit old timer came up tae me an said he kent jist how Ah must be feelin. Funny thing, Ah felt a whole lot mair like takin a swing at him than Ah did the bus driver.

Ah didnae cry at aw at the funeral, which made me feel guilty. A couple i women were snifflin a bit. Ah couldnae see them cos Ah wis right up at the front. Mrs Donaldson sung a song an she wis huvin trouble keepin it together. She wis a friend i ma Mah's. She sung a lot at the church, an when she did, me an Jeff Baxter aye hud a good laugh cos she wis kinda fat wi huge tits, an when she breathed in they'd rise so far up ye'd swear she hud tae fall backwards. But she nivir did, an Ah think it wis a tribute tae her high heels that acted as a counter balance. Ah wisnae laughin the day though an probably nivir wid again. Ah suppose Ah should've been grateful tae Jeff cos Ah hud stayed at his place so ma Granda could go up tae Oban in the car. But Ah didnae want tae talk tae him.

Mah nivir hud ony brothers or sisters. She hud two cousins in

Australia. Melbourne, Ah think. But they nivir even exchanged Christmas cards or wrote letters. Ma Gran showed me a picture once. Ah cannae remember what they looked like, except that they were wearin sunglasses an leanin against a car. Couldnae even tell ye what their names were. Ma Dad jist hud the one brother who wis a few years older than him. Uncle Archie. He showed up at the funeral wi Aunt Mabel an Ronnie, who wis a few years older than me. Uncle Archie seemed a bit uneasy, shiftin aboot in his seat. Might've been because he wis in a church, or mibbee because he wis thinkin aboot the accident, but mair than likely he wis jist restless because he needed a drink an he wisnae used tae wearin a tie. Onywye, efter the service the three i them came up tae me, an Uncle Archie said how awfie it wis an that Ah'd jist huftae make the best i things, cos they certainly couldnae take me in even though they wish they could, whatever that meant. Ronnie looked completely uninterested the whole time, didnae even huv the decency tae stare at his shoes. Aunt Mabel nivir said onythin. But then she nivir did as far as Ah could remember.

"Jimmy, on behalf of the entire school, we want to extend our condolences," said the heidmaister as he thrust oot his hand as if Ah'd jist won a scholarship tae the Royal High.

"It's a terrible shame," offered Mr Galloway. There followed an awkward silence fir them, but which seemed as nae consequence tae me. Finally, Mr Galloway gied me a brown parcel.

"It's an important year," he started, "and there's no sense falling too far behind, and so I brought some work for you to do."

So there Ah wis surrounded by a lot i people hell-bent oan appearin carin in front i their friends, an clutchin a bundle i books wrapped in brown paper an tied wi string. Ah'll say one thing though: at least bereavement offers the luxury i remainin silent.

It came as a big relief when ivryone finally went hame. Aw Ah really wanted tae dae wis go tae ma bed an be alone. Of course, it wisnae ma bed, but at least Ah wis alone. It wis still light ootside, but late enough tae be quiet. Ah could see the picture oan the wa opposite me. It was nuthin special. Jist a vase i flowers; but if ye looked closely at it ye could see that it wis made up i hundreds i postage stamps. A collage. The Queen's heid, Canada geese, an assorted other images hud been cut up intae wee pieces tae create this vase i flowers. It wis a far cry fi the picture i Dennis Law that hung oan ma bedroom wa at hame. Dennis thrustin his heid forward, the veins in his neck lookin like they would soon burst, as he latched his foreheid ontae the ba, aw the while huddin ontae the cuffs i his shirt like he did. Oan the far wa there wis a photie i their daughter. Ah think her name wis Elaine, an she lived in London now. She looked awfie serious, like her lips hud been stuck together. Ah missed ma ain bed an the pictures oan the wa, then Ah felt guilty cos Ah should be missin ma family, so Ah started tae think i the cold black loch again. Ah hope Granda held ontae Davy an Shona.

"Jimmy, come on in and have a seat," said the minister. Ah'd nivir been in his study before. The whole room wis surrounded by books, save for where the door wis an the windie. Ah couldnae help but look aroon.

"Do you like books, Jimmy?"

"Some books, aye."

"What do you like to read?"

"Onythin as long as it's interestin."

"Well, you might find something interesting to read here."

"Is that why ye wanted me tae come in here, Mr McCrae?"

"Actually Jimmy, we need to talk about where you will be living."

"Ah'll be livin wi ma Gran when she gets oot the hoaspital."

"Ah yes well, I'm not sure that's feasible really. Your

grandmother is still quite ill and I don't think we can reasonably expect you will be able to live with her in the near future."

"Here's the tea," said Mrs McCrae as she walked right intae the study.

There wis a tray wi three cups an saucers, an a plate wi three Jacob's Club biscuits surrounded by about a dozen Rich Teas.

"Would you like tea or milk, James?"

"Tea, please."

Mrs McCrae was old, about forty-five Ah'd guess. She hud a really nice smile, even although she hud slightly buck teeth. Ah think that at some point long ago she'd decided that her misshapen teeth wirnae goanni prevent her fi smilin. It wis hard tae get used tae seein her without a hat oan, cos she always wore one tae church. Somehow Ah jist expected that she'd wear one at her hoose. Mr McCrae wore his white collar aw the time, even when he sat an read the paper efter tea.

"What kind of biscuit would you like, James?"

"Jacob's Club please."

"I thought you'd say that," she said as she handed me one.

"As I was saying, Jimmy; arrangements have been made for you to live at a home for young people. There will be other boys in similar circumstances to you."

At that he leaned forward, inter-locked his fingers together, and placed them oan his tidy desk.

"Unfortunately your uncle is … unable to have you stay with him."

Mrs McCrae nodded deliberately.

"It'll jist be till ma Gran gets hame right?"

"Well, as I said, perhaps you shouldn't build your hopes on that."

Ah wisnae too concerned. He didnae ken ma Gran as well as Ah did.

"I know that this is a lot for you to think about now, Jimmy."

Actually Ah wis thinkin aboot how someone could possibly be eatin a Rich Tea biscuit when they could've hud a Jacob's Club, but there he wis dippin it in his tea. Ah wis wonderin if when ye goat old ye felt obliged tae pass up chocolate biscuits, or if ye really preferred tae huv a Rich Tea. Ah wis glad old age wis a long way oaf fir me yet.

"Can we still go up an see ma Gran oan Friday, Mr McCrae?"

"Of course."

Mr McCrae drove a shiny, black Sunbeam. It wisnae very new, but he kept it up nicely. Ah dinnae ken how onyone could paint a car called a Sunbeam black, but there ye are. When Ah wis younger we used tae sing a chorus at the Sunday school: *A sunbeam, a sunbeam, Jesus wants me for a sunbeam*. It wis ages before Ah realised it wis talkin aboot a ray i light. Ah hud no idea why Jesus wanted me tae be a family car. Ah wonder if onyone else wis thinkin that? Probably no. What an eejit Ah wis. Mrs McCrae wis wavin fi the garden. She'd been straightenin up the peonies that lined the path.

"Not the best spot for that kind of flower really."

"Why's that, Mr McCrae?"

"They need to be in a bigger bed where it doesn't matter if they spread out, or fall over. They're just clogging up the path there."

"Ah suppose so."

Ye'd expect an old minister tae drive slow, like he hud aw the time in the world. No this one. He'd gie Jackie Stewart a run fir his money. It wis a bit strange really cos he talked slowly an deliberately, sometimes turn an look at me. Ah wished he wouldnae.

"I know you'd prefer to live with your Gran, but I think you'll find Logan House a very nice place. I suppose what I'm trying to say, is that I hope you give it a chance. I think you'll find over time that it'll be a place where you can grow and learn."

"Hmm."

The long driveway wis sheltered oan either side by tall rhodedendron bushes at the height i their bloom. Admittedly it wis very nice, an even Mr McCrae felt compelled tae slow doon an take it in. Logan House emerged at the end, as if detached fi the rest i the city.

"Stuart Logan made his fortune in the tea trade in India."

"Oh aye?"

"Yes, well it seems he himself was a … well an orphan, and he left a sum of money for this home."

An orphan. Orphan. Ah hudnae really thought i masel as bein an orphan, but Ah suppose Ah wis. Orphan. It sounded strange. Sounded mair like the name i a car. Ladies an gentlemen, Ford unveils the brand new Ford Orphan. It would be a small car that goat good mileage.

It wis indeed a large hoose, covered in white stucco, an surrounded by mair purple rhodedendron bushes an huge trees, except tae the east side where ye could make oot a fitba field through the gap. Ah wis gainin interest.

"It's a nice big hoose, Mr McCrae."

"That's the spirit, Jimmy."

He rubbed his hand oan the top i ma heid. Ah hate that.

In we went through the front door. The lobby wis huge an hud a sittin area wi couches. In the middle there wir wooden stairs, nicely carved, that led tae the second floor. The floor wis a kinda scruffy red an white linoleum that robbed the place i any chance i passin fir classy. There wis a strange smell tae the place, that wis a combination i too many shoes lyin aboot, kitchen food, staleness, an a wee bit i perfume fi the rhodedendrons that wis sneakin in. Sounds in the distance hud a sort i hollow, echoey feel like when ye go intae a hoose wi no furniture or carpets.

"I'm going to introduce you to Mr Wilson. He's a very old and good friend of mine."

Before we goat tae his office, Ah heard a confident whistle, *Onward Christian Soldiers,* Ah think. Ye must be jokin. Turnin aroon Ah saw this tall gangly bloke, who hud tae be aboot the same age as Mr McCrae. His brown troosers were a bit short, drainpipes, an he wore a pair i black shoes that came tae a point. He hud a green cardigan over a tatty white shirt that turned up slightly at the collars. The blue tie wis a complete waste i effort.

"Mr McCrae," he bellowed oot, bringin the soldiers tae an abrupt halt.

"Mr Wilson, so good to see you."

They shook each other's hands forcefully, an Mr Wilson patted Mr McCrae oan the back. Ah dinnae ken what it is aboot adults that keeps them fi usin first names when they're in the presence i onyone under the age i sixteen. They've kent each other fir donkey's years, but because Ah'm stahnin there they huftae call each other by their surnames. Like the whole security i the hame wis dependent oan the secrecy i the maister's first name.

"Well, well, this must be Jimmy McPherson."

At that he placed his hands oan his hips, airms stickin oot tae the sides, an strained his neck as he looked me over. Ah half expected him tae break intae a John Cleese, Ministry i Silly Walks impersonation.

"Hullo."

"James likes football," offered Mr McCrae.

"Is that right?"

"Aye."

"Well then, you'll have to play with the other boys. They play every night after tea, and now that summer holidays are upon us there are lots of activities planned."

Ah jist nodded.

"Here is the folder," said Mr McCrae, an he passed it tae Mr Wilson. As they made the exchange, oot popped ma report card an Mr Wilson scooped it up wi his bony hand. Lookin at it he smiled an said: "You've done very well Jimmy, especially in English."

"James is an avid reader," offered Mr McCrae.

"You're all set for secondary school in September then?"

"Aye, Ah suppose so."

Chapter 9

Terminal Three of Pearson International Airport was a new experience for James, and despite Karen's assurances that she had driven there before, he periodically offered directions, more to alleviate pre-flight stress, than to be of any actual help to Karen. It wasn't that he was afraid of flying, rather the travel experience in its entirety was the antitheses of what James sought to embrace. The lack of familiarity, the crowds of people, and the necessity of placing oneself in the hands of others was a major source of concern.

Toronto International Airport, as it was formerly and more aptly named, while perhaps not the biggest in the world, shared the frenzy and chaos associated with large airports. Some years ago it had been re-named Pearson International in honour of Canada's fourteenth prime minister, who despite many other endeavours is best remembered for being in office when Canada first raised her own flag in 1965. If that act was expected to inflict a sense of nationhood on a post-colonial dominion, it must be said, from the dawn of a new millennium perspective, that it has struggled to do so. Not failed mind you. But struggled. Similarly, if the re-naming of Toronto International to Toronto Pearson was intended to inflict a sense of order and identity, then it has failed. Not struggled to do so, but failed. Yet as James entered the new Terminal Three, it appeared as a veritable oasis of serenity, a million miles, not metres as actually was the case, away from the pandemonium of Terminal One. Terminal One, where, invariably, extended families numbering forty-seven individuals, having mortgaged their home to park for the day, waited impatiently for an aged grandmother to emerge through the sliding doors signalling the end of a harrowing flight from the old country, whether it be Poland, Greece, Italy, or Sri Lanka.

"I wish I was coming with you," offered Karen in an obligatory fashion. James smiled. This was a trip that had to be undertaken alone, and Karen knew that.

"Well goodbye, good luck."

"Thanks ... I ..."

"Let's move it along," blurted the fascist traffic cop with the permanent scowl.

"You love me, I know, and I love you. Call me."

James planted a kiss on his wife's lips. He stood there dutifully for a moment and watched Karen weave her way around a stretch limousine and disappear into the sea of vehicles, as if she had been sucked into the giant vacuum that drew everyone back to Toronto.

It was seven thirty, a full ninety minutes before his plane was due to take-off. That would be a lengthy wait for James, but as far as the airline was concerned, James was cutting it close. Being an international flight, the airline's valued customers were technically expected to arrive two days prior to departure, or at least some obscene length of time which would make it easier for the airline, but guaranteed a hellish spell of boredom for the would be passengers.

The interior of Terminal Three fulfilled what the pristine exterior had promised, a vast crystal palace that was fresh and new, and had there not been the obvious reminders, you had the sense that you were entering an upscale mall. The abundance of luggage being toted here and there, the odd airline staff member walking briskly, and the occasional muffled announcement across the intercom spoiled the illusion of the piazza. A fountain would have topped it off, thought James as he managed to locate the Canux Airlines counter.

There was by now only three people ahead of him, the novices who had trustingly arrived shortly after lunch having been processed and were by now no doubt milling about the departure lounge door, waiting to get in, lest the plane leave without them. James stepped up and was met with the expected transparent welcome from the well-groomed clerk. Tall and shapely, perfect teeth, though on the large side, and a Caribbean accent, this was surely who Elton John had in mind. Evidently arriving ninety minutes prior to an international flight did not warrant a chastising. James stood there working on the appropriate facial expression in deference to the professionally effusive clerk, who having perused James' ticket was busily punching entries into the computer.

"Mr McPherson, you have been upgraded to business class," declared Island Girl, with an even fuller smile.

"Are you sure?" asked James, rather taken aback.

"Quite sure. Can I have your bags sir?"

"Actually I just have a carry on bag."

"I'll just put this on," she said as she affixed a red "priority" sticker, that stood out rather pretentiously on his black bag.

James was handed his boarding pass and directed by the ever smiling clerk to the VIP lounge. Karen had tried to persuade him to fly business class, but he had resisted, governed as he was by his parsimonious and careful nature. James smiled on the inside as he made his way to the lounge, thinking how pleased Karen would be with her devious self as she made her way back across highway 407.

Approximately twelve seconds into the VIP lounge it became abundantly clear to James there could be no going back to cattle class ever again. He fixed himself a double Chivas, promptly slunk deep into a plush leather armchair, actually relaxed. His obligatory reading material, ironically Alan Spence's *Way To Go,* never leaving his side pocket. The announcement for boarding came almost as a disappointment, but James managed to find the departure gate and promptly boarded the dubious mechanical contraption that seemed to be emitting altogether too much noise for a stationary position. Past the point of no return he was ushered into his seat by a slender young woman who assured James that his comfort was of her utmost concern, and to that end she proffered an impressive array of beverages. In fact it became very evident that the flight attendant had been sincere, as before the plane had left the ground, James had managed to weigh into a third glass of a very credible Bordeaux. This was far more pleasing than enduring the emergency procedure demonstration that the stewardess was perfunctorily performing to the cretins in economy. Business class passengers, it appeared, were deemed to be literate and therefore directed to peruse the instructions in the manual located in the pouch of the seat. James decided to forego this educational opportunity in favour of devoting his full attention to his wine, which along with the Chivas was beginning to produce the desired effect. Besides, in the event of an actual emergency, James was convinced that the best plan would be to wrap the pillows around his ears to muffle the screaming that would likely be the most distressing feature of any calamity.

James was awakened by the captain's baritone voice over the intercom, informing the passengers that the flight was on time and would be arriving in a fog shrouded Glasgow airport at 8:30am. It came as welcome news as James' sleep had been fitful and sporadic, fuelled as it was by alcohol; it had been punctuated with fragments of dreams that made little sense. The pilot didn't actually say "fog shrouded," as that could have been translated as alarming to those passengers who actually had paid attention to the safety demonstration, some six hours previous. The phrase used was more benign: rather cloudy and light rain. James speculated there was probably a little guidebook for airline staff designed to eliminate any vestige of terminology that, while being more apt, could be construed as liable to create panic. Wind shear was probably described as, "rather breezy conditions," and thunderstorms as, "intermittent light and periodic significant moisture." In fact, being a pilot in this day could be considered an excellent precursor for a career in Canadian politics. A pilot by the age of say forty-five, would have become quite adept at gilding his language and delivering meaningless sound bites in a relaxed comforting manner, all the while pretending to fly a vast aircraft, when in actual fact a computer did most of the significant work, yet keenly aware of the indicators, ever ready to change course should that prove to be a popular decision. The day would surely arrive when pilots would outnumber lawyers in the House of Commons.

One deep breath wasn't enough to dissuade James' heart from its increased tempo, as the inevitability of his destination became apparent. Here he was, some twenty-two years since his departure, about to return to the land of his birth. A glance out the window revealed only that the captain's forecast was accurate, in an understated sort of way, yet he was reluctant to withdraw and continued to attempt to catch a glimpse of land through the clouds. Nothing could be seen until suddenly the runway was visible and almost immediately the plane had touched down.

The millisecond the seat belt light had gone out a queue emerged pressing against the exit, as if their life depended upon it. James scanned them briefly, attempting to imprint a memory in the hopes that the next time he saw one of them, they would be lingering around the baggage terminal, anxiously awaiting their battered bag, which hopefully would be the last one to appear on the carousel.

"Business or pleasure?" enquired a rather disinterested official without looking up.

"Aah … pleasure, I suppose."

This less than convincing response was enough to cause the retirement-nearing official to glance at James, but he seemed satisfied that there was no threat to national security and waved James through with a well practised gesture of the arm that made James feel like an annoying child pestering his elder.

The car rental went relatively smoothly. A red Mondeo was the result. Standard transmission. This was the only drawback, as James would have preferred automatic, in deference to the challenge of driving on the left. Upon entering the car, the prudent thing to do prior to embarking on a journey in rainy, misty, conditions in an unfamiliar land where vehicles drove on the opposite side of the road, would have been to familiarise oneself with the car's controls and perhaps peruse a map. However James possessed a Y chromosome which by design prevented him from doing any of the above. New gene therapy held future hope, but for the time being, he was off and cruising, attempting to become accustomed to the clutch as he headed in a vaguely eastward direction.

Chapter 10

"It's very rarely this quiet in here, Jimmy, very rarely indeed," said Mrs Wilson as we climbed up the stairs, which wir well worn in the middle. Likely Mrs Wilson, or matron as Ah wis supposed tae call her, wis the most responsible fir this state i affairs. She wis as fat as Mr Wilson wis skinny, but very cheery. Her smilin mooth wis bordered by red cheeks that gave her a kind i Santa Claus type i look. Obviously there were no white whiskers, but given a few mair years, they would likely appear. There wis awready somethin above her lip that wisnae left over fi a glass i milk, if ye ken what Ah mean. As she made her wye up the stairs she emitted a funny sort i whish, wheesh, wheesh sound that as near as Ah could tell wis due tae excessive rubbin noises comin fi underneath her dress. But it didnae bear thinkin aboot too much cos it wisnae long till dinner time.

"You can have this bed here Jimmy," she said, restin her meaty hand oan the toap bunk near the door.

"Ye mean Ah can huv the toap bunk. It's no taken then?"

"It's all yours Jimmy. You can put your clothes in this drawer here," she said smilin aw the mair, but she wis probably jist happy tae be up the stairs an gie her thighs a chance tae cool doon.

"The bathroom's down the hall on the left. The other boys will be back shortly and they'll show you the ropes. Well, good show," she said an oaf she trundled. Ah didnae really think people actually said: "Good show," ootside i prisoner i war films, like Trevor Howard, but it seemed tae go wi matron.

"You, Jimmy?"

"Aye."

"Ah'm, George. Ye've tae wash yer paws before dinner."

Ah followed George doon the hall.

"This is the boys' bog. If ye make a mess, ye've tae clean it up. Ye huftae wash before ivry meal, an sometimes they check."

The other boys were lookin me over as Ah washed ma hands, which wirnae really clarty, but it didnae seem tae matter.

Dinner wis a serve yersel type i deal. Mince an tatties. The peas were awfie hard, but they didnae make ye eat them aw. Matron probably ate the leftovers. There wis even jelly. A wee square i green jelly wi a squirt i white cream oan toap, which hud been put oan too soon an hud started tae melt an run doon the side. Better than Ah'd expected though. Mr Wilson came over.

"Is George showing you the ropes, Jimmy?"

"Aye, thanks."

"George," he said, "Jimmy likes to play football, so perhaps you can see that he gets in the next game."

"Aye, Mr Wilson," said George. "Y'any good?"

"No bad," Ah said, no wantin too build masel up too much.

"You wantin that?" he asked, pointin tae ma jelly.

"Aye, Ah dae."

Ah pulled it over closer tae masel, an as Ah looked round, Ah could see a lot i eyes lookin back in ma direction. Ivryone seemed tae be finished their dinner except fir me, even the girls oan the other side i the hall. No wantin tae hold ivryone up Ah jist wolfed doon ma jelly, which wis too bad cos Ah always liked tae eat jelly slowly, meltin it in ma mooth before Ah swallowed. Tae make matters worse Ah burped up some gas, which tasted i mince, right when Ah wis chompin doon ma jelly. As soon as Ah wis done, Mr Wilson stood up again an gave oot the announcements. Somethin aboot a trip tae the seaside, which ivryone seemed awfie pleased aboot. When he wis finished he dismissed us, an up we goat wi oor dishes. George nivir said onythin so Ah jist copied him. Cutlery in the big grey tray, efter ye hud scraped oaf yer plate an put it in the white tray.

"We're no allowed tae play till half past one," said George.

"So what dae we dae now?"

"Yer supposed tae read a book in the dorm, but naebdy does."

"Whadye dae then?"

"Jist grab a book fi the library an sit oan yer bed till half one."

George showed me where the library wis then went upstairs. It wisnae a very big room but it hud a lot i books an magazines. Ah grabbed a National Geographic an went up tae the dorm. The rest i the boys were awready there, sittin oan their beds wi a book or a magazine. George hud the toap bunk across the room fi me. He wis probably the oldest boy in the room. Certainly wis the biggest; no jist tall but thick too. Looked like he'd be pretty tidy, so best tae stay oan his good side. He wis right aboot naebdy readin. Ivryone wis jist talkin back an forth. The book wis jist fir show, in case matron checked in. Mind you, they could probably hear her comin wi the sound her thighs made, an they'd huv plenty i time tae pretend they were readin.

Ah kinda glanced at ma National Geographic. It wis old but it didnae really matter. A piece aboot New York. Seventeen inches i snow one day in the winter. That would be somethin tae see. There wis an alarm clock oan the table that hud two drums oan toap, wi the wee hammers seemin anxious tae let loose an explode wi noise, but time seemed tae be goin awfie slow, cos Ah wis keen tae play fitba. But at twenty efter one, a boy near the big windie let a right loud fart go, an that goat ivryone laughin. It wisnae long before the whole dorm wis echoin wi the sound i farts, an we aw laughed aw the louder. Next thing we kent, Mr Wilson popped his heid in an told us aw tae be quiet an read or we'd huftae stay in till two. The laughter quickly subsided, but one i the younger boys in the bunk next tae George's couldnae help himsel an he let oot first a snicker, then a laugh. Ah could see him shakin tryin tae keep fi laughin oot loud, an then he let oot a rippin fart fir a wee laddie, an we aw were near pishin oorsels laughin again. Ah didnae want tae, what wi Mr Wilson stahnin there, but Ah couldnae help masel. Mr Wilson eventually clapped his hands twice loudly, an said: "Right you give me no choice. Two o'clock it is," an oot he went. We aw laughed oor erses oaf fir a couple i minutes mair. Enjoy the crime; dae the time. Ah dinnae ken why he didnae find it funny, but mibbee it reminded him i matron fartin, an that wouldnae be funny if ye were married tae her. Be dangerous probably.

Two o'clock came eventually an we aw barrelled doon the stairs, through the hall an oot the back wye tae the field. It wisnae a full sized pitch, an the goals wirnae regulation, but it did huv painted lines. It wis oor dorm against the other, except fir one girl, Alison who ivryone called Ally, but she went oan the other side.

"Jimmy, ye go in goal," said George.

"Ah'm no very good in goals. Better if a play oot."

"Jist go in goals the now, cos yer tall."

"Well, jist fir a wee while then."

In Ah went, an stood there fir aboot ten minutes before Ah hud onythin tae dae, till finally a pass back. Instead i pickin it up Ah played it oot the box, but oot i nowhere came that Ally lassie an took the ba oaf me. She didnae waste ony time tuckin it in.

"You're useless," said this boy oan ma team. Wisnae sure i his name.

"You go in then, if ye're so good."

"Ma granny could huv stoaped that, ye spastic. Beaten by a lassie."

"Put yer granny in the goals then."

"Fuckew," he says, an he pushed me back.

So Ah shoved him, an that wis it. He came right up tae ma face an Ah thought he wis goin tae gie me a shove again, but before Ah hud a chance tae dae onythin he stoated me wi his heid. As Ah fell back Ah felt the sting spread aw over ma face, an then the taste i warm blood roll back ma throat. Ah started tae get up an felt ma eyes start tae water, but Ah could see him stahnin there lookin doon at me. Awready the chant i "fight, fight, fight," wis oan. As Ah goat up Ah spat a mouthful i blood, which near as Ah could tell wis comin fi ma nose, an through ma bleary vision Ah could see him smirkin at me.

"Right ya bas'," Ah says, an before Ah wis stahnin, Ah took him doon wi a rugby tackle. What he did fi that point Ah cannae remember. All Ah mind is jist swingin away, as hard as Ah could at his face. Next thing Ah kent Ah wis bein pulled oaf i him by Mr Wilson an some other man.

That wis ma first real fight. Ah'd hud scraps before, but Ah'd nivir really felt like hurtin onyone, always lettin up a bit. Ma Dad hud showed me how tae fight, well, box really. Lead wi the left. Jab, jab, jab, then come in heavy wi the right when ye hud the openin. Trouble wis ma Dad nivir told me that a fight would start wi some bastard stoatin me in the heid. Ah'd always thought it wid be a square go like.

"Tut, tut, tut … my word. That is a nasty mess." Ah nivir said nowt, while matron dabbed away at ma face wi a damp cloth, like she wis soakin up the gravy wi a slice i breid.

"This simply won't do will it, Jimmy?"

It didnae seem worth answerin. What would Ah huv said: "Actually, yes it will do"? It wis like sittin in the chair wi a chatty dentist, askin ye stupid questions while it feels like he's tryin tae jam the Forth Road Bridge intae yer mooth. For a while ye try an make an effort, mumblin an movin yer eyes until ye think: what's the point. She might've gone oan forever dabbin an tut tuttin tryin tae make me think aboot what Ah hud done, but as Ah lay there aw

Ah could think aboot wis that ma earlier suspicions hud been confirmed as she definitely hud the beginnin's i a moustache.

"I was hoping that you would have been introduced to Mr Adams under more pleasant circumstances Jimmy, but I'm afraid that his first encounter with you involved pulling you off another boy."

"Aye, sorry aboot that, Mr Wilson."

"Mr Adams runs the summer programme here."

"I don't like to see fights, son," piped in this Mr Adams as he slid oaf the desk that he'd been sittin oan. He hud a funny voice, too high fir a grown man, but no like a woman. Mair like a wee laddie. His black hair coulda used a good wash, an that's mibbee why he wis wearin a cap indoors. Ma Granda used tae wear his bunnet in the hoose, but that wis tae keep his bald heid warm Ah think. Ma Mah used tae say that it wis caulder inside his flat than it wis ootside.

"You know when we have a problem with someone else, we need to try and talk it out, hmm. Violence is really no solution to any problem now is it?"

That wis it. The cap wis what reminded me. Put this Mr Adams in short troosers an a stripy school tie an he wis Jimmy Clitheroe.

"Now is it, Jimmy?"

"Ah suppose so, Mr Adams."

Mr Wilson wis sittin at his desk occasionally gently noddin in agreement wi Jimmy Clitheroe. As he nodded he looked through me unaware i how daft he looked contortin his lips while his two index fingers did push-ups against each other. Finally he goat up. "Usually it would be six of the strap."

There wis a silence fir a minute while Ah assume he thought Ah would be crappin boulders.

"But since you're new and not fully aware of our rules, I'll make an exception today."

He stoaped the finger push-ups an looked right doon at me as if he wis peerin below make believe glasses. It wis as if at that moment he'd wished that he would've worn his glasses fir extra effect. If he thought Ah wis aboot tae kiss his erse in gratitude he wis sadly mistaken an Ah jist sat there. Not an hour before, Ah'd jist aboot hud ma nose pushed intae the back i ma heid, an his strap didnae trouble me too much. He wis so skinny onywye it would probably huv been a sham.

"Well then, off you go to the dormitory, and let this serve as a warning."

Ah goat up tae go an started oaf doon the hall. Before Ah wis oot i earshot Ah could hear Jimmy Clitheroe.

"Remember, my door is always open to talk."

Aye that'll be right, we'll invite Bill an Ben an Sooty an huv a party.

Naebdy talked tae me at teatime, except Ally who asked if Ah wis okay. She wis awfie nice lookin, but Ah didnae feel like talkin much right then. But efter, when Ah wis jist hangin aboot behind the hoose, a wee guy came over tae me.

"How's the beak?"

"Ah'll live."

"Ah'm Charlie."

"Jimmy."

"Where you fi?"

"In the toon. Doon Drylaw wye. You?"

"Ah'm fi Aberdeen."

"What ye dain here then?"

"Ma Mah's deid an ma Da's away the now."

"Away where?"

"Jist away, ken."

Charlie hudnae moved. Stood there wi his hands in his pockets, heid oan an angle. It dawned oan me that his Dad wis in the nick.

"What did he go away fir?"

"Chorin. Well chorin fi banks."

At that he cracked a smile an ye could tell that he was kinda proud i his old man. He came closer an Ah could see he'd been in the wars himsel. He hud two big plasters oan the back i his heid, both in the shape i an "H."

"What does that stand fir? Haggis Heid?"

"Split ma heid open last night when Ah, eh Ah fell oot the toap bunk. That's why ye goat the toap, cos matron says that Ah hud tae stay oan the bottom bunk fir now."

"How old are ye?"

"Thirteen," he said. It wis hard tae believe cos he wis quite wee an thin.

"Shh."

Ah woke up. Didnae ken what wis up, or where Ah wis fir a minute. Ah could jist make oot what Ah thought wis Charlie's face in the dark. Sure enough. He took his bony wee hand oaf ma mooth.

"Ah jist need tae use yer bunk fir a minute," he whispered.

"Ah didnae figure ye fir a poof, Charlie," Ah said.

"Dinnae be daft."

At that he hoisted himsel up an pushed the trap door oan the ceilin open, an moved it tae the side. He wis up in the attic in no time. Ah stuck ma heid up the hole only tae see him crawl oan the beams, torch in his mooth. Ah could hear somethin below, so Ah quickly wis doon an under the covers, but it wis only Raymie tossin an turnin, no doubt still feelin the doin Ah'd laid oan him in the efternoon.

Efter aboot fifteen minutes, Charlie stuck his heid through the hole.

"Aw clear?" he whispered.

"Aye."

He wis doon in a flash, replaced the trap door, an wis aboot tae climb doon the ladder when Ah grabbed his airm.

"What the …"

"Shh, Ah'll tell ye the morn."

At breakfast Ah sat next tae wee Charlie, playin wi ma porridge, tryin tae choke doon the odd spoonful.

"Tools."

"Eh."

"Ah needed some tools fi the janny's oaffice."

"What fir?"

"Chorin. Dae ye want tae gie me a hand?"

"Ah'm in enough trouble awready."

"Ye'll no get caught. The key is tae take stuff they'll no miss fir a while."

"Says who?"

"Ma Da."

"This the same dad that's in the nick?"

"Bad luck, that's aw."

"Aye, well count me oot."

"Ye'll no shop me will ye?"

"Course no."

He seemed satisfied, an Ah didnae think that he thought Ah wis scairt, so Ah went back tae mushin ma porridge aroon the bowl.

"Jimmy, could you come with me to my office please?"

It wis Mr Wilson, wearin the same clothes as yesterday, except he'd switched tae a blue shirt that looked like it hud a bit mair life in it, an he didnae huv the cardigan oan cos it wis fairly warm the day. Somethin hud tae be done aboot thae brown drainpipes though.

Ah thought mibbee he'd changed his mind an decided tae gie me the belt, but when a goat tae his office, Mr McCrae wis there.

"Mr McCrae, Ah thought it wis tomorrow we were goin tae see ma Granny."

"Perhaps you should sit down, Jimmy."

The last time someone said those words rushed back tae me. Now Ah kent why people said it. When Ah wis told aboot ma family, he said: "Sit down, son," so Ah did. Now Ah kent it didnae mean sit doon; it meant bad news wis comin.

"What?"

Mr McCrae put his airm aroon me.

"I'm afraid that your grandmother passed away last night. I'm very sorry."

"We're all so very sorry," threw in Mr Wilson.

Ah hud heard it aw before. Ivryone wis so very sorry.

Chapter 11

The drizzle had transformed into a steady rain adorning the bright-red, double-decker Glasgow buses with a gleam that seemed alien on such a dreary dull and wet June morning. Despite this James felt somewhat revitalised as he quickly became accustomed to driving on the left, and feeling no worse for his limited sleep the abbreviated night before. The volume of traffic was such that it rendered any temptation to drive on the right unthinkable, and it was only when he decided to slip off the highway that it felt like an effort to stay on the appropriate side of the divide.

Having absolutely no real time commitments was a luxury that James seldom enjoyed and the sign for Loch Lomond, in this set of circumstances, proved too much of a temptation to resist. But as he headed toward the famed body of water, unsure if he was on the high or low road, the rain came down with ever increasing purpose. What at first seemed to be a good idea degenerated into an endurance test as sightseeing ventures often do. The rain's accompanying mist, rather than serve to enhance or romanticise the loch, merely irritated James as he attempted fleeting glances. Driving quickly became a task again rather than a pleasurable endeavour. And as much as he still thought it was a good idea to view the fabled loch while he was in the vicinity, it was the unforeseen experiences that managed to kindle in him memories long relegated to the corners of his mind, never to be revisited unless pried loose by a visual or olfactory cue.

A lone pheasant at the side of the road seemingly oblivious to the presence of the car as it sped by, or the ever watching cat's eyes delineating the road's centre line, which as a concession to the reliance on snow ploughs in Canada were a rarity there. Sights such as these were an unexpected key to a past, which had in James' mind been obscured by larger, more oppressing baggage that had formed a cloud in his head, ever threatening to release its poisonous load. James, constantly cognisant of its presence, had been careful not to do anything that might seed the cloud and he was well aware, at least on the unspoken level, that this trip had the potential to burst the cloud. Despite this knowledge, and despite the fury with which the rain came down, it was the sight of such things as gorse bushes set upon the unique Scottish landscape, or even otherwise prosaic features such as road signs, that captured James' imagination and he continued his journey with a sense of hope he had not enjoyed since Don Hutchison scored for Scotland in the first half against England at Wembley.

Old Archie, Ronnie, and Edinburgh still had to be dealt with, but for the present James was content to revel in what would be trivial and meaningless items to virtually everyone else on the planet. The sign for a lochside hotel was an invitation he felt obliged to pursue in the event its contents or ambience might offer up more gratifying reminiscences.

After a brief altercation with the gear stick, James managed to reverse the car into the parking spot. It was always best to back into a spot, he reasoned, in the event that conditions would alter and make extrication difficult. This was a lesson he had shared with Lisa as he was teaching her how to drive. A task that like so many others had been placed on hold for the present. But as he sat in the car it did not appear that the ample parking lot was likely to become crammed. Nevertheless, James lived by a litany of personal rules designed to free himself of unnecessary worry, so he would have backed the car into the spot even if it had been the only car left on the British Isles. In one sense his plan worked in that he felt more comfortable about trivial mundane issues, such as his ability to make his escape from a parking lot, or where his keys and wallet were located, but it tended to free his mind to worry about weightier matters. Granted, they were only weighty to James, but significant none the less.

The rain was still uncharacteristically heavy for this temperate part of the world, and in deference to James' belief that it was unlikely to continue, and the very real possibility that he would be forbidden a cigarette on the premises, he lit up in the car. Even with the window only slightly open however, the rain found its way inside. So rather than close the window he resolved to extinguish the source of the fumes and re-commit himself to a life without smokes. He hadn't so much planned this as he thought it would be a good idea when he first saw the "No Smoking" sign upon alighting the airplane. James thought that completely different surroundings might be an opportunity to quit, and in so doing greatly please Karen. But it wouldn't happen with half a pack in his jacket pocket, so as he entered the hotel he deposited the package into the wastepaper basket located just behind the vacant front desk.

With no human in sight and the dimly lit establishment appearing to be abandoned, James followed the arrow on the wall that promised to lead to the tea room, and with some luck a kilt clad local with a delightfully lilting accent ready to accommodate a lone tourist. But as James waited at the entrance to the tea room, he had to resort to clearing his throat in an effort to elicit a response, all the while wondering how long it would take him to fire someone should this ever occur at his restaurant. Finally, a young woman, a girl really, appeared from what presumably was the kitchen.

"Can Ah help you?" asked the waitress, head tilted seemingly permanently to one side, to the degree that she appeared flummoxed. Her brown hair was tied back severely, although she was attractive enough to get away with it; high cheekbones and a smattering of freckles on her small nose were sufficient to make James wonder if she was old enough to serve alcohol.

"*Yes, I was wondering if I could get a haircut*," James was tempted to say, as he wondered why his presence should be dealt with so obliquely.

"I was wondering if you serve lunch, or perhaps tea, in this tea room?"

Head straightening, finally, to reveal that she was not the victim of some strange affliction, she wiped her hands on her apron, and muttering something under her breath, presumably referring to obnoxious American tourists, she pulled a menu off the cabinet and proceeded to stride to a small table, which commendably was nicely appointed beside the fireplace. Without a word she headed for the safety of the kitchen, leaving James alone, which was very much to his liking. The fire was not lit which might have been due to the fact it was not yet noon, or perhaps because it was June, but certainly not because it was warm. James resolved should the young lady deign to reappear then some hot tea was in order.

"So what can Ah get you?"

"Hmm, how about the soup of the day. What is it today?"

"We don't have any yet. Our first bus isn't due in till one," said the expressionless waitress.

"Okay, perhaps you can tell me what you do have," said James.

"Well, there's just really scones for now. There might be a mince pie."

"How about some tea and a scone then."

James handed the menu back, wondering why it was given to him in the first place, barely managing to conceal a smile. As he waited alone, and as patiently as was possible for James, he privately wondered if he didn't prefer this kind of service to the superficially over-friendly North American brand. After all, he only wanted some food and drink, which back home seemed to always entail the server attempting to initiate a personal relationship with the customer. It was no longer possible to order so much as a soft drink without some bubbly waitress, serotonin pulsing through her brain, telling you her name, and what a great pleasure it would be for her to serve you. If current trends continued the typical restaurant would insist that prior to placing an order, you would be required to lie down on a couch and listen to the server's life story and then reciprocate by stating your problems. Presumably it was to make the customer comfortable, but more often than not, James felt that it put just as many customers ill at ease. For that reason he insisted on politeness, but not effusiveness at his establishment. It was a nice blend between over-board American culture and overly reserved British gentility, which was how he felt about Canada as a whole. It was a balance that he sought to maintain in the Pentland Gardens. Any efforts by his managers to alter this aspect of the business met with James' disapproval and probably a lecture on the follies of attempting to appropriate American culture and foist it upon unsuspecting Canadians, who only wanted a nice quiet meal and to mind their own business. It was a lecture James had given often and it usually finished with a caveat, warning that most customers were much more concerned with clean washroom facilities than the first name of their waitress.

The tea arrived and unfortunately so did the scone, which, had David used it against Goliath, would have felled him immediately, such was its density. Unwilling to risk a visit to a dentist on this trip, James let the piece of granite sit threateningly on his plate, and sipped his tea in solitude. Upon finishing, he foraged in his pocket and found enough change to cover the cost and left the hotel.

The rain had let up and was back to a more traditional pace. Intermittent mist and raindrops accompanied James as he made the short drive, by North American standards, across the country to the capital, resolving not to evade his destination any longer. By the time the Pentlands and the T-woods were in sight, the rain had all but abated, and there were some rays of sun finding their way through the clouds. So, rather than head for the city centre and a hotel, James bypassed the old neighbourhood and headed for Swanston Village at the foot of the Pentlands. There was something comforting about places that appear timeless, like the village with its thatched roofs and the hills themselves, adorned with sheep that always seemed so blissfully oblivious to everything around them. The scene took him back to summer days many years ago when he would spend the day climbing the hills, eating his lunch on the summit overlooking the city. On a good day it could be an invigorating experience; the warm winds seemingly wafting the spirit within, building the required strength to deal with the trials that awaited two thousand feet below. He would have to take a lunch to the top on this trip, only this time he would take the ski lift.

James followed the path for a few hundred yards, searched in vain for his initials that he was sure he carved into a tree back in 1975, then slowly made his way back down to his car. A crow cawed overhead loudly, then quieter as it soared eastward, then its sound was completely muffled by the drone of the wind. The hills would be there tomorrow, and the next day and for a thousand years hence, unchanging, no matter what they encountered.

James managed to find a parking spot near the bridges, but the incline was such that it made parallel parking an adventure. Nevertheless he was in. Placing his faith in the handbrake, he left with his meagre luggage, mentally congratulating himself for taking out the extra insurance. The first hotel was full, but the second had a room available and despite what seemed an exorbitant fee, James decided to take it at least for the first night. He managed to convince the bell boy that he was quite capable of carrying his own bag, such as it was, but the eager young man was not easily dissuaded, and felt it necessary to question James' decision every couple of minutes.

The room was larger than it appeared, as the presence of two double beds robbed it of any open space, and there was a pervading dimness despite the long June day, which had by now thrown off any predilection for rain. The bell boy turned on a lamp to compensate for the limited light that was passing through the undersized window and, after advising James that the room was equipped with a mini bar, made his way gingerly to the door, at which point he affected an expectant expression. Bewildered for a moment, James quickly recovered and managed to find what he felt was an appropriate monetary compensation for the ardent young man, whose thankful smile prompted James to wonder if he hadn't over done it and would pay for it by being pestered for the duration of his stay.

At the sight of a comfortable bed, James suddenly felt the toll of the travel, and decided upon a nap before dinner. The mini bar was appropriately well stocked with scotch, and James poured himself a drink, but after seeing the price of the tiny bottle, made a mental note to purchase a replacement before it was added to his bill.

James was quickly asleep and dreaming. It was a dream that was not new, but whose visits were infrequent. He found himself back in the woods near where he lived as a teenager. It always started out well enough, walking through the field of wild daffodils that led up to the woods skirting the neighbourhood. But once in the woods it quickly deteriorated as he made his way to the small clearing to the west of the old abandoned house. As he got closer he could hear the crackle, then see the orange flames wriggling upward, then the face of Ronnie, his dark eyes fixing on James as he emerged from the woods into the clearing. James awoke, perspiration on his brow and short of breath, his anguish compounded by not immediately knowing his whereabouts. A dream, that was all. Hotel room. Edinburgh, Y2K. And yes, scotch. James sat up on the bed, his pillow propped against the headboard for comfort, and finished his drink. He contemplated a call home to Karen, but given the difference in time decided to put that off until later. He found the remote for the television and soothed himself with the sound of an unfamiliar voice.

Chapter 12

Ah'd always dreaded the first day i school before, but despite Ronnie's warnin's that Ah wis liable tae get a doin ma first day, cos it wis tradition, Ah wis nivir mair keen tae start an get away fi the hoose. Ronnie said he couldnae walk wi me, cos he hud tae meet his mates at the Com. Ah wisnae too interested in goin by the Community Centre onywye. It jist wisnae a place ye wanted tae hang aboot. It wis hard man central, an ye were liable tae become victim tae the run an the boot, jist fir the sport i it. Ronnie hud goat awfie big over the summer, no that he wis wee tae begin wi an he ran wi some right nutters. They aw looked the same. Doc Marten boots, stay-pressed, sky-blue troosers, an a black Harrington jacket, an long sideburns if they could manage it. In the winter the jacket would be replaced wi an Abercrombie overcoat. They wouldnae be caught dead in the school uniform, but they followed their ain dress code mair strictly than the toffs did at Stuart Melville or the Royal High.

Ah wis up an away before Uncle Archie hud woken up, which wisnae hard. Ronnie wis awake, but no up yet, but he'd mumbled somethin aboot stayin near the front i the school next tae the biology pond and Ah would be awright there. Aunt Mabel wis sittin in the scullery suckin oan a cigarette, her mind away somewhere else. When Ah said cheerio she nivir said onythin, jist sat there starin intae space.

When Ah goat tae the school it wis still early an Ah didnae ken what tae dae wi masel. At primary school there wis aye a fitba game goin, before school, at playtime, an at dinner time. No here. Efter a while groups i people started tae gather near the doors. Catchin up wi each other fi the summer. Some hud the whole school uniform oan, an some didnae. Ah hud Ronnie's old blazer, an it didnae fit too bad.

"Ah wouldnae hing aboot there."

"George. How ye dain?"

"Ah'm awright but Ah wouldnae stand there if Ah wis you."

"How no?"

"Cos yer liable tae get thrown in the pond, it bein first day n'aw."

"Aye, right."

"Go over tae the blue door. That's where ye go in when the bell goes."

"Aye, thanks, George."

Ah moved away fi the pond feelin a bit lucky an a bit stewpit.

"So how come ye're no at Logan House any mair? Dinnae like us?"

"Naw, a liked it there, but efter ma Granny died ma Uncle said Ah hud tae live wi him."

At aboot quarter tae nine Ronnie an his mates showed up over by the biology pond, an it wisnae long efter that they grabbed a new, first-year boy an threw him in. They aw thought it wis hilarious. The pond wis only aboot a foot and a half deep, but it caught him so much by surprise that he fell backwards an goat completely soaked. Once he hud found his glasses, an collected his bag, he climbed oot, his face streamin wi tears. Ronnie gied him a boot as he tried tae get by, an a couple i his mates followed, their shiny DMs gettin their first action i a new season. The boy made his way tae the blue door where the first years were aw by now waitin. Naebdy dared go near him. That would huv been suicide.

A few minutes later the same thing happened, except this boy didnae loose his balance, an goat away wi only wet shoes an socks. He didnae greet or onythin, an jist tried tae laugh it oaf when he made it over tae his pals an the door, but ye could tell he wis pissed oaf. A crowd i younger hard men in trainin started tae gather near the pond, tryin tae get a better view, but they kent no tae get too close in case one i them goat jumped. It wis kinda like watchin one i thae animal pictures that sometimes came oan the telly. The young wildebeest that strayed away fi the herd an goat too close tae the hyenas, an the younger ones waitin in the wings fir their turn.

The next tae come over the bridge wis a first-year girl an naebdy touched her, but right behind her came this dippit lookin boy whose ma hud jist dropped him oaf in her brand new Renault. He wis aw decked oot in his new school uniform. He even hud a shiny new satchel. He might as well huv hud a sign oan his back that said: "Kick the shite oot i me, please." The poor bastard didnae see it comin at aw, an the hard men were gettin rougher, throwin in a few boots fir good measure. He wis jist twelve or thirteen, an couldnae huv hud an older brother or sister at the school tae warn him, so it wisnae his fault. But it made ye wonder what his ma wis thinkin aboot, dressin him up like that, droppin him oaf in a car, an especially a satchel in this place. The clueless sod started tae greet before he goat oot, fumblin fir a hanky tae stoap his nose fi bleedin, but he wis saved some mair Doc Marten action, cos the janny came oot tae break it up. The young hard men in trainin blew their dignity an ran away fi the scene, but Ronnie's crew jist sauntered away, except, that is, fir Ronnie.

"Move away fi this pond, right this instant."

Ronnie wisnae goin onywhere, an fir a second there wis a rumble i excitement in the expectation that he wis goanni take oan the janny. Jist when it looked like somethin wis aboot tae happen the bell rang, an face wis saved.

Ah didnae huv ony money fir dinner, so efter school Ah went straight back tae the flat tae make a jam piece, but when Ah goat there aw Ah could hear wis Uncle Archie yellin at the toap i his lungs. At first Ah jist thought he wis huvin a go at Aunt Mabel, but when Ah went intae the scullery, there she wis still sittin where she wis eight hours ago. She hud a right blank look tae her. The only thing she seemed tae dae wi any enthusiasm wis tae suck oan a cigarette. She didnae even make tea onymair since uncle Archie didnae come hame fir it very often. He wis usually at the pub early these days, huvin spent the afternoon at the bookie's, which wis only aboot a hundred yards fi the pub. Ah kent it wis a risk comin back early, but Ah wis starvin an Ah wis sure that he would huv been doon the bookie's by this time.

"Can Ah make a jam piece, Aunt Mabel?"

Slowly, she looked up in ma direction, as if it wis the first she noticed me bein there, an inhalin deeply she drew the last i her cigarette an shrugged. Ah took that as a yes, an quietly went aboot spreadin the jam oan the bread. Ah wis hopin tae make it, clean up, an get back ootside before Uncle Archie kent Ah wis there, but as Ah put the knife back in the drawer, the noise fi the front room goat louder an then came that familiar dull thud as Uncle Archie's boot caught Ronnie in the mid-section. At that Aunt Mabel shook in her chair as if it wis her that hud been hit, but then she jist reached fir another cigarette an went back tae dreamland.

Ah wis oot the door quickly, careful no tae make a noise when it shut. It wisnae like Uncle Archie tae lay intae Ronnie. Aunt Mabel wis another matter. The odd time he'd smack me around a bit, but the next day he'd say he wis awfie sorry, an he didnae ken what hud goat intae him. There were times that it wis best tae avoid him, like when he didnae huv ony money, or if Hibs lost. It wis too bad he didnae support Celtic, cos they hardly iver lost. On Saturday evenins, Ah jist assumed Hibs hud lost unless Ah heard different. Sometimes he could be okay. One time in the summer

Ah jist happened tae be walkin past the bookie's, an oot he came an gied me ten pence. Told me tae go an buy some sweets fir masel, an oaf he went tae the pub wi his mates. Must've won big oan a horse. But he wis at his best when he hud a coupla drinks in him, but before he goat drunk. It wis a small windie i opportunity if ye needed tae ask him somethin.

From what Ah could make oot fi his yellin, Ronnie hud caught shite fir what went oan at the school this mornin. Uncle Archie kept sayin that he wis headin fir the Borstal if he kept it up. Onywye, the whole timin i this wis bad cos Ah hud wanted tae ask fir money fir school dinners, but Ah thought Ah would jist bide ma time an wait fir the right moment. Ah'd make another piece fir tomorrow.

When Ah came back at half past six, Aunt Mabel hud managed tae park hersel in front i the telly, an Uncle Archie must've been at the pub. Ronnie wis lyin oan his bed.

"Y'awright Ronnie?"

"Aye, why would Ah no be?"

"Ah jist thought that the old man stuck the boot in, that's aw."

In a flash he wis up oaf his bed an grabbed me by the neck.

"Listen, ye wee shite. He didnae dae nowt, an if Ah hear ye sayin different Ah'll kill ye."

Then came a loud gurgle fi the depths i his throat an he horked in ma face. He held me tightly by the collar an laughed at his handiwork, then threw me against the wa, an then he wis gone oot the front door. At school ye hear "Ah'm goanni kill ye," aw the time, an it disnae really mean onythin, but wi Ronnie ye wirnae jist too sure.

By the time Ah wis half way intae the third week i school, Ah hud pretty well sussed oot what wis up. The classes were nae bother really. The real work wis figurin oot where ye could hang aboot at break time an especially dinner time, which fir most first years wis one hour i survival. Generally speakin ye wanted tae stay wi the pack, especially when ye were oan the move, like when ye wir headin tae the dinner hall. Of course, Ah couldnae go there cos Ah nivir hud ony dinner tickets. Ah did ask Uncle Archie if Ah could huv some money tae buy dinners, but he said he didnae huv ony money the now, but tae remind him at the beginnin i the month. He always seemed tae be flush at the beginnin i the month. No ivryone hud school dinners. There wis a chippy that came an parked jist oaf the school property every day, but only the hard men tended tae go there. They wirnae the only ones wi money tae spend, but there wis only one lane tae the van, an if ye were headin doon there, yer chances i makin it without losin yer money were virtually nil. If ye wir wearin the full school uniform as well, ye could likely bank oan a doin tae boot.

Some i the boys an girls that lived in the nice hooses that were jist tae the east i the school went hame fir their dinner. No many, but some did. When they came back jist before one, they hud tae get past the young boot boys in trainin, who usually hung aboot the area that wis jist above the path. The odd time one would get a doin, but usually they were jist gobbed oan, an asked fir money. They wirnae robbed so much as accosted, an asked fir money.

"Gies a lane i a penny," wis the constant line, which ye could hear anywhere, but in particular oan this path at the end i dinner time. The worst thing ye could dae wis tae iver gie them onythin, cos then ye would be hounded mercilessly. It's too bad no one iver hired them tae work fir Oxfam, cos world hunger could huv been solved in no time!

Ma particular problem wis when the others were in huvin their school dinner, Ah would be alone, but there were wyes tae be careful. Usually Ah would jist wait in the queue, which could take up tae half an hour, especially if yer last class wis away doon in the science wing, an ye were late gettin in line. Jist before they wid gie in their ticket, Ah would peel away an find a place tae eat ma piece. At least it wis warm an dry, but it wis hard tae smell the food, an then at the last minute no get tae eat it. Aw ma mates were aye moanin aboot how bad the food wis, but nane i them iver wanted tae swop their ticket fir ma piece'n jam. Oan Fridays Ah quickly learned no tae bother queuein up wi them cos they hud the most coveted meal oan the menu: bridie, beans an chips, or BBC as it wis referred tae, an it smelled absolutely brilliant. They hud it some other days as well, but ye could pritty well count oan it oan Fridays.

There wis always a menu at secondary school, which wis a nice change fi primary, where there wis only one thing fir ivryone, but one i the items wis always a salad which didnae really count. That left a choice i two, which wis still okay as long as ye goat in the queue early enough. When BBC wis oan the menu, it changed the whole complexion i the school day. It wis easy if ye happened tae huv maths before dinner, cos ye could smell that distinct aroma comin fi the kitchen which wis only a sixty yard sprint doon the hall. The art department wisnae a bad place tae be either cos it wis located oan the floors directly above the dinin hall, an the smell i the chips in particular wis a signal fir ivryone tae be oan their marks. The problem wi huvin art right before dinner though wis although it wis close, it's hard tae barrel doon stairs as fast as ye can run oan the flats, an, tae boot, some i the art teachers hud their heids up their erse half the time. The bell wid come as a complete shock tae them, an then they'd insist oan ye helpin clean up before ye could go. There wis a whole lot i swearin that would accompany the clean up when that would happen. As a result, ivryone who hud English, or wis even in the Languages wing felt like they hud a realistic shot at BBC.

There wis even some game lads who would try an cover the six hundred yards fi the rec complex or the science wing in world record time, but that wis unrealistic unless ye managed tae somehow get oot before the bell. The odd time it would happen too. Mr Colqhoun who seemed by aw accounts tae be a bit soft in

the heid, an wanted tae be ivryone's friend, wid sometimes let ye
oot i science early. One time a remember sittin in history, an fi the
windie aw ye saw wis a pack i boys go flyin by, on their wye tae
the dinin room. A look i utter delight oan their faces at the prospect
i BBC when they hud probably written their chances oaf. The
history teacher, Mr Harkness, strained his neck through his
starched collar tae look back at where they were comin fi, expectin
tae see some masked gunman chasin them. There wis no point in
askin Harkness tae let us oot early. He nivir let ye oot till efter the
bell, an he made sure ivryone walked doon the stairs, which pritty
much relegated ye tae a salad. The Harkness monster he wis kent
as, an it fit him well. It wis widely rumoured that he hud been
kicked oot the S.S. fir excessive cruelty, an his belt wis generally
felt tae be the hardest in the school. It wis aw a bit daft. Ah dinnae
ken why they didnae jist make mair bridies an less salad. That
would've made too much sense. Mibbee Harkness hud somethin
tae dae wi it.

It's funny how a lot i things were the opposite tae primary
school. At primary ye were always lookin tae be the one who goat
tae take somethin doon tae the office fir the teacher, but at this
school it wis best tae avoid that sort i thing. The first time Ah hud
tae dae that, wis when Mrs Jess in English telt me tae take an
envelope doon tae the main office. She wis actually quite nice an
Ah dinnae think she realised what she wis askin, but ye couldnae
say no tae her. She aye wore mini skirts an high heels, an she wore
lotsa perfume. Right sexy like. Mike Black said she probably
wisnae married, an jist called hersel Mrs, but she did huv a ring
oan her weddin finger.

Ah stepped oot intae the hall, an moved one step doon the
corridor so's she couldnae see me through the wee windie, that wis
heid height. It wis awfie quiet. Way doon the corridor Ah could
see a lassie stahnin beside another door, an she wis clutchin a big
brown envelope as well. It seemed safe tae go but it wis risky, cos

before Ah could get ootside Ah would huv tae pass by the boys'
bogs, but Ah wis feelin adventurous an Ah didnae huv ony money
oan me onywye so Ah decided jist tae go fir it. Ah passed the
cloak room area where in the whole history i the school naebdy
hud ever hung a coat, an as Ah came up tae the boys' bogs it wis
awfie quiet an Ah actually thought aboot goin in fir a pee, cos Ah
wis fair burstin, but Ah quickly came tae ma senses. That would
huv tae wait till efter dinner, when Ah could go oot behind the
metalwork shop. Hardly onyone iver pished where they were
supposed tae, cos the lavvies were considered tae be an easy trap.
Kinda like the first antelope tae make it tae the waterin hole that
gets dragged in by the hungry crocodiles. That wisnae true
ivrywhere. Ye could pish wi a fair degree i safety in the Language
wing, cos the hard men didnae hang aboot there too often, cos they
didnae take French, an especially no German or Spanish. Usually
they were in the thicky classes an they hud enough trouble wi
English; nivir mind French. So if ye hud tae pinch a loaf; couldnae
hud it till ye goat hame like, then that wis where ye went. Mind
you Keith Murry once shat oot back i the metalwork shop, but he
wis a daft bastard an wis aye lookin tae dae somethin that wid
make ivryone laugh an contribute tae his reputation. He always
insisted that ye called him mental Keith fi Dalkeith cos that's
where he came fi. Wiped his erse wi wee Dave Duncan's snot rag
that he pulled right oot his pocket. Fir days efter that he felt the
need tae go back an check the progress i decay. Ah'm sure if Ah'd
suggested it he could an wid huv talked Colqhoun intae makin it a
science project fir the whole class. Another year an he'd likely be
runnin wi the hard men.

It wis goin pritty well an the doors tae the ootside were within
sight, when Ah could make oot some boys jist ootside. The
unmistakeable uniforms i stay-press troosers an black Harringtons
could be made oot through the dirty glass in the door, so Ah
decided tae hang oan an wait fir a teacher or a janny tae walk by. A

few minutes went by, an Ah wis thinkin that Mrs Jess would think that Ah wis jist goin fir a right skive, but it seemed best tae wait. Eventually, a man teacher wearin a three piece tweed suit came briskly walkin doon the corridor, goin in the direction i the main office. He wis probably oan his wye tae the staffroom. Behind him wis the lassie Ah hud seen before, still clutchin oan tae her brown envelope, an another boy who Ah think wis in second year walkin behind her. Ah quickly knelt doon an pretended tae be tyin up ma shoe laces, an then Ah jist fell in behind them. Before we goat tae the doors tae the ootside, another boy hud joined in behind me, huvin jist made like he hud jist come oot the classroom, an we passed through the doors an oan tae the main office without incident. The teacher at the front i oor wee line seemed oblivious tae it aw, an so did aw the teachers really, cos ye would often see lines like this goin doon corridors, an across the common. Ye would think that they would huv wondered how come it took so long fir ye tae deliver things an make yer way back tae the classroom, when some folk could make it fi the science wing tae the dinin hall in eighteen and a half seconds, whereas it took them a half hour tae go tae the office an back. Mrs Jess certainly nivir said onythin, but Ah wis sure she thought Ah wis skivin. It wis always a delicate balance cos ye hoped the teacher didnae think ye were skivin, but ye wanted yer classmates tae think that ye hud milked it fir aw it wis worth.

It would be better if ye were older, but that seemed a long way oaf fi the first year perspective. Primary school wis nivir like this; even when ye were younger. It wis only oan Remembrance Day ye hud tae be careful. Most i the boys who went tae Cubs or Life Boys wore their uniforms oan that day, an at playtime or dinner it aw goat a bit tribal. Rovin bands i Life Boys or Cub Scouts terrorised the non uniformed who didnae answer appropriately, or strays wi uniforms. Ah'm not sure that's what the spirit i the day intended, or what they were supposed tae be learnin when they went tae the meetins, but that's what usually happened oan November eleventh. But it wisnae too serious. No so much doins as roughin folk up an pushin them in the mud.

Fightin wis very different at secondary as compared tae primary. There appeared tae be a distinct absence i square goes at secondary school. In primary, fights were often discussed an planned in advance, an ivryone kent when an where a fight wis goanni take place. At the very least there would be fair warnin by way i a lotta pushin an shovin, an fuckews. Then a good fist fight would go until one i the lads hud hud enough. It wis very different at this school. Fights would spring up suddenly an take ye by surprise, like seein a car accident happen. They were usually over jist as quick as a car accident too. But what ye noticed efter a while wis that the winner wis the one who goat the first boot in. It seemed that the most successful technique wis tae boot the man in the baws so hard that he doubled over in agony; ye then grabbed him by the hair an started tae boot him in the face. We aye called it Marquis of Queensferry rules.

Sometimes challenges could be deflected by sayin "up the Com the night," makin like it wis too dangerous tae fight an settin it up fir later. If this worked, then usually the fight nivir took place, cos by that time it would huv been ancient history. Ah wis aye careful, but there were a few lads who hung wi me cos Ah wis connected tae Ronnie, who wis considered tae be one i the hardest men in the school. They thought that made me an untouchable, but Ah kent better.

Chapter 13

"Jimmy. When are ye goanni come doon the toon wi me?"

"Charlie, huv ye no been nicked yet?"

"Ah'm tellin ye, Ah ken what Ah'm dain."

"Aye mibbee soon."

"Ah'm goin doon the toon oan Saturday. Come wi me."

Ah thought aboot it fir a while as wee Charlie stood there, an Ah really couldnae come up wi a reason tae say no.

"Aye, Ah will."

When December arrived somethin went oaf in ma heid that said enough wis enough. Uncle Archie wis drinkin mair than iver, an although he'd gied me some money fir dinners, it wisnae regular an Ah wis gettin tired i it aw. Charlie wisnae in ony i ma classes, but Ah did see him aboot the school. He hud been put in wi the thickies, but he wisnae sae daft. He wis jist bidin his time till he wis old enough tae leave Logan House an join the family business. His invitation tae go doon the toon wi him oan Saturday seemed like a good idea. Ronnie went chorin jist aboot ivry Saturday an as far as Ah kent, he nivir goat caught. It wis a wonder, cos they aye went in packs an the shopkeepers must've been blind or somethin no tae suspect them. Ah mean did they think they were in there tae shop fir ties?

By dinner time oan Friday, instead i feelin sorry fir masel, as Ah normally would huv been, cos Ah found masel in maths right before dinner wi nae money fir a ticket, Ah wis kinda lookin ahead tae Saturday mornin an goin oan the chore. As much as Saturdays were a break fi school, they wirnae much fun now that it wis winter. Ah usually jist stayed in the bedroom an read a book Ah hud goat fi the library van, mibbee catch Sam Leitch's fitba preview oan Grandstand, if the livin room wis clear. As long as Ronnie wis oot an Archie wis sleepin oaf the night before, an Ah hud a decent book, it wisnae that bad. Aunt Mabel nivir bothered anybody. She could've fallen oot the back windie, an no one would've missed her until the next time Archie wis lookin fir somethin tae hit.

The library van sometimes hud some good stuff, but the wifie that ran it aye thought she would dae me a favour an help me oot choosin a book. The books she always tried tae gie me were aye aboot some boy at an English boardin school. Jennings at school, Jennings and the Midnight Adventure, Jennings at Large. If this Jennings prick hud come onywhere near ma school he would've goat his heid kicked in, an as much as Ah didnae really go in fir that sorta thing Ah probably would've stuck the boot in anaw. Jennings Gets the Shite Kicked Oot i Him; now that's one Ah would've read. There were nivir ony books aboot real schools where real people went, so Ah tried tae read a lot i older books. Some were good, some were awfie, but Ah tried tae get through them unless they were pure shite. Moby Dick wis pure shite, an Ah didnae get through that one.

Ah hud ma alarm set fir eight but Ah didnae need it, cos Ah wis awake since quarter tae seven. It wis jist as well, cos Ah didnae want tae wake Ronnie up an piss him oaf. He didnae half come in smashed the night before, an he wouldnae huv taken kindly tae bein wakened up before he wanted. The room reeked i sick, cos he must've boked oan his clothes that were lyin oan the floor. He hud a mate who worked in a licensed grocers an ivry Friday night when he wis workin there, a bunch i them would hang aboot the back door fir the free bevvies. This went oan aw over Edinburgh as far as Ah kent. Jist aboot ivryone kent someone who worked in a licensed place, so it wis nae bother if ye iver wanted somethin.

Ah wis oot the door by quarter past eight. A bit early, but there wis nothin keepin me there. Ah pulled the door shut quietly an turned the key slowly, but no matter how hard ye tried it always snapped right at the last an made a loud click. Only Aunt Mabel wis likely tae hear it, an she wouldnae huv cared. She didnae seem tae care aboot onythin at aw, as long as she hud her fags.

"Mornin Mrs Simpson," Ah says, but she kinda took me by surprise cos she wis stahnin directly across the hall fi me. She nivir said nowt, jist bounced her face oaf her first chin, mooth turned doon at the corners. She wisnae a friendly woman, an she didnae seem tae trust onyone. Lived by hersel except fir a big Alsatian dug, which she sometimes let run loose. The back green wis covered in its shite, but that wisnae the dug's fault an Ah nivir heard i it bitin onybiddy. She shuffled in wi her paper an rolls that smelled awfie good. Swayin enough as she went in the flat tae see her saggy tits shake oot i step wi the rest i her flabby, old body. Her fat tits were always aboot a half second behind the rest i her. They seemed tae go aw the way doon tae her waist. Ah wis thinkin how good a set i tits could look an then how ridiculous they could look. It wis like she didnae ken what tae dae wi them anymore an hud jist given up. She might've tried tae braid them or somethin, cos naebdy needed tae see thon. But stand her next tae Avril Maxwell who wis in ma French class an ye could be excused fir thinkin they were a different species. Avril Maxwell hud the nicest set i tits, melons, hooters, wallies, knockers, bazookas call them what ye like. It's funny how there's lotsa names fir tits, but only one name fir eyebrow. Anythin tae dae wi sex hud lotsa names, an the names goat less an less fir other body parts. Legs, pins, gams; Ah heard gams oan an American film oan the telly once. There were quite a few names fir legs, but no as many as there were fir tits. Avril wis jist average at French, but she wis definitely way ahead i the other girls in the class when it came tae tits.

Ah've always hated waitin fir the bus. In fact Ah've always hated waitin fir onythin, but particularly this mornin. Ah stood alone in the bus shelter waitin fir the number four bus. Charlie hud said tae be sure an take the number four, so's he would ken Ah wis oan that an he could meet me. Ah could've taken the sixteen, or twenty-seven. Ony one would've taken me tae Princes Street. Ah could've even walked over tae Buckstone an caught the eleven or the fifteen. The number four wis the best choice though cos they wir usin the new buses that hud the automatic doors wi jist the driver who took the fares as well. There wis nae chance i skippin yer fare this wye, but the buses kept warm in winter cos they wirnae open at the back. Onywye there wisnae any real chance i skippin yer fare oan a trip aw the wye intae town, an especially at this time i day, cos the bus would be near empty until it goat further intae town.

Ah stood in the shelter watchin the number twenty-seven in the terminus across the road gettin ready tae leave, its lights still oan cos the sun wisnae really up yet. A Christmas tree that hud been put up a wee bit early in one i the hooses next tae the shelter, flashed its coloured lights. Someone hud forgotten tae turn them oaf last night before they went tae bed. Still it wis probably warm in that hoose, an early or no Ah wis thinkin how it would be nice tae huv a Christmas tree, even if it wis a wee silvery one like the one in the hoose. The wind wis whistlin right through the shelter cos there wis a lot i glass missin. There wis a couple i new holes probably fi last night cos the shattered bits i glass were still oan the ground. They looked like big pieces i sugar an Ah liked the crunchin noise they made when Ah stood oan them. Ah put the hood i ma parka up tae keep the cauld oot an started tae chew the furry bit. It wis a good coat, Ronnie's old one, an it would come in handy the day, what wi aw the pockets. Ah hated tae think that Ronnie probably sucked oan the fur before me, but Ah couldnae help masel. It wis like a scab that hud tae be picked.

Finally the bus came, an Ah stood ootside the shelter so's the driver wis sure tae see me, an when Ah goat oan the bus Ah wis glad tae part wi the fare in exchange fir the warm petrol smell an ma pick i the seats oan the near empty bus. Charlie wis waitin at the stoap jist ootside Logan House, that wis lookin a bit bleak at this time i year. Aw the leaves were doon oaf the trees an there wir nae flowers left oan the rhodedendron bushes.

"Jist dae what Ah tell ye an we'll be awright," said Charlie.

"Nae bother," Ah said tryin tae look like Ah meant it.

"Your job'll be tae keep shoatie."

"Aye, awright."

We didnae talk aboot much else other than fitba. How Scotland needed a decent centre forward, an how could Malcolm MacDonald be English wi a name like that. That kinda stuff. But Ah did ask him how Ally wis dain. Ah kent fine well how she wis dain cos Ah saw her at school, but Ah jist wanted it tae get back tae her that Ah'd asked aboot her.

"Ah'll tell her yer wantin tae get oaf wi her then," said Charlie tryin tae hold back a smile.

"Dinnae be daft," Ah said, but Ah wouldnae huv minded. At gym class we hud tae dae two weeks i Scottish dancin an aw the boys made like they hated it, but dependin oan who ye goat tae dance wi, it wisnae bad. Ah hud made sure that Ah wis stahnin near Ally, who wis wi a bunch i her friends. They tended tae hang in bunches, ivry now an again a cackle i giggles escapin. Aw the boys hud tae go an ask a girl, but there were less boys than girls an the teacher made the ugly an fat ones that were left dance wi each other. It wis nice tae be close tae her. Tae smell her talcum powder against her milky white skin. When she swirled aroon sometimes her long black hair would brush against ma face an Ah felt like Ah wanted tae jump in an hide in her hair. Ah always tried tae wear the baggiest pants Ah hud oan the days we hud dancin, cos ma pecker disnae seem tae huv any sense i occasion, an Ah wis liable tae get a steamer jist by seein her across the gym, never mind dancin wi her. But ivryone else seemed tae huv the same problem. It wis jist somethin tae be dealt wi. Kenny Henderson didnae seem tae think it wis a problem, an he goat the belt fir coppin a feel i Avril Maxwell's tits. Really fancied himsel did Kenny, an he aye wore this poofy purple shirt the days we hud dancin.

We goat oaf the bus oan Princes Street which wis startin tae get busy wi ivryone dain their Christmas shoppin, but it wis still early. Ah jist walked along wi Charlie, tryin tae dodge aw the gobs oan the pavement until Ah came tae cross the road an Ah hud tae look up tae make ma wye through the crowd comin the other wye. Ah wis amazed how it always jist seemed tae work oot. Ah mean there wis aboot two hundred folk oan one side an another two hundred oan the other an when the wee lighted man appeared allowin ivryone tae walk, they aw managed tae get tae the other side, which wis kinda miraculous really. It wis like American fitba that Ah hud seen oan a Jerry Lewis film once, except naebdy goat flattened.

Charlie headed tae this wee café an bought us both a bacon piece.

"Ye cannae go tae work oan an empty stomach," he said.

Ah wis up fir it now. The sandwich seemed tae gie me the bottle. Ah wis tired i no huvin ony money, an Ah wis feelin lucky that Charlie hud asked me tae come along.

"The thing is Jimmy, tae be tidy. Dinnae make a mess. If ye can get what yer efter without onyone kennin ye were there, then that's the best wye."

Ah nodded as if Ah awready kent. Charlie seemed right intae

it, movin his hands when he talked. It wis like when the manager puts the sub on wi ten minutes tae go in the match, an needin a goal tae tie it up. Ah wisnae totally new tae this sort i thing. Jist up fi the primary school there wis a wee sweet shop that wis pritty easy tae chory fi. There were two old biddies that manned the shop at lunch time when the store wis busy, but the best time tae nick stuff wis at mornin playtime. Naebdy wis supposed tae go oaf the school property but there wis a bunch i us that did. At that time i day there wis only one i them in the shop an the first boy would ask fir somethin that wis kept in the back. Then ivryone else would huv a five finger discount. Ah did that a coupla times but Ah kinda felt sorry fir the old woman cos she wis always so nice tae ivryone, that it didnae sit well nickin sweets oaf i her.

"We'll start oaf easy," said Charlie as we made oor way intae Woolworth's at the east end i Princes Street, jist doon fi the Mound. Tae ma surprise Charlie headed straight tae the perfume counter. Ah wis jist thinkin that it wis a bit suspicious two thirteen year old boys lookin over the perfume an make up, when Charlie smiled at the sales girl an asked her what she thought would be the best kind tae get fir his ma fir Christmas. She took one look at us an suggested the lipstick. She didnae even get oaf her stool, which wis probably a good thing cos if she hud've moved too fast her face would probably huv cracked. She wis caked in make up an reeked i perfume. Ah jist followed Charlie's lead who wis lookin over aw the lipstick carefully. Efter a while he walked back along the counter an announced tae the sales girl that he wis goanni check oot the scarves.

"Okay, we jist hing fir a minute here, an when we go back she'll jist think that we're shoppin fir a present fir oor mahs."

"Sounds like a plan."

"Ah'll snag the stuff. Your job'll be tae stahn between me an her, awright."

Ah jist nodded. Charlie wis in his element. There's nothin like watchin a true professional at work, an Charlie obviously kent his trade.

Sure enough when we went back tae the make-up counter, the girl jist glanced over tae us then went back tae sortin a display i Channel No. 5. Special Christmas package. Ah stuck ma hands in ma unzipped coat pocket an pushed oot a bit tae make like a curtain, but no too obvious. Charlie grabbed a bunch i lipsticks an then went right fir the nail polish. He wis done so quickly that Ah dinnae think Ah wis really necessary.

"What were ye dain wi yer jecket? Ye looked like a seagull aboot tae take oaf."

Apparently Ah wis a bit mair obvious than Ah thought.

"Jist relax."

"Aye, awright, Ah wis jist bein sure, that's aw."

Charlie's pockets were pritty full an he emptied some i them intae mine, an then he wis oaf tae the sweets section.

"Same thing, awright."

He did the same thing, askin the woman behind the counter if she thought chocolates would be a nice gift fir his ma, cos she wis aboot the same age as his ma. She seemed quite taken by Charlie who looked very thoughtful as he carefully inspected the selection, an she told him that chocolates would make a lovely gift. Again Charlie said that he'd like tae go an check the price i scarves first an oaf we went. When we came back, the woman wis busy takin care i an old man an she didnae seem too worried aboot a nice boy like Charlie. This time Ah jist stood there in front i the selection boxes, packed wi aw ma favourites, an it wis hard tae pay attention tae what Ah wis dain, but Charlie wis quick liftin some big Cadbury bars.

Before we left Woolie's we each bought a wee chocolate bar an walked oot nae bother.

"See, nice an tidy," said Charlie.

"Naebdy'll even notice onythin wis missin."

"Nice touch buyin the chocolate Charlie," Ah said.

"Well, they're no goanni come efter ye if ye pay will they?"

"True enough," Ah said, "but Charlie there's somethin botherin me."

"What?"

"It's jist that the first day we met at Logan House ye were tryin tae get in ma bed, an now yer chorin nail polish an lipstick."

"Right funny bastard, you. Ah sell that stuff tae the lassies at Logan House an the school, but mostly at Logan House."

We walked fir a bit along Princes Street, which wis by now very busy. Passed the Sally Ann. Ah aye liked the sound i thae brass instruments. Ah mean they wirnae T Rex or nuthin but it sounded good there an then, an we stopped fir a minute an listened tae *Hark the Herald Angels Sing*.

"Ye would never go in there," said Charlie as he casually jerked his thumb in the direction i Jenner's.

"Stick oot like a kafflick at an Ibrox board meetin."

"Exactly. They'd be watchin ye like a hawk the whole time," said Charlie, who seemed pleased that Ah wis catchin oan.

"Mind an make sure thae chocolate bars dinnae melt."

"They'll no melt, it's too bloody cauld fir them tae melt."

Ah must've hud six large bars in ma pockets an enough lipstick tae keep Danny LaRue goin fir a year.

We went doon tae Rose Street next an walked by aw the parked cars lookin fir one that wisnae locked an hud somethin worth liftin, but there wir always a lot i people around. Efter a while we gave up an went fir one i the wee lanes back nearer tae Princes Street. Charlie spotted a nice car, Volvo Ah think, parked there oan a double yelli line. Quick as a flash he hud the door unlocked wi a coat hanger. He'd done that before, that wis fir sure. He grabbed the handbag oan the front passenger street, removed the purse, then put the bag back exactly the wye it wis oan the seat, locked the door an we were oan oor wye. Ah wis a bit taken aback, an Ah kent no tae run, but it wis aw Ah could dae tae walk at a normal pace. Even Charlie wis lookin a wee bit unnerved, which surprised me.

We crossed over tae the gardens an found an empty bench. There wisnae onyone near except fir the iver present pigeons, walkin aboot peckin at scraps like their heids were oan wee springs.

"That wis a stroke i luck," says Charlie smilin fi ear tae ear. It wis the first either i us hud spoken since the Volvo. Ah couldnae help lookin around every few seconds cos Ah half expected the polis tae be right oan oor heels.

"Relax will ye," goes Charlie. "They'll no even notice till she looks fir her purse. She'll probably think she left it at hame."

In ma heid Ah kent he wis right, but still Ah could feel ma heart beatin aw the wye up ma throat, mostly fi fear, but partly fi excitement.

"This is the best part," said Charlie, "like Christmas."

He wis right. Ah wis filled wi anticipation, although Ah couldnae help masel fi still lookin aboot, but Ah wis certainly cooler aboot it now. If Ah smoked Ah would've casually pulled one oot like James Garner in the *Great Escape*.

Charlie opened the purse wi his right hand still in his pocket an lookin in Ah could see it wis thick wi bills.

"Yes!" goes Charlie as he removed the cash fi the purse.

A quick count revealed there wis forty-eight pounds an some loose change as well.

"Twenty tae ye," he says, which Ah felt wis mair than fair since it wis really his score, an besides it wis mair money than Ah hud iver seen. He dumped the brown purse in the bin next tae the bench that said, "Keep Britain Tidy." It seemed a waste, but it made sense.

"A hud better get back tae the home. Supposed tae be back fir dinner time at half twelve."

"Aye awright," Ah said an Ah gied him aw the stuff Ah'd been huddin, except fir one chocolate bar. Fruit an nut.

"Ah think Ah'll jist stay fir a while. See ye Monday."

"Dinnae hing here but," goes Charlie an he nodded tae the bin, then he wis oaf, pockets bulgin as he walked away.

Ah made ma wye back up tae the street an crossed over tae the shops side, an walked along jist lookin at aw the people, ma left hand never leavin the bills in ma pocket. Ah walked an walked, up Lothian Road until Ah found masel aw the wye tae Tollcross. Ah passed a few cinemas until it clicked that Ah could afford tae go in an see a picture, but the timin wisnae right so Ah jist went an hud a fish supper, which didnae even put a dent in ma money. Hud a pickled onion as well. After that Ah went intae Goldberg's an looked around, an warmed up a bit. They went aw oot oan the decorations. Even hud a merry go round fir the bairns in there. Ah didnae buy onythin although Ah wis tempted tae buy a pair i trainers cos Ah wis startin tae get a hole in one i mine, but it wis oan toap so Ah didnae get wet feet or onythin. They were awfie comfy an Ah wis rememberin what ma Granda hud said aboot money. Ah wis keen tae find a wye tae use it tae make mair money, but Ah wisnae sure how Ah wis goanni dae that jist yet. Trouble wis when Ah thought aboot ma Granda Ah goat tae thinkin how disappointed he'd be if he kent what Ah'd done the day.

Ah went back doon tae the ground floor in the lift. The whole time the lift operator wis lookin me over like Ah wisnae supposed tae be in there, but mair people goat oan an then he couldnae see me so well at the back i the lift. Some nerve he hud tae stare at me when he wis wearin this daft maroon suit. Ah wis thinkin what a borin job that would be tae work a lift aw day. He didnae look too happy either; jist hangin oan till retirement likely. Hud a lot i wrinkles oan his face; thin an gaunt like an no much hair left. If Benny Hill hud goat oan the lift he would've slapped him a few times oan toap i the heid.

Before Ah went back ootside Ah wis lookin at a display i scarves, thinkin Ah should get Aunt Mabel somethin fir Christmas, an thought Ah'd branch oot oan ma own, so Ah asked the sales clerk if she thought a scarf would be a good gift fir ma Mah. Worked like a charm, cos she said she thought it would be a terrific present an what a nice laddie Ah wis tae get ma mother a gift. Ah looked a wee while longer an then telt her Ah wis goin tae check the perfume first. Away Ah went pritty pleased wi ma performance, except Ah wis feelin guilty cos it wis like Ah wis usin ma Mah. Ah felt like she wis lookin doon at me shakin her heid an tsk tskin. Nivir mind, Ah waited till an old woman went up an when she wis blabbin away tae the wifie Ah picked oot a nice silky, dark blue scarf an reached fir it nice an smooth.

"Jimmy?"

Aw shite, Ah thought, an Ah felt ma throat go instantly dry, then it occurred tae me that Ah hudnae done onythin wrong. No in Goldberg's onywye.

"Jimmy. It is you isn't it?"

Ah turned round an tae ma great relief it wis Mr and Mrs McCrae.

"Hullo."

"Well, fancy seeing you in here," said Mrs McCrae, beamin a smile.

"It's nice tae see ye too."

"And how are things at the new school, and with your Aunt and Uncle?"

"Oh jist fine," Ah said. It jist naturally came oot.

"I called a couple of weeks ago and left a message with your cousin. Ronald, isn't it?"

"Aye, that's right. Sorry, Ah nivir goat the message."

Ronald sounded aw wrong fir Ronnie, like he wis a barrister or somethin.

"Well, I just wanted to make sure everything was all right."

"Aye, fine, Ah suppose."

"Perhaps you could come for a visit over the Christmas holidays. Would you like that?" asked Mrs McCrae.

"Yes Ah would," Ah said, mibbee soundin a bit too anxious.

"Wonderful," said the minister like he really meant it too.

"I'll telephone you closer to Christmas and arrange to come and pick you up."

"Ah could get the bus. It'd be no bother."

"Well we'll work that out when I call you, all right."

At that he stuck oot his hand an we shook, which wis definitely a step up fi gettin ma heid rubbed. Mrs McCrae jist smiled a lot, an then they were oaf. Ah nivir bothered wi the scarf efter that an jist decided tae head oan back tae Oxgangs an the flat, hopin Hibs hud won or at least managed a draw. So Ah caught the bus an Ah found a seat up the stairs, but it wis a struggle tae weave around aw the people an parcels, comin back fi their day i shoppin. But ivryone seemed pritty happy wi it gettin near tae Christmas. It wis efter four now an dark ootside which normally can be a bit depressin, but a few folk hud their Christmas trees in their windies, coloured lights, some flashin, some no. The whole time Ah kept ma hand oan the wad i bills in ma pocket which in turn made me feel good an then guilty, but Ah relieved ma guilt by thinkin that it wis an awfie nice car an mibbee the woman wouldnae miss it too much onywye. Mibbee if she kent Ah'd be eatin a decent meal ivry day next week at school she'd even be happy aboot it. Mibbee no happy, but no so angry onywye. But then what if she'd jist collected that money fir a charity like starvin children in Africa or somethin? Then again starvin children in Oxgangs wisnae a bad charity tae start. Ah worried too much Ah told masel.

When a goat back tae the flats Ah could hear a dug barkin an it seemed tae be comin fi the wee storage room oan the ground floor, which wis usually kept locked. Sure enough, when Ah goat over tae the door, there wis definitely a dug in there, but Ah wis a wee bit hesitant tae unleash some mad dug intae the hallway. Efter it yelped a few times though, Ah decided tae risk openin the door, an oot jumps Mrs Simpson's Alsatian, so excited tae get oot it knocked me flat oan ma back. Its mooth open, it went right fir ma face, an Ah wis near shitin ma pants, but it jist wanted tae lick me. Ah patted it an played wi it fir a while an this dug that Ah hudnae been too sure aboot wis aw i a sudden ma best friend in the world.

Ah took him up the stair wi me an knocked oan Mrs Simpson's door. She took an age tae finally come, an then only opened the door a crack.

"Adolph!" she said.

"Naw, its me, Jimmy," Ah said, but then Ah realised she meant the dug.

"Where've ye been, ye daft dug?" she said rubbin it aw the time behind the ear.

"Actually, somebdy hud put him in the storage room doonstairs, an Ah let him oot."

"Thanks, son, he seems tae like ye."

"Aye he's a nice dug."

"C'moan in wi him."

Ah wis a bit taken aback since it wis the most words she'd iver spoken tae me the whole time Ah'd lived there, but then when Ah thought aboot the rest i who lived in the flat, then mibbee she wisnae that unfriendly tae ivryone, jist whoever wis connected tae Archie, an ye couldnae blame her fir that. So Ah went in an sat doon wi Adolph who hud gone an laid doon in front i the gas fire. Pattin his thick coat. He'd gie me the odd lick oan the hand, then jist roll his heid back doon flat oan the rug, as if it hud at that instant goat too heavy tae hud up.

"Ah'll put some tea oan."

"Grand," Ah said, an Ah took ma parka oaf.

It felt strange tae be in a place that didnae reek i cigarette smoke. Ah'd huv thought she would've been a smoker cos she hud such a deep throaty voice. Ye could've mistaken her fir a man, unless of course ye'd seen her, in which case the big fat tits were a dead giveaway. She really needed tae open a windie though cos there wis a right stagnant smell that wis a mixture i the dug an too many fry ups. The walls were pritty bare save fir a picture behind the settee. Nothin in particular. Hills, sheep an a ruined castle. But the mantel above the gas fire wis cluttered wi photies, wee ornaments, pens, an a few Christmas cards. The settee an armchair hud been covered in an old sheet tae keep it good fir a day that would nivir come. She even hud some Christmas decorations up which surprised me. A couple i thae bells that are made i coloured tissue paper an fold oot, an the budgie cage hud some lights oan it, but no tree.

"Here ye are, son."

In she came wi a tray perched against her shelf. Teapot an some shortbread.

"Mrs Simpson?"

"Aye."

"Ah wis wonderin why ye called the dug Adolph."

"Och," she goes wi a chuckle, "that wis ma husband Jock, an awfie man. He wanted aw the bairns tae be feart i the dug."

"Aye, well it worked."

"Died three year ago, he did."

"Ah'm very sorry," Ah kent what tae say.

"Aye well, Ah jist huftae muddle along without him, that's aw there is tae it. He aye said that since he hud a dug's name, he'd gie the dug a man's name, an now Ah'm left wi him but Ah cannae walk him any mair cos Ah've a bad leg. So Ah jist let him oot himsel now an again."

"Ah could take him fir walks sometimes. Huv ye a leash?"

"Oh aye, there's a leash ben the room there."

"Well, mibbee the morn then, cos Ah think he's hud enough fir the day."

"Aye, right ye are, son."

Ah drank ma tea an ate a bit shortbread, even though it hud dug hair oan it, an Ah talked tae Mrs Simpson fir a while. Talked aboot livin in Aberdeen in the twenties an how ye could go doon tae the fishin boats when they came in an they were practically givin the haddock away. She put the telly oan efter we chatted, an Ah heard the fitba scores. It wis the best i news an the worst i news. Hearts hud lost, an Hibs hud won. Dependin oan how Ah wanted tae look at the situation, it wis a no win or a no lose set i results. But now that Hibs hud won onywye, hopefully the highlights would be oan Scotsport tomorrow efternoon, which would keep Uncle Archie in a tolerable mood, cos it wis the one day he generally spent at hame.

Chapter 14

School holidays arrived an Ah hudnae heard fi Mr McCrae, so Ah went doon tae the shops an called fi the phone box. Ah didnae huv his number, but Ah found it in the book, which wis lucky, cos like the kiosk itsel it wis less than intact.

"Mr McCrae, hullo."

"Hullo. Who is this?"

"It's me, Jimmy," Ah said.

"Oh hullo there Jimmy; we were about to give up on you."

"Well, Ah wis jist waitin cos ye said ye'd ring, but then Ah thought that mibbee ye forgot."

"I see," said Mr McCrae.

When he said that a wee light went oan in ma heid. Mibbee Aunt Mabel hud forgot tae tell me, or mibbee Ronnie, but of course Mr McCrae hud called, cos he said he would.

Ah took the bus doon tae Granton an jist met Mrs McCrae at the door i the church. Two days before Christmas an it wis cauld enough fir snow. Ah remember it snowin once when Ah wis wee oan Christmas. We woke up tae everythin lookin white an pure. It wis a wet snow an it hud stuck tae everythin – cars, every branch i the trees, even the side i the tenement across the road. We hud aw made a snow man an by Boxin Day that wis aw that wis left.

"Merry Christmas Jimmy," said Mrs McCrae, an she looked merry fir a cauld mornin.

"Hullo," Ah said. Ah couldnae bring masel tae sayin, "Merry Christmas," cos it would've sounded daft. There wir a lot i familiar faces that Ah hudnae seen since the funeral, an when Ah walked doon the aisle tae take ma seat near the front wi Mrs McCrae, some folk looked at me an half waved, screwin up their faces jist enough tae let me ken that they still felt sorry fir me. Two days tae Christmas an Ah hud tae look like ma family hud jist died again cos that's what people expected. They forget that while they might huv given the whole thing the odd thought over the last six months, Ah've hud tae dream aboot it, live wi it ivry minute, an get used tae it aw.

Jeff Baxter kinda nodded tae me an Ah nodded back. Mrs McCrae kept inchin her wye tae the very front, huvin a wee word wi some folk as she went. It felt as if ivryone wis starin at me an the feelin intensified as Ah goat nearer the front. It wis aw a bit unnervin an Ah didnae dare look but Ah wis convinced Ah wis flyin at half mast. When we finally goat tae oor seats in the second row, the first thing Ah did wis tae check, an tae ma great relief Ah wis fully zipped. Mrs Donaldson turned around an before she could say onythin, she started tae greet a wee bit. A big tear started tae run doon the side i her cheek, until it met wi too much resistance fi her powdery make-up, an it formed somethin like what's left in the bottom i a cup i hot chocolate. She ended up jist puttin her chubby hand on ma face. Ah hope it made her feel better cos it didnae dae onythin fir me.

It wis strange bein in this place again. Even though there wis a Christmas tree an there wis a festive air i anticipation in the pre service church murmur, Ah couldnae help but think i the funeral, an what if there hudnae been an accident, an how different this Christmas would be. But it's a game ye shouldnae play, cos it's harder tae come back tae what passed fir reality now. So Ah tried tae look around the church, aw the time hopin it would jist get started. Ivrywhere Ah looked there were eyes lookin back at me, an Ah felt masel feelin the need tae look appropriately tragic. Ah flipped through the hymn book fir privacy an saw aw the old hymns that Ah nivir sung onymair, but then Ah started tae feel guilty aboot ma chorin. *Blessed assurance, Jesus is mine. Why do Ah nick things all of the time? Heir of salvation, purchase of God, Ah'm walkin aboot like a lightnin rod.*

Finally it starts an we sing some carols, an it aw feels right again an safe an a long wye fi where Ah huftae call hame now. Mr McCrae comes oan an introduces the special Christmas programme, an then we're intae it. Mary an Joseph in the stable. As usual Mary hus trouble keepin her heid gear oan, an Joseph forgets his lines. Girls are much better at this sort i stuff. But aw in aw it goes along well till the shepherds start tae get a bit restless an one hauls oaf an punches the other in the side i the heid. He hits back, wi the lamb doll he's huddin an then the first one's big brother forgets fir a moment that he's supposed tae be a wise man an he comes over tae stand up fir his wee brother, an right when aw hell is aboot tae break loose a coupla the indignant teachers jump in an restore order. Christmas in Granton. The play goes oan. Life goes oan. Ivryone jist makes the best i it aw. Work hard, play hard. Mental.

Mrs McCrae laid oan a nice dinner. There wis another family there too, who talked aboot how they were movin tae Canada in the new year, so Ah didnae huftae talk much. Canada sounded like a great place. This Mr Galbraith hud a job lined up in Toronto wi the polis. Said they were goin tae buy a hoose. Land i opportunity. Ah resolved tae find oot mair aboot Canada. Mibbee see if they hud a book aboot it oan the mobile library efter Christmas.

Ah told Mr McCrae that Ah'd take the bus back but he wouldnae hear i it.

"I thought we could have a little chat on the way back Jimmy," said Mr McCrae. He'd better make it quick at the rate he drove.

Silverknowes tae Oxgangs wouldnae take long fir him oan a Sunday.

"I don't know too much about your Uncle and Aunt. So I was just wondering if everything is … well … is going all right for you there."

"Aye, its okay Ah suppose, but Ah quite liked Logan House."

"Would you have preferred to stay there then?"

"Aye Ah think so. No that there's onythin wrong wi where Ah am now. Ah mean it's okay like."

"Yes, you said that. It's okay, that is."

Mr McCrae seemed quite serious, an fir a split second Ah thought aboot tellin him aboot Archie an his drinkin an beatin oan Aunt Mabel, but then Ah kent Archie wouldnae like that an it aw might backfire.

"Well, when you're seventeen, you can leave on your own. It's my understanding that at that time you will be eligible to inherit the remainder of your grandmother's estate."

Mr McCrae pulled the Sunbeam over tae the side i the road.

"I want you to know that if things aren't going well, then you can give me a ring. Your Uncle is the official guardian, but remember at seventeen, you will be able to set out on your own. If that's what you'd prefer … understand?"

It wis like he wanted tae tell me mair, but that he'd told me too much. He drove oan, an we didnae really talk onymair. Ah thought aboot a lot i things. How much hud ma Gran left me? Ah hudnae really thought aboot it, but Ah suppose there would've hud tae be somethin there.

"Is that why ma uncle wanted me tae come live wi him then? Ah mean does it huv somethin tae dae wi the money?"

"I don't think you should worry about these things too much at this stage. Just remember that when you turn seventeen, then you are in charge."

"Where in the hell huv you been aw day?" wis what Ah heard when Ah goat in the flat.

"Oot."

"Ah ken ye were oot, but that's no what Ah asked wis it," he persisted.

"Ah went back doon tae Granton tae see some folk, that's aw," Ah said hopin it'd be enough.

"Yer no seein that daft minister are ye? Fillin yer heid wi nonsense."

"Naw, Ah didnae see him the day," Ah lied.

"Aye well jist make sure ye dinnae or Ah'll huftae set ye straight. Ken what Ah mean," he said, his left hand poised in the backhanded strikin motion. Then somethin caught his attention oan the telly an Ah took the opportunity tae move oan tae the bedroom. So Ah sat there. The most depressin time i the week. Sunday evenin. Disnae matter what ye dae there's no gettin past it. Ah mean Ah hud a good day, an it wis Christmas oan Tuesday, jist found oot Ah hud some money comin tae me in four years, but Sunday night jist hus a feel tae it that ye cannae shake.

Christmas day arrived wi no expectations oan ma part. Ah hud thought that at best ivryone would exchange fivers an mibbee a decent nosh. Archie would be smashed by the time the Queen spat oot her speech at three. Tae ma surprise there wis a chicken wi Brussels sprouts an roasted spuds. The four i us sat roond the table together wi the telly oaf. There wis even presents. Ah goat a selection box fi Uncle Archie an Aunt Mabel goat perfume an a new coat an a carton i cigarettes. Be aboot a two day supply fir her. She didnae say much but she seemed awfie happy. There wis a glimmer there that ye rarely saw. Mibbee, she wis thinkin that he really loved her an that he'd turn things around. It's hard tae believe that onyone could be that stewpit, an Ah'd huftae say that she probably jist gave hersel the luxury i believin it fir one day i the year. Ronnie even hud presents tae give oot. He gave Archie twelve cans i beer. Somethin Archie needed like he needed an extra ersehole. Gave me five quid, which he probably nicked oaf me in the first place. Ah wis glad Ah hud bought ivryone somethin though, an Aunt Mabel seemed tae like her scarf. Ah gave Uncle Archie a wee shavin set. No that he wis too regular in that department, but it would come in handy if he felt the need tae shave his tongue the mornin efter a booze up. Ah gave Ronnie a book oan fitba. Lotsa pictures; no much readin.

It wis aboot the best day Ah hud in that hoose, but by the time her majesty made her appearance, Archie wis well oan his wye, Mabel hud stoaped kiddin hersel, an Ronnie hud gone oot tae be wi his mates. Ah wis left tae sit oan ma bed wi ma selection box, an makin the mistake i rememberin last Christmas, an the one before that. It aw made it harder tae come back when Ah wis done daydreamin. It wis jist me an Cadbury's an the thought that one day Ah would be seventeen.

Chapter 15

James arrived back at the hotel, his stamina bolstered by a nicely done steak, the appreciation of which was enhanced by a respectable bottle of red wine recommended by the waiter. He had hoped to enjoy the sight of the castle lit up against the night sky, but being the month of June it was not yet dark despite the lateness of the hour. Nevertheless, the walk was exactly what his much-travelled muscles had needed, and the bed in the room was a welcome sight when at last he returned.

A check of his watch, which he had kept on Toronto time, suggested that it was time to call Karen, and that is what he did, slightly inebriated as he was.

"Hello."

"Hi Val. It's Dad."

"Hi Dad," she said enthusiastically. "How's Scauwtland?"

Val liked to attempt to imitate what was left of her father's accent.

"Scauwtland," said James playing along, "seems to have gotten along just fine without me. Is your mother home yet?"

"Yeah, but Dad guess what?"

"I'm really in no position to guess, Val."

"Remember Cindy's dog had puppies?"

"Yes, and I remember saying that we weren't going to take one."

"But Dad, there's only one left, and my birthday's coming up, and I'd never ask for anything else ever again," stated Val.

"Put your mother on will you?"

"Okaaaay."

"Hi hon, everything alright?"

"Sure, great. I assume you were responsible for the business class ticket."

"Did you like that?" enquired Karen, smiling all the way through the telephone line.

"It was nice, very nice actually. Thank-you," said James demurely.

"Did Val talk to you about the whole dog thing?"

"As a matter of fact she did, and I trust that you're backing me up on the negative position," said James.

"Oh I love it when you talk dirty, James."

"Seriously, Karen, I just don't want her to get her hopes up when we both agree it would be a bad idea."

"Well actually, I was thinking it might not be such a bad idea to have a dog around here. I'd feel better when you're away with a dog in the house."

"It's not that I'm away that often you know," implored James, who was starting to feel at a bit of a disadvantage being three thousand miles away.

"But it's the cutest thing James," said Karen with emphasis on the *cutest*.

"You mean you've seen it then." James knew his strictly canine free household rule was now in serious jeopardy. Karen was capable of real empathy for a hamster, let alone a puppy.

"Well, you know Val. She managed to get me over there to look at it, and you know, James, she really has always wanted a dog and it might be good for her to have the responsibility."

"Well … well what do Lisa and Sarah think?"

"Lisa's keen and Sarah hasn't really expressed any feeling one way or the other."

"Hmmm," mused James.

"So that's a yes then," said Karen, and James heard a triumphant echo from Val in the background. He had lost this argument. The one item that he had stood resolutely firm on, he had lost.

"Just make sure one of Sarah's friends doesn't eat it or something."

"James," exclaimed Karen in horror.

"Thanks, Dad!" Val had hijacked the receiver from her mother.

"Just remember there's a lot of responsibility in owning a dog."

"I know, I know," interjected Val. "Like walking it every day."

"Well, yes," said James, "and looking after it, keeping it, you know, safe, and well just looking after it properly."

"Yes Dad, I know, but we can't take it home yet 'cause it's too young still, so I'm going to get a book and read up on dogs, and oh Dad I'm going to call it Prince. Thanks, Dad, I love you, bye."

"Bye Val, I love you too."

"Hi it's me again," said Karen. "Hotel okay?"

"Yeah it's fine. They don't allow dogs. Is Sarah home?"

"No, not right now. Neither is Lisa actually, but I'll tell them you called."

"Thanks," said James. "Well I guess I'll call in a couple of days when hopefully I've got something to tell you."

"So you haven't contacted anyone yet," said Karen.

"No, not yet. Tomorrow's another day. But when I do call, please don't tell me that we're the proud owners of a pony or something."

Karen laughed heartily at the suggestion, knowing that it was James' way of telling her that he wasn't angry for the way she had taken advantage of his absence.

"Okay goodbye then. I love you," exclaimed Karen.

"Bye, I love you too," said James weakly, protected as he was from intimacy by three thousand miles.

A dog, thought James as he searched in vain for his cigarettes. There was no going back now though. It would have crushed Val, and anyway, maybe Karen was right about the whole guard dog concept. There had been a number of break-ins throughout the neighbourhood recently. Already he was beginning to rationalise how feebly he had folded under the pressure, and yet there was something tugging at him suggesting to his subconscious he had become weak. Suddenly he remembered why he couldn't find his cigarettes; he had quit for the seven hundred and fifty sixth time. Too tired to go looking for a pack at such a late hour, he resigned himself to going to bed.

James set out just after nine o'clock feeling well rested and generally positive as he bypassed the little gift shop in the foyer that proffered all manner of cigarette brands and made his way for his first great challenge of the day. Difficult as it had been to park the car on such an incline, extricating it would be even more of a challenge given that the two cars immediately in front and behind had left a total combined space of about two and a half inches between bumpers. Regardless, James wasn't about to let anything spoil his mood, braced as he was by such a promisingly warm, by Scottish standards, June day. It proved to be the challenge he anticipated, but with the precision required of an astronaut and the sort of patience that is always easier to produce early in the day, James successfully managed to engineer the vehicle onto the thoroughfare. Granted there was some minor kissing of bumpers involved but not enough to elicit any concern from James, who would not have felt any obligation anyway given the position the other parkers had placed themselves in.

Although James was full of good intentions as far as accomplishing the task at hand, he felt seduced by the opportunity at independence and anonymity presented before him. Without looking in the rear view mirror he was confident his frontal lobe was adequately concealed by hair, and the feel of the gear stick in his hand on such a day as this seemed to infuse him with excitement. To this end, any attractive woman who happened to glance in his direction had, in James' mind anyway, amorous intentions, and any man who did likewise had to be admiringly jealous of this handsome single man in a red sports car. So rather than head for the old neighbourhood, James decided on a circuitous route that he rationalised would serve to re-acquaint himself with the city.

After driving around the old town for some time, James found himself headed for Holyrood Park, and while stationary in the traffic of the Royal Mile, his attention was caught by a rather attractive thirty-something woman in a small car that found itself stopped in the opposite direction. Realising that she was looking at him, James suavely rolled the window down all the way, and smiling confidently, greeted the woman with a North American, "Hi there."

"Ye tryin tae blind me wi thae headlights?"

Stunned for a moment, James managed a mumbled apology and the woman drove off shaking her head, muttering something about the stupidity of allowing Yanks to drive cars. James quickly located the switch and turned off the lights, slunk down a few inches in his seat and felt his short-lived confidence leave his once again middle-aged shell. Finally the traffic was moving again and James was able to relieve his feeling of claustrophobia by driving around the unique landscape of Holyrood Park. But he did not linger at the base of the extinct volcano, much as he enjoyed seeing it again, and after a lap he headed to the south of the city.

It was remarkable to James how naturally he seemed to find his way around, given that he had never driven there prior to leaving for Canada as a young man. Granted, there was little of any real substance that had changed in the city, at least outwardly. This was a real contrast to his adopted home of greater Toronto, which had expanded aggressively to accommodate the growing population over the last quarter of the twentieth century. Farms and golf courses that surrounded Toronto in the early seventies, understandably beguiled by successive real estate booms, had succumbed to suburban development, where new homeowners worshipped at the altar of consumerism. Suburbia, where discarded, cardboard, appliance containers left on the boulevards for the weekly trash pick-ups would dwarf the feeble sticks that passed for trees; maple trees that would eventually reach a reasonable height just about when the new homeowners were about to enter homes for the aged. Staked against the elements, the trees symbolised the hope that one day mortgages would be retired. But they could submit to the ravages of disease, be snapped in two by an erratic driver, or fall victim to stormy weather.

Blessed with antiquity, Edinburgh's streets and neighbour-hoods held a charm that North America was on the whole unable to reproduce, save for a few exceptions like Quebec City's old town. But given the choice, as devoid of character as Toronto's new subdivisions were, James felt they were much the lesser evil than the "schemes" of Edinburgh as they were euphemistically known. Certainly they were homes to almost unique micro-cultures with their own identities, but there were some that could also be described as soulless, and as James approached the old neighbourhood, he felt the despair he had known, and despite the simple charm of the day, there was a cloud forming overhead.

The school appeared to have been captured in time, unchanged in spite of the passage of years, and James felt sorry for the occupants, despite knowing that everyone from his era had moved on. It was as if because the buildings hadn't perceptibly altered, then the same people must be within. In his head he knew differently. He knew his fellow classmates had all entered their forties and had moved on to careers, families, other places. It was a comfort to James to know that his contemporaries, although he had not seen any of them since his departure, were ageing at the same rate he was. Of course, some would not have the privilege of growing old and seeing their grandchildren. Car accidents, AIDS, cancer and the like would have by now inflicted a significant cull. Maybe there was a young man who "fell" in Northern Ireland during the "Troubles."

There were always attempts to soften the impact of war and death. The plaques on the walls of churches commemorating the victims of the great wars invariably said "those who fell," presumably because it was more palatable to the widows, and besides it sounded more romantic than "killed." James sat in his car in the parking area of the school and remembered the day when there was an assembly for all the boys, and an army officer spoke in an attempt to recruit from the economically depressed area. He reflected on the question and answer period after the officer spoke, and how most of the questions pertained to why the potential recruit had to have his hair cut off. The recruitment officer had answered dishonestly by plucking a particularly bushy haired young man from the front row, and installed the traditional army hat on his ample yet dishevelled coif producing howls of laughter from the proles. It was, he explained, simply because it was not an appealing sight, and, in fact, looked somewhat ridiculous. He didn't say it was because it was their intent to rob the recruits of their identity.

James remembered that day and how he wanted to ask a more biting question, but he was never given the chance. When a boy finally asked a decent question, it had irked him how the officer was dismissive of the potential for harm if one was dispatched to Ulster and the "Troubles." In his history class no one had referred to the Spanish civil war as the "Spanish troubles."

Some would have enlisted out of desperation, or excitement, or the prospect of a steady pay cheque, or simply the opportunity to get away. Some day soon James speculated, with the internet, you would be able to find out what became of just about anyone you had ever been acquainted with. He was unsure if that was a good thing.

James drove on and weaved his way through the old familiar streets where he would walk with the dog; up past the community centre, site of more fights than Madison Square Gardens. He paused at the Church of Scotland, whose white walls were still waging a losing battle against the graffiti artists. The names had surely changed, but that was all. Then a memory that had needed visual coaxing returned. The large church was the site of many weddings. There were periods in the summer months when they were weekly events each Saturday. Scores of children and youths would lurk around the front of the building and then jostle for position in anticipation of the scramble, or "pooroot" as it was more traditionally known because the guests were expected to pour out the contents of their pockets. When the bridal cars would leave, loose change would be thrown from the windows and the scramble was on to scoop it up. An athletic youth could collect a tidy sum as well as a significant amount of cuts and bruises during the mêlée that would ensue. It was always more profitable if there was a bus laid on for the guests to go to the reception. This became less common as people acquired their own cars, but in the early seventies it was not unusual. James sat and smiled as he recounted a day when he had learned of three weddings at different churches, and managed to be at the scramble for all three. But they were not assured. Much ado had been made about the inherent danger of the custom, as the odd victim would get caught under the wheel of a bus, and by the early seventies there would often be weddings without pooroots. The happy occasion in such an event would be showered with boos by the expectant youths who had come to see it as their right. James wondered if they still had scrambles.

There was a phone booth at the little shopping concourse that housed the betting shop, site of Archie's profligacy, and James pulled out the sheet of paper that contained Ronnie's telephone number. As he punched in the number he was somewhat taken aback by the trembling in his hands, and despite the time it took for Ronnie to answer, James had not sufficiently composed himself, yet he resisted the temptation to hang up.

"Hi, it's me, James," he managed.

"Jimmy, well well," said Ronnie, rather surprised. "Have ye changed yer mind. Are ye goanni come over?"

"Ehh, yes I thought I would," said James evasively.

"Aye well he still asks fir ye."

"Ronnie, I meant to ask before. Your Mum. Eh, is she still alive?"

"Aw naw, Jimmy. Been gone ten year now. Heart trouble like."

James was not surprised. It was what he suspected; it was only the manner of her death that modestly surprised him. Lung cancer had seemed the most likely, or a broken neck, the result of a "fall."

"Yes, I'm sorry to hear that," said James managing to inflect a sympathetic tone despite having absolutely no feeling of bereavement.

"Aye, well," said Ronnie awkwardly.

"So where is your Dad then?"

"He's in this place oot Corstorphine wye. When are ye thinkin i comin then?"

"Not quite sure, Ronnie, but while I've got you on the phone, perhaps you could give me the address of that place," said James having recovered his composure enough to trouble himself on a subconscious level at his ability for prevarication.

"Aye, jist a minute an Ah'll get it," and Ronnie, evidently not sufficiently acquainted with the establishment as to have the address committed to memory, was off to rummage. James was left to make sure he had done everything required of him by British Telecom, so that a voiceover would not suddenly become audible and blow his cover to Ronnie. He had not intended to feign he was still in Canada, but when the opportunity had presented itself it had seemed like the best tack to take. Ronnie eventually returned to the phone with the name and the address of the home, and James had promised to call Ronnie when he arrived, which as far as Ronnie knew was still undetermined at this point.

Chapter 16

Seein Mr 'n Mrs McCrae again an aw the folk at the church hud made me rethink ma brief attempt at a life i petty crime, an when Ah turned Charlie doon three weeks in a row he pritty much gave up oan me an Ah didnae see too much i him efter that. Mr McCrae hud told me tae phone him ony time Ah wanted an sometimes Ah did, but we didnae talk too much aboot what Ah think we both kent wis goin oan at the hoose. Ah would take the bus doon the odd time oan the weekend an they wir always glad tae see me, an it wis a nice break. Sometimes Ah'd go tae church there an Ah would sit wi Jeff Baxter an it would seem sometimes fir a few seconds that it wis jist like before, but no fir long an Ah kent it could nivir be like before. Things hud changed an there could be no goin back an Ah kent that it would be best tae get away fi onythin that kept pullin me back tae the wye things wir. So over time Ah didnae bother goin back, an Ah stoaped callin, an Ah didnae hear fi Mr McCrae cos we hud the phone disconnected cos Archie hudnae been payin the bills. Didnae matter much tae him onywye cos he wis hardly iver hame. Ah did get at least one letter fi Mr McCrae, cos Ah happened tae notice it in the rubbish bin. It hud been torn up, but Ah wis able tae put it back together an read most i what it said. The McCraes hud jist said how they missed seein me an that Ah could visit onytime. The same sort i thing that he would've said oan the phone. Still it wis nice i them an Ah thought aboot callin them, but Ah nivir did.

Ah managed tae get a job deliverin the newspapers ivry efternoon except Sundays, an oan Saturday mornin's Ah hud a job helpin oot at the grocer's shop. It gave me enough money tae make up fir the food Ah wisnae gettin at hame, an between the jobs an keepin up wi ma homework it kept me pritty busy. Ah quite liked workin at the shop, an Saturday mornin would go by quickly. Emptyin boxes, sweepin up, an sometimes Ah would get tae help folk carry their groceries an mibbee get a tip. When Ah delivered the papers Ah would go an get Adolph an take him fir a walk wi me. He wis good company, but try as Ah might tae get him tae come tae "Addie," he jist wouldnae, an Ah aye felt a bit conspicuous when Ah hud tae yell "Adolph," tae get him tae come. One time he wandered away when Ah wis oan ma route an at the top i ma lungs Ah hud tae yell: "Adolph, ADOLPH," but he couldnae hear me fir the noise i the traffic an the rain, but this old codger, who wis half bald but hud a black moustache, came runnin efter me. Ah tried tae tell him Ah wis callin the dug but he wisnae huvin ony i it. Started tae hit me wi his brolly an there Ah wis fendin him oaf, tryin no tae laugh too hard. When Adolph saw aw the commotion he came runnin up tae us an started tae bark an snarl at him. He took a bite oot i his coat before Ah could pull him away. Ah nivir heard ony mair aboot it, which wis a bit i a surprise since it wouldnae huv been hard fir him tae find oot who Ah wis, bein that Ah wis deliverin the papers. He wis probably too embarrassed tae dae onythin cos he did kinda look like Hitler.

Mrs Simpson wid get me tae go tae the shops fir her sometimes cos her legs wir bad, but she aye wanted tae pay me. Ah could nivir take it fi her, so Ah'd let her make me tea an it would let her huv a wee chat. It wis a one way chat, mind ye, an it wis aw Ah could dae tae nod at the appropriate times, or if Ah felt energetic Ah wid massage ma chin an lightly nod ma heid tae look thoughtful. But Ah felt sorry fir her cos she wis old an didnae really huv onyone. She did huv a son in Australia who she talked aboot a lot. An one time Ah wis there when he called oan the phone. But it nivir really came oaf very well cos she wis rushin her speech an wisnae makin too much sense, aw oan account i her tryin tae save her son money, cos, as she told me later, the call must've cost him a fortune. Ah suppose that's why he didnae bother callin too often, but he did write her letters an Mrs Simpson wid aye read them tae me, an it wis aboot the only time ye could say she looked happy.

When it came tae a part aboot her grand daughter, she wid often stoap readin an ye could tell she wis visualisin her at her ballet, or swimmin in the pool. Then she'd read oan an Ah'd pretend tae be very interested, an she'd keep it oan the mantel until the next one wid arrive, an then she'd put it in a shoe box wi the others she kept under her bed.

One Saturday Ah left the flat an knocked oan Mrs Simpson's door tae get the dug cos Ah wis aboot tae dae ma papers, but she said she hud let the dug oot awready, which wisnae oot i the ordinary. So Ah didnae think too much aboot it an usually he would find me an walk the route wi me onywye. In the back i ma heid though Ah wis a wee bit concerned cos Ah hud caught Ronnie an his mates throwin darts at it fi the second floor windie. There wisnae much Ah could dae except get Adolph away fi there. One i the darts hud caught him in the thigh an he wis yelpin aboot, no kennin what hud hit him, an Ah wis worried that he'd turn oan me when Ah pulled it oot, but he didnae, an he didnae seem the worse fir wear efter a wee while.

Ah finished ma route an there wis no Adolph in sight which wis unusual, an Ah started tae think mibbee somethin hud happened tae him. Run over oan the busy road or somethin, an so Ah quickened ma step an took a short cut through the woods even though Ah hud been paid fir the week an it wisnae the wisest move tae walk through there oan yer own wi money in yer pocket. But Ah seemed tae get bigger by the day an felt like Ah could handle masel in most situations, but it wisnae the square go that ye hud tae be concerned aboot. There wis always the possibility i bein jumped by the likes i Ronnie an his mates, but in the woods if ye kept yer wits aboot ye, then ye could stay oot i harm's wye.

Ah didnae see onyone, but as Ah approached the clearin Ah could make oot a bonfire goin. Cracklin orange flames in the dusk reminded me i Guy Fawkes night, but it seemed an unusual place tae huv a fire nivir mind that it wis naewhere near November the fifth. There wis a group i aboot six around the fire, an as Ah goat closer Ah could see a dug tied up oan a stick jist like ye'd roast a pig. Ah started tae run cos Ah wis sure, aye, it wis definitely Adolph.

"STOAP, STOAP!" Ah wis yellin an runnin, but they couldnae hear me, an they hoisted the dug ontae the flames an Adolph wriggled violently, an as Ah goat closer Ah heard him yelp, a noise that Ah'll nivir forget. Ah finally goat there aw oot i breath. The twitchin an writhin hud mercifully stoaped, an Ah hud tae stumble back fi the heat gaspin fir breath, an greetin.

"You fuckin bastards," Ah wis yellin an Ah took a swing at Ronnie an missed, an the momentum made me fall in the mud an empty beer cans. Ronnie jumped oan me an stuck his knee in ma back, pulled oan ma hair till Ah thought it hud tae come oot, pushin the back i ma heid intae ma spine.

"Jist calm doon, jist calm doon," he wis sayin. "The dug bit me. Somethin hud tae be done," he said, as if that justified the cruelty. He let me up an through ma tears Ah could make oot what wis left i the dug, ma dug, but the sickenin, bitter smell i the burnt hair made me retreat. Ronnie's accomplices were by now starin intae the fire, cuppin their hands around their cans i beer, havin lost interest in drinkin onymair. Even they hud been appalled at the spectacle, except, that is, fir Dave, who hud helped wi throwin the dug tae its horrible end. He wis snickerin as he cracked open another can an Ah made a lunge at him, but Ronnie intercepted me an aw three i us rolled around in the mud, fists an boots flyin. He hud done mair damage tae me, but Ah hud goat mair satisfaction fi the few shots Ah goat in.

"Gawn hame now!" said Ronnie an Ah did. Limpin an bleedin an ma right eye swollen so much Ah could hardly see oot i it, Ah went back tae the flat. As Ah walked away Ronnie wis mumblin oan aboot how, "it wisnae right that a dug should be bitin folk an shitin aw over the back green. Hud tae be stoaped. Hud tae be stoaped." His voice tailed oaf. He wis tryin tae convince himsel, an keep Dave fi comin back at me at the same time.

As expected Archie wis oot at the pub, an Aunt Mabel wis sittin in the livin room, smokin in the dark wi the radio oan softly. Ah went straight tae ma room an lay oan the bed, an tried tae think aboot what Ah wis goin tae tell Mrs Simpson, but ivry time Ah would try an shut ma eyes, aw Ah could see wis the dug writhin in agony an the sound i that yelp stung through ma brain.

Chapter 17

James decided to give up his room at the downtown hotel in favour of the more regal comforts of the Braid Hills Hotel, which was nearer to the area of town he was most familiar with. It had not been James' intention to opt for premium accommodation, but after making two enquiries at bed and breakfast establishments in Morningside, he had realised that such arrangements would necessarily entail social interaction with kindly, elderly proprietors. This was something James sought to avoid. So he found himself casting off the shackles of his normally parsimonious nature. It was definitely a trend that seemed to have arrived at about the same time as he reached the age of forty, and in truth he felt it to be a positive direction he seemed to be embarking upon. He had long felt that his frugal ways were the result of too long watching every penny, and whenever he bordered on frivolous use of finances he felt physically sick afterward. And while there was a part of him that wanted to chastise his extravagant ways, there was also an emerging side of him that was privately pleased, like a child who had just learned to tie his own shoe laces.

Also, his apprehension about visiting the neighbourhood appeared to James in retrospect to have been unjustified, for he now realised it had always been with him. As a result, James felt he was ahead, and although there was still an obligatory visit to old Archie, there was only reticence in place of dread. It did trouble him however that the trip would, therefore, not be the cathartic experience he had faintly hoped it would be. Perhaps, he felt, he was consigned forever to dream dreams he would rather not. On an intellectual level, he reminded himself of his impatient nature and so he told himself that it was only one day. But on a visceral level he still felt very damaged.

The distinctive red-brown sandstone of the hotel with its ornate architecture was something James, on a subconscious level, felt he needed to conquer. He had delivered the newspaper there more than a quarter century ago, and never in his wildest dreams did he ever think that one day he would return as a guest. The starchy gentleman at the front desk, who seemed to have cornered the local Brylcreem market, announced matter of factly that Mr McPherson was very fortunate they indeed had one room left. However, after James saw the rate, he certainly didn't feel very fortunate, but he took solace in knowing Karen would be pleased when he told her about it. She would think that he was making real progress. Any thoughts he had harboured about apologising for the window that he and Neil Scott had broken via a stray stone all those years ago also soon dissipated as he made his way to his room. The sound of the glass breaking had been exquisite. Like a mini car crash in which no one had been seriously hurt, viewed from a sixth floor apartment.

The still-strong rays of sunlight broke through the thick pane illuminating the particles of dust that seemed in a constant cycle of motion, apparently defying all physical laws of nature. James sat on the plush armchair, sinking so deep he appeared like a child with a flotation device, his head being forced up above the water. He stared at his luggage on the bed before him, wondering why he felt so tired, given that he was technically on holiday. Pondering on the reality, James reflected on how he once worked so long and hard and on the realisation that was no longer possible. It would be too difficult to go back, and slumping in the comfort of the armchair, James started to question himself. Was he becoming soft? It was the kind of moment better shared with Karen, as she always knew exactly what to say in reassurance. But alone and far from home, James' mind started to run away with itself and he imagined himself a corpulent sybarite by the age of fifty.

James decided to forego the opportunity to dine in the hotel alone, and after foraging in his travel bag for his most casual clothes, he changed his appearance to one more in keeping with how he felt, and opted for the privacy of his rental car which he was becoming rather fond of. The travel bag was left on the floor next to the ample chest of drawers. James never unpacked when he stayed in a hotel, no matter how long the stay, preferring to live out of his suitcase. His jeans and tee shirt garnered a few condescending glances as he made his way out of the hotel, with Brylcreem Boy's the most incriminating, well practised, as it must have been. So any thoughts of knocking back a pint in the lounge before leaving were quickly abandoned.

Fish and chips, though not the healthiest of choices, was what James opted for. He rationalised the consumption of fats by convincing himself he wouldn't have the opportunity to experience real fish and chips, the way they were meant to be eaten, when he returned to Canada. But he was less than satisfied as the chips were crisp and not mushy as he remembered they had been. Perhaps, he thought, traditional fish and chips had fallen victim to concerns of health, and justified as that may be, there seemed to be something almost sacrilegious about it. James attempted to drown the food in vinegar and brown sauce in an effort to recreate the taste and texture sensation he had remembered. As he lingered at the counter, eating and soaking in vinegar, he made a mental note to himself that should he revisit this or any other chippy during his stay, he wouldn't order the pizza. What passed for pizza was a round hunk of dough with traces of cheese and sauce that prior to consuming apparently had to disappear in a bubbling vat of boiling fat. He had heard you shouldn't order pizza when in Italy, but clearly it was downright dangerous to do so in Scotland. The alleged pizza was served up with a large dose of chips to an overtly pimply, chubby specimen destined for an early grave.

James stayed in the establishment to finish his meal. The muffled sound of the radio struggled over the volume of bubbling fat. Just as he was following a news item on the barely audible radio, the line of the story was broken by the noise of another batch of chips being condemned to the vat. A steady stream of customers provided adequate entertainment for James though, who attempted to determine what each face represented. It was never possible, of course, but eating alone as he was, it was something to keep his mind occupied.

As he was finishing the last of his fish supper and about to slide off the stool, a man about the same age as James entered the premises. Short and stocky, with an aged tattoo on his exposed right forearm, the naturally curly hair not yet tainted by grey, there was something familiar about him to James. He stared a little longer than social convention allowed, but it elicited no response except annoyance, and James left the shop. Perhaps it was someone he had gone to school with. Perhaps not. It didn't seem worth exploring, so James made his way to the parked car, his mind still working furiously to at least ascertain the identity of the man, when suddenly he heard his name called.

"Jimmy? It is you isn't it?"

James looked around on the second enquiry, assuming the first had been in error.

"Ally?"

"It is you," said the tall statuesque woman who had just passed by, but then stopped upon recognising James. Her long black hair was now shoulder length, but to James that was all that had changed. He didn't notice that some minor wrinkles had crept around her green eyes evidencing the passage of time.

"You look great," said James abruptly, meaning it completely.

"You look great yourself," responded Ally in kind. She then placed her lithe arms around James and hugged him right there amidst the pedestrians of Morningside Avenue, who probably attributed the proceedings to the fact that it was tourist season. James was at once relieved and disappointed that the embrace did not include a kiss.

They stood back for an awkward few seconds inspecting each other until James finally said: "How've you been, isn't going to quite do here, is it, Ally?"

"No," she laughed nervously. "I haven't been called Ally in a long time. Are you alone?" she enquired.

"Yes, actually," said James, "all alone." He wondered, now that he had answered, how she had meant the question.

"Would you like to go for a drink or something?"

"I'd love to ah … ah … Alison," said James, which made her laugh.

"Alright, but you, Jimmy, will have to call me Ally."

"Alright, Ally. Where to?"

"I know a little place near here. Come on." And they were off, James bubbling with excitement. As they walked, the man who had seemed vaguely familiar to James emerged from the fish and chip shop.

"Ally, do you recognise him?"

"Ken Henderson. Married Avril Maxwell after getting her in the family way. Divorced four years later," she said, matter of factly.

"That's it," said James, "Kenny Henderson. How the mighty have fallen."

"Thought he was God's gift to women."

"So how do you know what became of him?"

"Avril was a friend for a while."

"Ah yes, you babes ran in packs. I remember," said James, and she smiled the perfect smile James recollected only too well. He had explored every one of her teeth with his tongue on a few occasions, the memory of which made him grin. He also recounted the clumsy gropes of adolescence he and Ally had shared, and that made him feel self-conscious.

It was with some relief to James that Ally led him to a place that was more of a restaurant setting than a bar, thereby enabling them to talk without competition from a relentless dance beat.

"So did your dreams come true, Jimmy?"

"In what way?" said James, somewhat puzzled.

"You know. You couldn't wait to get out of here."

"I wasn't running away from everyone. I missed you terribly," said James anxious to make himself clear on that point.

The drinks arrived and neither felt it appropriate to continue in the presence of the waiter. James fumbled with his napkin, and when the waiter had left the table, he seized the opportunity to move on to a discussion of Ally's life. She diplomatically omitted their awkward parting of ways and opted to discuss her post Edinburgh, post Jimmy experience.

"So I went down to London, when I was eighteen."

"And what were you running from?" James regretted saying that as soon as it had left his lips, but it was too late. Ally gave little visual indication she had been stung, but responded in a forthright manner.

"Nothing. But then there was nothing to keep me here."

"I know," said James. "I'm sorry." And he reached out his hands and held Ally's. She smiled.

"So you went to Canada."

"Yes, I went and stayed."

"So this is a visit."

"Oh yes. I'm just back because my Uncle is apparently near the end."

"You came back for him." Ally was incredulous. "I thought he was one of the main reasons you left."

"Well, yes. That's true, but …" James squirmed. Recovering he said: "Tell me about you."

"Did some modelling in London," said Ally, with a shrug of her shoulders that revealed her bashful reluctance.

"I have absolutely no trouble believing that," said James who was starting to enjoy himself again, allowing the possibilities that were dancing in the back of his brain to filter into his imagination. "When did you come back here?"

"Just last year. I decided to leave London, and my husband, behind."

"Oh," was all James could manage, hoping Ally would expand. But she did not. "Any children?"

"No, no … no," said Ally as if the idea was preposterous. "No! Actually we were only married for four years. It was a mistake. He's quite a bit older than me and then he has a great deal of difficulty with the whole monogamy concept." Ally shrugged in an effort to bring her discussion of the issue to a close.

"How could someone have difficulty with monogamy if they were married to you?" enquired James attempting to appear munificent despite his own personal falterings in regards to his commitment to monogamy at this moment.

"Because he's a man!" stated Ally with emphasis on the *man*, and she thrust her head and lean neck across the small table to accentuate her point. They both laughed. James did so to relieve nervous tension and Ally laughed in an effort to introduce some levity to the discussion.

The waiter returned as James had devoured his beer, but Ally declined on his behalf and when the waiter left to prepare the bill, she invited James back to her flat. James' pulse rushed a little faster, but he attempted to appear pensive before acquiescing to what he had hoped she would ask. So off they went. James was pleased to open the door of the car for Ally, externally appearing debonair in spite of his casual attire, but internally waging war with his conscience. As they headed toward the centre of the city the conversation progressed in a lighter vein. Reminisces of yesteryear and what became of some of the people they had known. Ally never did enquire as to James' family and this made it easier for him to allow the game he was playing to continue.

Ally's flat, as she referred to it, was housed in a spacious Georgian building that looked stately in the reluctantly fading light of a long June day. The interior delivered on the promise intimated by the majestic exterior, as it was appropriately outfitted in period décor. And as Ally drew the heavy curtains, denying the remnants of natural light, James felt himself transported in time as well as distance from all that was his reality. Without speaking, Ally turned to the impressive array of electronic gadgetry and the room was infused with soothing jazz. She looked in James' direction and smiled as he perused the apartment like a wide-eyed child, and still feeling a little under-dressed he stuck his hands in his pockets trying to appear casual.

"The bar's over there," said Ally pointing in the direction of an elaborate cabinet, and James instantly welcomed the opportunity to head for a task in which he felt comfortable.

"What can I get you?"

"Double gin and tonic please," said Ally, as she arranged some CDs on the carousel, but it was another cue that James chose to interpret as an invitation. He was thinking with a brain that seemed to be located in his groin and though he was aware of that on an intellectual level he chose to run with it for the moment. As he neared Ally it was all he could do to keep the ice from rattling around the glasses betraying his nervousness, which was heightened by Ally's decision to plant her still nubile body on the couch instead of the armchair. Ally took her glass and offered a toast to "us," and James gulped his scotch while Ally sipped her drink.

"How do you like the music?" asked Ally. But James needed a moment to think as he had hardly been paying attention to the soft sounds emanating from the background.

"Great," he said giving himself time to tune into the sounds. "Steeler's Wheel. That takes me back."

"They're all from the seventies. Steeler's Wheel, Elton John, Gilbert O'Sullivan, Fleetwood Mac, and Supertramp."

"Perfect," said James.

One drink led to another and another, and they talked, intermingling reminiscences with probing questions they answered honestly. James even felt compelled to tell her about his family and, despite the volume of alcohol consumed, he felt himself withdrawing from what he had so recklessly contemplated earlier in the evening. The familiar sounds of Elton John and Kiki Dee transported them instantly back to the summer of nineteen seventy-six, a time full of future promise. But just as Elton and Kiki were unlikely to have broken each other's hearts given subsequent revelations, so too it became evident that James and Ally could not turn back the clock to an earlier time of innocence and freedom. They had adult baggage. Some welcome; some not. Perhaps he had been seduced by the opportunity to escape convention or the chance to experience youthful excitement once again. Whatever the case, James felt relieved that he had not done anything to tarnish what he had so recently sought to escape.

Chapter 18

My birthday had always been a virtual non-event in Archie's household, and, as far as he was concerned, my seventeenth would be no different. There was to be no last minute effort to entice me to stay with my inheritance. The drink had long since numbed his senses and his grip on reality, so he may not have been totally aware his monthly subsidies from the estate, intended for my upkeep, were about to become extinct. Archie's abysmal record as a handicapper had been periodically punctuated with some big wins, which had subsequently been squandered at the pub, but he largely lived his life on a monthly cycle that revolved around a cheque arriving at the beginning of each month.

Ronnie and I had nothing in common, with the exception of our contempt for Archie's repugnant life. His rare triumphant moments aside, Archie was a nobody, a nothing. He did know that much, and we knew that because of his frequent need to have dominance over something, or more aptly, someone, in his life. As first Ronnie, and then myself got to be bigger than Archie, the focus of his violent episodes became almost exclusively Aunt Mabel. For my entire stay at the flat she had remained a pathetic creature unwilling to leave or seek help and Ronnie seemed to hold her in as much contempt as he did his father. She had no meaningful friends and rarely ventured outside, seeming to draw all her mental sustenance from cigarettes and television.

The fact that she was willing to live a kind of second hand existence through a nineteen inch black and white box of electronics by no means made her unusual, but it was the extent to which she did so that was troubling. On occasion, Archie would, in a fleeting moment of generosity by virtue of an unlikely winner, give her some money and she would go to get her hair lacquered into that stiff style women of her age always seemed to settle for; or she would venture out to the bingo in search of a paltry win that would accommodate the breadth of her dreams. But she rarely showed any emotion and she weathered her abuse like a roofing tile on an abandoned cottage long since vacated.

On those rare occasions when I happened to be in the flat at the same time as Archie, he would refrain from lashing out in a physical way at Mabel, but would often substitute with verbal assaults in redundant efforts to belittle her to a level beneath where he had sunk. I suspect there was a time when Mabel would have found that more difficult to bear than the beatings, but it was long since gone, and it was hard for me to ever imagine a time when that was the case.

If you were to ask Ronnie he would tell you he left school because it was a waste of time, but in reality there was some dispute as to whether he left or was expelled. Either way he was another angry young man woefully unprepared to face the world. He was still officially staying at the flat on the occasion of my seventeenth birthday, but he was often gone for extended periods. His world was one of petty theft and dole fraud. But he was too thick to pull it off and it was only a matter of time before it would catch up with him. The best I could hope for Ronnie was that he wouldn't get some poor girl up the stick and perpetuate the misery on another generation.

The money arrived with the suddenness that had caused my condition five years ago, and though it wasn't a fortune, it provided a foundation for the larger dreams that had been my sustenance, but with its arrival came a sense of responsibility and opportunity. Few people knew of this development. Mr McCrae, of course, knew, and he had helped me with the legal formalities even although I had latterly not kept in touch. A teacher at the school, who had long encouraged me to drop my dialect, in favour of what passed for Standard English in Edinburgh, and apparently impressed with my academic promise, had convinced me to stay on and take my Highers, was also privy to the information.

Then there was Ally whom I loved more than I ever allowed myself to reveal to her, and it was only recently she had learned of my improved prospects. I had kept the knowledge from her for fear it might influence the course of our romance, but that had been unnecessary as Ally had the determination and ability to take her wherever she wanted. That had been made clear to me the first time I had seen her as she had stolen the ball from under my nose and deposited it in the goal.

Even after five years there's not a day goes by I'm not forced to think about my family. Stupid little things that are of no consequence to anyone else have the ability to hurl me back in time and inflict that sense of loss again and again, and I don't imagine that will ever change. I can be watching some half-arsed film of the week on the television, assigning the ten percent of my brain that's required to follow what passes for the plot, and an insignificant character's name is Muriel and then I'm thinking of my Mum, and off I go into the past. The way she brushed her hair; the perfume she wore on Sundays; making dinner in the kitchen; and she's gone. Sometimes I find myself getting off on ridiculous tangents. Like watching an American movie or a James Bond film, and when you're forced to endure the obligatory car chase, I start to think that maybe Dad could have done better and avoided the bus or something if only he was a better driver. But that was daft and futile. Sometimes I'd play the if only game. If only Gran hadn't got a heart attack then they wouldn't have had to drive there, but that was like blaming Colin Stein for the Ibrox disaster.

I moved into a large flat with some other blokes who were older than myself, and who I didn't know. A teacher at school had set it up for me in an effort to have me complete my education, and it just felt like the right thing to do. It was a complete shambles of course. Dishes were washed on an as need basis and it didn't pay to stock up on food as it was deemed fair game by the other flatmates. The place reeked of stale beer, cigarettes, socks and the remnants of curry takeaways, but it was a world away from the stress I'd almost become accustomed to. Yet it was here I began to smoke. I felt relaxed and there was always my own room to escape to should I find the mess overwhelming.

I'd like to say that I was careful with my money, but that would be an understatement. I was tight with it and hated to deplete it in even the slightest amount. But the odd time I'd spend some. I liked to get out of the city whenever I could, so I'd head down to Waverly Station and jump on a train and head north just for the day. It was better if Ally came with me but sometimes I'd go myself.

Girls came and went and it always made me wonder what they found appealing in men. I mean it's men who are often accused of only being after one thing, but in reality the opposite is true. A lot of the women who came in were interesting to talk to, they went to great lengths to make themselves look and smell attractive, and they seemed to be genuinely interested in knowing how I was doing. They had lofty goals for their lives and career aspirations and I always had the sense that their apartments were not likely to be plagued by stale odours and untidy piles of soiled laundry. The men who shared this flat on the other hand were uninteresting and boorish. To them, a well-rounded man was someone who knew who the current Prime Minister was and was likely to use deodorant at least three times a week. But by dint of well practised dance moves and the ability to whisper pure bullshit at the appropriate times, they were often able to bed these superior beings.

In their defence, some of the women probably really believed that there was a potentially meaningful relationship to be had. If only she could save him from his debauchery, there was a caring and loving man she could share her life with. But if they actually believed that, then when they quietly ventured into the bathroom the morning after, to do whatever it is women do in there, surely the magnitude of the squalor to be found behind that door would cure them of that misguided conception. But generally I did not subscribe to that theory. They couldn't be that dense. It was easier for me to believe that it was they who were only after one thing.

Archie never made any efforts to contact me, but on occasion Ronnie would drop by looking for a "sub" until his fortunes improved. The late teens can be a time of great influence and people often undergo life-changing experiences. It can be religious, or marriage, or even a desire to go to some foreign land to improve the lot of an impoverished people. Ronnie became a skinhead. I tolerated his periodic visits because my time was short and as soon as school was finished and the details were completed, I was off for Canada. The land my Grandfather never went to would be my destination. A fresh start where no one knew who or what I was.

Chapter 19

Muffled sounds and coffee smells intermingled with the curious dream James was experiencing, until they superseded the quickly forgotten illusion and James was awake. Ally stood before him with a coffee and a smile. It was a smile that appeared to have interpreted James' sexual reluctance as a magnanimous gesture in deference to her recent unfortunate experience with men. It was just as well. For prior to James succumbing to his alcohol induced slumber, he worried Ally might be disappointed he had not at least made a token gesture in that direction. Even now as he gratefully accepted the coffee, he hoped his hair successfully straddled the rugged look without being too bad as to be described as unkempt. It was a fine line, and for some reason he hoped that he hadn't crossed it.

Ally was fully dressed and she announced that she had to go to work.

"So, when shall we get together again?" said Ally assuming this was a given.

It quickly dawned on James that, by chickening out of a dalliance, he had fallen into that most unfortunate of positions; he was to be a platonic friend to a beautiful woman. But what could he say to dissuade her? *Look, I had thought that we might have a shag for old time's sake, but I had no intention of becoming best pals.* No, that would never do. She would hate him. He would hate himself.

"I'm going to be busy today, but perhaps dinner tomorrow?" That would buy him some time until he could figure out how he wanted to handle the situation.

"Great. Call me," said Ally and she handed James a card with numerous telephone numbers. Cell phone, pager, office, and home; she had it covered. She kissed James on the forehead, instructed him on how to lock the door upon leaving, and she was off.

James lay back down on the couch, counting on his bladder to hold out for a few more minutes. Beer before bed was never a good idea, but it certainly wasn't the worst decision he could have made last night. He thought of Karen and the girls and how close he'd come to jeopardising the domestic bliss that often drove him crazy, but which he knew he treasured and couldn't do without. As he showered, his brain undertook the task of visualising the many scenarios that might have unfolded. After mentally exploring the rabbit in the pot paradigm, James decided that he was getting carried away as he was wont to do, and so he tried to move on.

The car was sporting a rain spattered ticket on the windscreen indicating a parking violation, and James removed it with some disgust. He would have to peruse the fine print in the rental agreement to see if he was responsible for paying. It was always worth reading, but he strongly suspected that once he got down to the really small print, indeed he would be accountable, as well as, for that matter, numerous other items that he hadn't thought about. By the time he was through they'd probably pin the kidnapping of the Lindburgh baby on him.

James headed south, back to his hotel, which he wished now he hadn't bothered to check into. Of course, he couldn't have known that but it still bothered him he had in effect wasted his money. He would go and get changed and then head on over to the old folk's home or whatever it was where Archie was residing. As he drove he allowed his mind to wander and think of Ally. The way she was; the way they were, like Robert Redford and Barbra Streisand, although that wasn't right. Ally was much better looking than Barbra Streisand. Still, he tried to imagine what a life would have been like with Ally, but then it was hard to imagine his life without Karen. Ultimately he felt a little responsibility for Ally's unfortunate marriage. That was insane, he knew, but then he had been playing the what if game for a long time and it was hard to break the habit.

After changing, James sat down to a leisurely breakfast, the type he'd always planned to have on Sunday mornings, but for one reason or another it never could be managed. He read the paper and sipped his tea, distracted only by the odd traffic sound, which prompted him to look out of the window, casually identify the source, then turn back to his newspaper. By the time he was finished he decided that it would probably be too close to lunch time at the home, so he postponed going till later in the day.

The intermittent light rain that had plagued the morning seemed to have abated and James embarked on a drive to Hillend and the ski slope. He took the lift up to the top and, deciding that he should get some exercise, undertook to climb to the summit and enjoy the view. A check of his watch indicated that he should really be heading over to the home, but once at the summit he was reluctant to rush back. In this manner he managed to piss the day away. Certainly, he attempted to rationalise in his mind there was no hurry, and this was one of the things he had wanted to do, but he knew he was avoiding a task he had to accomplish.

Next morning, James checked out of the hotel, his thinking being, if he was to be Ally's friend, then he might as well sleep on her couch again. If not, he could find another room elsewhere. Today he would definitely go and see Archie. Get it over with and move on. But not immediately. The afternoon would be better for that sort of thing, and so he headed for the north end of the city. He didn't know why, but he felt the need to drive around and see the house he had lived in prior to losing his family. It appeared dark and small and it somehow seemed inconceivable that some other family lived there now, indeed that the terraced house still existed was strange.

Cars lined the narrow street such that a football game would simply not be possible. Besides, kids today played football on computer screens rather than the real thing. The primary school still stood behind the ostentatious wrought iron gates that someone thought would be a good idea to paint powder blue. Although it was no longer a primary school, but the centre for some kind of community social service department, James drove through the gates and made the circle around the driveway. He smiled in recollection at his greatest achievement as the large room that was once used for school dinners became apparent. It had been there as a nine year old he had successfully propelled a particularly mushy Brussels sprout onto the ceiling, where it had stuck fast. It had been deemed a fine accomplishment in the eyes of all his mates and when the dinner monitor had accused him, he could hardly have denied it given his instant cult status. He had got the belt for it as a matter of course, but it had been well worth it, and he had by his actions started a craze that made lunchtime somewhat hazardous. Boys who were older than him took up the challenge and he had proudly demonstrated his technique, placing the sprout in his spoon which was balanced over the fork. When the fist was applied to the other end of the spoon the Brussels sprout sprang upwards to the high ceiling. To his knowledge no one else managed to actually stick another Brussels sprout to the ceiling, but it wasn't for want of trying. When sprouts were not on the menu, eager young lads would substitute, often inappropriately, and the results were not always pretty.

As all fads do, that one came to an end, but not before a good three weeks that almost drove the dinner monitor to a nervous breakdown. James' Brussels sprout had remained there long after however, although its size diminished through dehydration until it appeared to be a giant piece of snot that in years to come people would wonder how on earth had got there.

James was tempted to go in and see if it was still affixed to the ceiling, but decided against it because he wasn't sure if he would be able to explain his curiosity if a staff member challenged him. There was no way a forty-year-old man could make such a request appear reasonable and sane, so he drove away.

James dutifully headed for Corstorphine as the noon news came on the car radio. Nothing much was happening in the world so it tended to be overly weighted with insignificant economic news and prognostications that on busier days wouldn't have got a sniff. The rain became audible as it smashed against the windscreen, hurled as it was by the gusty wind. Whether that was enough to distract him, or perhaps just his familiarity with the city had faded over the years, he found himself having overshot his destination and had to backtrack at the site of the slaughterhouse, and taking a little longer than he had anticipated, he succumbed to logic and pulled out the map.

After locating the street on the map, James managed to navigate his way to the home. It was set amidst large properties, all rather similar in style. Heavy, dark, stone houses softened by a mature landscape belonging to another world that existed before the war, when servants' entrances were required. Most had been converted to guest houses, a few to retirement homes. James located the home easily as it had large white numerals painted neatly on the stone pillars that marked the entrance, one of which gave evidence of a van having misjudged the width of the entry. It could have been another guest house, but was lacking the "No Vacancies" sign adorning the entrances of the majority of the establishments. A few of the larger houses had neon signs announcing the same news in a more obvious and garish manner that seemed inappropriate to the area. To be fair they were not as glaring as they might have been, but for the stately old homes it was like tarting the queen up in fishnet stockings.

James drove back to Corstorphine Road and managed to find a parking spot at a large hotel where he could get some lunch before the planned visit. It was loud and bright and far from the pub lunch idea he would have preferred, but it was convenient and he had already driven past a couple of pubs that would have necessitated parking half way to Glasgow. But as he sat awaiting his lunch he realised that convenience came at a hefty price. The place abounded with unsure tourists who tossed the restaurant into a state of perpetual slow motion. Waitresses were bogged down with inane enquiries concerning directions to Princes Street and menu questions dealing with minute details one would only ask if they didn't have to be anywhere. Babies wailed inconsistently and bratty children threw tantrums because they were denied ice cream; their flabby parents muffling their predilection to lash out with a smack, and smiling pretentiously when they came in contact with an elderly patron who was scowling in disapproval.

Despite the less than tranquil atmosphere, James resolved to resist drowning out the racket with alcohol and he rationed the beer in sips, not wanting to give Archie any kind of vindication should he arrive inebriated. He was in no particular hurry. Despite the noise, he attempted to think about what he would say to Archie. But it was as if he was cramming for an exam at the last minute, not knowing what area he should concentrate on, and he was unable to formulate anything in preparation.

Lunch finally arrived and was set on the table in a rushed manner, such that the side of the plate bounced once before coming to a rest, causing a couple of chips to slide onto the table cloth. The waitress apologised perfunctorily and James handed her the empty glass, signalling that he would like another. But this would be his last, he told himself. When he had finished, he had to wait for the bill and in his mind he attempted to revisit how he might articulate what he would say to Archie, but nothing seemed to materialise. Perhaps, he thought, he really didn't have anything to say. It would be easier if Archie turned up drunk and belligerent, but that was hardly likely to be the case in a retirement home and at his advanced years.

There was nowhere to park on the street, so James drove in through gates that seemed to be permanently left open as tuffets of grass had grown through the cracking asphalt and would no longer have permitted the clumsy iron gates to shut. The narrow roadway wound up an incline to fortuitously reveal an area reserved for visitor parking, and James backed in despite the fact that the angled parking was designed for cars to drive in. The mature trees swayed in time with the gusts as if they were giant wind instruments, and the lush emerald leaves of early summer glistened defiantly. Spots of rain came at sharp angles leaving marks that appeared as little rips on the large bay window at the front of the home, and James quickened his step to the front door in spite of his apprehension.

He made his way through the heavy front door that was left slightly ajar despite the weather, and then through a supplementary glass and oak door with a large brass handle. The ample foyer was deserted. James could have walked down either of the two corridors to the left and right, or he could have waltzed up the stairs ahead, as there appeared to be no one charged with a reception or security role. As he stood and waited for someone official to arrive, his eyes were led to a notice board advertising the upcoming social events. An outdoor tea, weather permitting, was to take place on Friday at three o'clock with music supplied by a local primary school band. That'd be right up Archie's alley thought James as he chuckled to himself. With a bit of luck he wouldn't be deaf yet and would have to endure the painful sounds of a bunch of ten year-olds murdering violas and flutes.

The notice board was also adorned with photographs, their corners curling up and drying out much like the inmates they portrayed. An Easter party had been the occasion, and several residents had been caught showing their false teeth, thereby demonstrating how happy they must be. James scanned the photographs in vain looking for one that might be Archie and just as he was about to initiate some exaggerated throat clearing noises, a stern looking middle aged woman appeared in a quasi nurse uniform.

"Can I help you?" she enquired, furrowing her brow as she gazed suspiciously at James.

"Ah yes. Actually, I understand that Archie McPherson, ah, resides here," responded James.

"Yes," was all the nurse/warden said which left James momentarily at a loss.

Recovering, he said: "I was wondering if I might see him, ah, I understand he's been asking for me."

"And you are?"

"Oh I'm James McPherson … his nephew … from Canada actually."

"Oh," she said, her mood finally brightening a little to a sub arctic glow, and turning, she instructed James to follow her.

James followed, attempting to maintain sufficient distance to allow the pungent perfume to dissipate. It was a futile manoeuvre, but he felt he had to make the effort as his recently deposited lunch was not sitting well and the offending whiffs were not in any way helping the situation.

"He's in here." She pointed vaguely into the large, densely-populated common room that was warm and smelled of unwashed clothes, boiled sweets, and perfumes from the same family the warden seemed to favour.

It wouldn't take long for a flu epidemic to decimate a room like this, thought James. A few played cards slowly and thoughtfully, and some listened to music that seemed to lose its impact in the high ceilinged, once elegant room. Many sat blankly staring at nothing in particular, perhaps lost in a time long past or perhaps wondering where they were. There was an eclectic collection of armchairs housing the crumpled frames of the residents, and it was difficult to distinguish where the chair began and the octogenarian ended. James was concerned that the warden had left him in this sea of years where most would have embraced him as their son, were he to make any gesture or enquiry. As he gazed through the frail mass assembled in God's waiting room, he was concerned that he would be unable to pick out Archie.

Such fears were immediately rendered groundless as soon as James laid eyes upon him sitting alone and off to the side. The years had certainly taken their toll, as well as the excessive drinking, but it was definitely him. He was thin and feeble looking. The only colour to speak of on his face was courtesy of an enlarged reddened nose. There was a reasonable complement of hair left for a man of advanced years, but it had all turned a very pale shade of grey. A long, thin wisp had fallen over his brow and hung down on to his nose making the end appear all the more red. He was, however, better dressed than he had probably ever been, save for the odd funeral or wedding he had been obliged to attend.

Glancing around the room, James noticed that a dress code must have been in effect. All dressed up and nowhere to go. Archie's blue striped tie was dotted with wayward splashings from spoonfuls that hadn't all made the target. Someone had attempted to wipe them off from time to time, smudging them deeper into the fabric.

James felt the eyes of the more alert upon him and there was a mumble from a few of the ancient commentators.

"Mr McPherson has a visitor," could be heard and it was accompanied by excessive nodding and facial skin movements.

"I think it's his son. He has a son you know."

More nodding, followed by tsk tsks when some old busy body commented on how infrequent the visits had been.

It was apparent that Archie was oblivious to what was going on around him, for as James approached he seemed to show no excitement at the prospect of something to break the monotony. He sat staring ahead and clutching something in his hands.

"Hullo, Archie. Archie McPherson."

To James' surprise Archie looked in his face, albeit with a look of bewilderment, and then looked down and fumbled with his hands revealing a set of yellowed false teeth. He then slipped them into his foul smelling mouth which was more than James' queasy stomach needed to experience, and with the warmth of the overcrowded room he had to make a real mind over matter effort to keep from launching his lunch all over Archie.

"It's me, James. Jimmy, your nephew."

No words, but his face brightened in recognition, and Archie raised his long bony finger and pointed at James, apparently shocked to see him.

"So how've you been?" said James.

But before Archie could answer, a young staff member approached and suggested that they might be more comfortable in the visiting room.

With some help, Archie managed to get off the chair and hobble along to another large bright room that ran off the foyer. Eventually they arrived at a table next to the bay window that afforded a pleasant view of the garden. James thanked the young lady for her assistance, and mentally speculated she could probably look forward to a chastising from the warden for actually being helpful.

"You comfortable, Archie?" asked James, but it was more of an effort to initiate some kind of conversation. What little momentum that had been achieved in the other room had been lost on account of the length of time it took Archie to struggle along the fifteen yards of hallway.

"Aye, Ah cannae walk, son. Cannae walk, ken."

"Yes, so I see. Are they painful? Your legs I mean?"

"Naw, naw. Jist Ah cannae walk, son."

"You know who I am don't you?" asked James, who thought he had been on to something, but they seemed to be getting bogged down.

"Aye, aw aye … Who are ye?"

"Jimmy. I've come over from Canada," stated James emphatically.

"Aw aye," and again came the point that seemed to signal recognition.

"Canada eh," said Archie and he blew an exaggerated puff of air through his dry lips instead of verbalising an adjective.

"Yes, Canada. It's been a long time though. But Ronnie told me you wanted to see me," said James, hoping to move things along. Archie leaned heavily on the arms of the chair and looked around the room, thinking that Ronnie was there, and when his eyes came back to focus on James it was apparent that he had to work hard to remember who sat across from him.

"Sweets anyone?" cried a jolly fifty-something woman, herself looking like a Liquorice Allsort, who had rolled into the room with a trolley laden with all manner of mints and confections.

"Would you like something, Archie?" asked James as the cart approached.

"Naw, naw," replied Archie screwing up his face in disapproval.

"Archie never has anything. Do you, Archie?" said the volunteer loudly and effusively as if she were talking to a three-year-old who had just successfully recited a nursery rhyme. Archie just shook his head obediently.

"Even when he first arrived and he had to give up that nasty habit he didn't even ask for mints."

She was now talking to James exclusively as if Archie were a piece of furniture, imitating the smoking action with her fingers just in case James was unaware of what she was referring to, and James surprisingly felt offended by that. He was also beginning to feel like a cigarette himself, but was glad that there were none available as he was pleased with his modest two-day smokeless streak.

The objectionable woman gone, James was anxious to elicit whatever it was Archie wanted to talk to him about.

"Mind the quarry, Dougie?" said Archie who much to James' dismay was now mistaking James for his dead father.

"No, Archie it's Jimmy. Dougie's boy. From Canada."

Again came the finger point and look of surprise on Archie.

"Mind that time doon the quarry, Dougie? Swimmin eh," he persisted. James sat back in his chair wondering if it was worth trying anymore while Archie rambled on about his boyhood and something about a quarry. It was hard to make any sense of it and James overheard a similar effort from an old woman talking to her son about when she was a girl in Caithness before the First World War. Her son, who was managing to stay patient and nod and uhhuh at the appropriate times, looked like a pensioner himself.

Archie finally ended his little soliloquy and began to gaze around the room, his eyes eventually fixating on the garden that lay beyond the bay window. It was still blustery and the June flowers had decided against revealing their colours in the absence of sunshine.

"Yon car there," said Archie pointing at James' rental car.

"Yes, that's my car," responded James not knowing if that was necessary. Then a thought occurred to him.

"Would you like to go for a run in the car?"

"Ah cannae walk son. Cannae walk."

"Is there anything you wanted to say to me? Before I leave."

James leaned forward hoping somehow to drag it out of Archie, his hands interlocked on the table and looking deeply into Archie's dark eyes. There followed a long silence peppered only by a forceful band of rain hurled against the window, and the intermittent ramblings of the well-dressed old lady at the next table. At another time James would have been interested in a social history of rural Caithness in the early part of the twentieth century, but not today.

"Soon be tea. Tea's comin soon. Tea's comin soon," mumbled Archie who started to shuffle about awkwardly in his seat. James hoped that he was just anxious he might miss the tea and biscuits, and that he hadn't shit his drawers.

"Well, I think I'll get you back in for your tea and then I'll be off," said James getting to his feet.

"Right then, Dougie," replied Archie pointing and nodding his head, which seemed to be his maladroit body language expressing approval. James commandeered a staff member to help Archie through to God's waiting room.

"Bye then," he said finally, but what was left of Archie's mind was now focussed on tea and biscuits as he struggled awkwardly down the hall.

James stood in the foyer for a moment attempting to digest what had just transpired. He was trying to resist a feeling of defeat, telling himself he came with no expectations, but he was feeling rather empty. Rather than marching out through the door he headed down the hall to the left where most of the staff members seemed to appear from. The door was slightly ajar, and female voices could be heard chatting light-heartedly. James knocked gingerly before entering.

"Oh hullo. I don't mean to bother you on your break, but I was wondering if someone could tell me something of Archie McPherson's condition?"

James' request was met with an awkward silence, though he did have the undivided attention of the four nurses. He wasn't sure if he was being viewed with suspicion or if he was being checked out, but remembering his experience on the High street the other day he decided not to allow himself the ego trip. After looking at each other as if they were school children who had just been caught in a lie, finally the one who looked like the youngest member of the railway children spoke up.

"We don't really know a lot about Archie," she said and then sipped her tea slowly and held it close to her lips with both hands.

"Well, I realise he's suffering from Alzheimer's, but his legs? I mean what's his prognosis?"

"We really couldn't say."

"Well does he get any visitors?" asked James attempting a different tack.

"Not really," said the spokeswoman. "Are you a relative?"

"Oh yes," said James apologetically, at last understanding her reticence.

"I'm his nephew. Visiting from Canada," he added.

"We're not really permitted to comment on any of the residents' medical conditions you understand."

"Ah yes," said James. "Well thanks anyway. Is there anything he needs?"

"No, everything's taken care of really," said the take-charge nurse with the long blonde hair as she got up and took her mug to the sink. With that, James acquiesced, backed out of the room, and made his way to the front door.

James got into his car muttering to himself. "Brain dead old bastard."

He drove off without looking back and turned on the car radio just for the sake of having some noise.

Chapter 20

As the large craft descended over the verdant city of Toronto, James strained to take in as much of the landscape as possible. Immediately he was struck by the preponderance of trees, that made the city look like one giant broccoli farm periodically punctuated by swimming pools. The flatness of the land made it seem as though the entire city was carpeted. To the south, beyond the skyscrapers and the giant phallic symbol, lay the vast lake dotted near the shore with triangular white sails on a warm summer's afternoon.

James' first impressions of Canada were both eclectic and non-traditional, a consequence primarily of when he arrived, and his predilection for noticing aspects others tended to overlook. He was immediately aware of a nation that placed a premium on straight teeth, enjoyed large powerful cars, and despite the fact that English was allegedly spoken, had different words for many things. The traditional image of a land of snow hardly held true arriving at the beginning of July, and James struggled to breathe the air as he disembarked the plane. It felt every bit the advertised ninety-three degrees, enhanced as it was by the surrounding tarmac and the sun radiating off the metallic craft. It was so hot the heat seemed to resonate with noise. James had never been south of the Scottish border before and so had never experienced anything close to the warmth and humidity of Toronto in the summer.

The terminal was flooded with anxious relatives, who by their body language suggested that they would rather spend a July Saturday afternoon anywhere but the arrivals area of an airport. There was no one to greet James, and as he waded his way through the crowds he was struck by the well tanned skin on view where it was not covered by halter tops, bell bottoms, or skin tight T-shirts. James felt extremely pale by comparison, but did share a desire to be outside the confines of the airport. As he lined up for a taxi, his eyes found a lone young man, possibly a little older than James, sporting a T-shirt that said: "I'm so happy I could just shit." In poor taste certainly, but it accurately reflected the opinion of most people there.

At any other time James would have been disturbed at the alarmingly rapid rate at which the meter was clicking on the taxi. But this day he was preoccupied with his surroundings, drinking in what was visible from Highway 401, and enjoying his respite from the stifling heat, sitting in the back of an air-conditioned cab. Factories and apartment buildings dominated the lands adjoining the highway betraying the leafy lush portrait that had predominated from fifteen thousand feet above. Brightly coloured cars whisked a mobile populace to and fro in comfort, and occasional glimpses of a concentrated towering skyline could be made out from time to time. Given the vast size of the available land in the country, the density of buildings sighted seemed odd to James. Occasional billboards advertised new cars that were alien to James, although he could already picture himself in the new LTD II as they rushed past the giant advertisement.

As the cab left the sixteen lane highway and headed south on Morningside Avenue, the sky had grown darker, and the distant rumblings of thunder could be heard over the drone of traffic. By the time the driver was weaving his way through the side streets in a less than convincing fashion, the rain was coming down in torrents, which immediately made James realise that Hollywood had not been exaggerating, as he had suspected. It really did rain like this, he thought. A loud peal of thunder was heard immediately after a fork of lightning seemed to strike only about a mile away, and James wondered if he would see a tornado. But the driver appeared totally unruffled and sensing James' apprehension he reassured him that the storm would be fleeting, and he was confident that they had not seen the last of the sun today. James was unconvinced, but by the time they pulled into the driveway of the Galbraith house, the storm had all but abated. To the west blue skies were visible.

James walked up the driveway, still wet from the rain and spattered with leaves from the ash tree, struck down in their prime by the whimsical power of the storm only a few moments earlier. His lone suitcase felt light though it held all he had wanted to bring, and as he set it down on the porch to ring the bell he reflected on how paltry his possessions were and that a new beginning was underway.

After the awkward introductions and superficial conversation, George Galbraith showed James the available accommodations in the basement of the house. He moved through the one bedroom apartment explaining almost apologetically the peculiarities of the set-up. James managed to maintain a sober demeanour, but on the inside he was ecstatic with the possibility of finally having his own space. A place he could actually call home. When the tour came to a close, Mr Galbraith, who was halfway dressed in his police uniform in anticipation of going on shift shortly, informed James of the terms.

"Now, Jimmy, I know we said we'd sponsor you, and that's something we're happy to do as a favour to Mr McCrae. But ... eh ... eh ... He did say that you'd be okay for money and well ... we do need rent for this place to help with the mortgage," said Mr Galbraith with less confidence than you'd expect from a police officer.

"Of course, of course," James broke in trying to put him at ease, and anyway he had been informed by Mr McCrae prior to his departure what the situation was.

Mrs Galbraith had by now appeared in the basement with a toddler clutching nervously at her pink, gingham summer dress.

"What do you think, James? Will it do?"

"Ah, oh yes, it's fine," said James momentarily taken aback by being called James.

"We were just about to discuss the rent," said George turning to his wife with a look that said you should have stayed upstairs.

"Oh sorry," she said nervously, but decided to remain now that she was already there.

"Well," started George, "we had originally expected to rent it to a young couple at three-hundred a month, but that would include utilities. So we thought two seventy-five would be fair."

James resisted the urge to snap up the offer with enthusiasm lest the Galbraiths felt they had surrendered too cheaply, so after a pause and feigning some mental calculations he nodded at first slowly and then confidently.

"Yes, I could manage that," he said.

"Good," said George, glad to have concluded the financial arrangements.

"Good. You'll have noticed that there's no separate entrance, so here's the key. You can use the laundry area on …"

"Tuesdays," interjected Mrs Galbraith, who had by now picked up the sweaty toddler who appeared very unsure of the new tenant.

Mr Galbraith pulled a piece of paper from his pocket, and checked his notes.

"Oh yes, if you get a car, you'll have to park on the street, and well … as long as it's just you, I mean we'd rather you didn't have a roommate, okay."

"Fine," said James. "How do you want me to pay the rent Mr Galbraith?"

"Well, first and last month is the custom," said George, "and please call me George."

"And I'm Fiona."

"Actually, while we're doing the name thing," said James somewhat sheepishly. "Could you call me James, rather than Jimmy?"

Although it was the basement, there were sufficient windows to allow a fair amount of daylight in, and James calculated that in an emergency he might just be able to squeeze through. The walls were of ersatz wood panelling that had started to ruffle and bevel in spots, but there was blue shag carpeting more or less throughout, that appeared to have been upstairs at one time as it was ill fitted and there were periodic oblong holes where the central heating vents had been. There was a shower in the small bathroom that despite the presence of a rather pungent air freshener still smelled of piss. The kitchen was really an extension of the main room; once a wet bar and now with a cooker and a compact fridge that sat on the bar. An old couch was the only piece of furniture, with the exception of a mattress set upon a box spring in the bedroom. Fiona had left some sheets, a pillow and a sleeping bag for James until he was able to buy what he needed, strategically placing them to cover the bulk of the inevitable urine stain which struck James as bearing a remarkable resemblance to the map of Australia.

Unable to register for university and unsure of what he wanted to do, James found employment as a waiter in the interim. George had occasion to visit the establishment during the course of his work and noticed that they were in need of experienced waiters with a thorough knowledge of wines, and preferably with a grasp of Middle Eastern foods. James, of course, had no such experience, but managed to convince the owner he was a quick study and he was hired; at first as a bus boy, then a waiter.

It was, however, a fair trip by bus and what with the late nights and the prospects for a transit strike, James bought a car. It was not a new car, as that would have significantly depleted his resources. Rather, it was a somewhat beat up 1971 Plymouth Fury, which he purchased for $850. Unwilling to part with his money, James had reasoned that it was better to opt for an eight cylinder engine as it was sure to last longer than the older model compact cars that were on offer. It was an unsightly relic rivalling the Queen Mary for size, but as it turned out, James was more troubled by the absence of an FM band on the radio, being forced to endure pop stations in an era that was slipping ever more dangerously down the path of disco. It was an unfortunate state of affairs, but he was committed to resist any temptation to part with his cash in an imprudent manner. It was as if James felt an obligation to his Grandfather to pursue a life that for whatever reason he had been unable, or unwilling to live.

The Omar Khayyam was an attempt at gourmet Middle Eastern dining that attracted a small number of people from that part of the world. The clientele was largely upper-middle class with a sense of adventure and a willingness to experience the various delicacies on offer. On Friday and Saturday nights when about eighty percent of the business was conducted, a belly dancer would periodically appear and weave her way around the restaurant, brushing by animated middle aged men, fuelled on alcohol, stuffing dollar bills into her exotic costume. Unable to compete, their proper wives sat sternly in their seats vowing to have no part in the fantasy when they arrived home. Generally speaking the dancers were proficient enough to label the proceedings as cultural, but for most customers it was a bit of fun. Very rarely was there a table of two or three grubby men who had mistaken the establishment for what is euphemistically known as exotic dancing; but it did happen.

On one such occasion, late on a Saturday evening, Michelle emerged for her final dance to the relentless music thumped out by the eight track above the bar, and as she glided through the room it was evident the two men who had come in for late drinks didn't particularly view it as a cultural experience. Abassi, the owner who also filled the role of host, had seated them anyway, even though he probably suspected their intentions. But it was a few more dollars, and that was all he really cared about. As Michelle gyrated her hips to the music they hooted and gestured wildly for her to dance at their table, waving five-dollar bills to entice her. When she chose to avoid their invitations, one of the men got up from his seat and waded over in her general direction with a stupid grin on his face. At that point James, who had been monitoring the scene, went over and asked the man to remain in his seat, and after momentarily stalling, he did so. James then remained close by to ensure they remained there.

After the last performance of the evening was completed, James moved through the floor taking care of his tables in a more thorough manner than he had been able to when Michelle was dancing. He kept one eye on the two men, but they quickly downed the last of their drinks and tossed down some bills contemptuously to cover the cost, leaving abruptly. Michelle retreated upstairs to change and gather her belongings prior to her departure.

Michelle waited for Abassi to pay her at the secluded table next to the bar, and when James appeared there to deposit two cheques into the till he noticed her and smiled rather shyly. Michelle smiled back and said: "Thanks."

"For what?" said James, though he knew perfectly well what he was being thanked for.

"In there," Michelle gestured tiredly with her head.

"Oh," said James feigning surprise. "That was nothing."

Michelle nodded and continued to smile at James, and that seemed to give him courage.

"Michelle, I ... eh ... know you don't really know me," he

faltered, "but I was wondering if you wanted to maybe get a drink or something." Very suave you idiot, James thought to himself who, once he managed to get the words out, would have settled for her not to scream for fear he was a serial killer. Michelle continued to smile at James, and for a few seconds that seemed like an hour to James, she did not verbalise an answer, but she did look at her watch. Oh, oh, thought James, she's forming an excuse, and he was about to go into his well it was just an idea act, which he would have ended with: "I'm really too tired myself anyway."

"Sure I'd love to," said Michelle.

James was momentarily taken aback as he had feared the worst.

"Great. I've just got a couple of tables who'll be leaving shortly."

"Fine."

Before leaving James went into the back to tip the kitchen staff who were cleaning up at the end of the night. He had noticed earlier that there was a new dishwasher, a young boy of fourteen or fifteen, whose job it was to load and unload the dishwasher and generally bathe in steam all evening. It was probably far more work than the kid had ever experienced in his short life, but that was never good enough for the merciless kitchen staff. Chuck approached him with a bowl of leftover rice and instructed him to go down to the basement to feed the camel.

"There's no camel down there," said the astonished dishwasher.

"Yeah there is, and it's your job to feed him at the end of the night, in' that right, James?" said Chuck with a straight face, the rest of the kitchen staff hiding in anticipation as they had money riding on the outcome.

"Oh yeah," said James. "That's not couscous you're givin' him is it," he said peering into the bowl, "because remember what happened the last time he ate couscous."

Chuck nodded at the befuddled youth.

"Shit all over the wall."

"Abassi was pissed!" offered James.

Fearing the prospect of losing his first job, the dishwasher reluctantly took the bowl and headed toward the door to the basement, walking slowly in the hopes he would be called back, suffer a little humiliation and then it would be over. But no such luck. There was too much money riding on the outcome. The rule was that if he went down four stairs then he was adjudged to have fallen for the prank. This unfortunate lad did and there were howls of laughter interjected with curses as money changed hands. James always felt bad for his role in the mendacious proceedings, but it did tend to ingratiate him with the kitchen staff and he could always count on his orders to come first, ahead of the waiters who felt that it was best to scream at the kitchen.

"Shall we call for a cab?" Michelle said.

"No, I've got a car outside," said James.

Michelle appeared surprised, but on seeing what passed for James' car, the look quickly left her face.

"It's not the greatest," said James seeing her disappointment, "but it gets me around."

James fumbled with the lock as Michelle started to make her way around to the other side.

"It's about a ten minute walk to the passenger door, or you can come in this way," said James hoping to introduce a little levity.

"It's fine," said Michelle chuckling as she shuffled across the bench seat, trying not to dislodge the brown seat cover as she went.

"So where can we go for that drink?"

"Actually, there's not too many places open now, but we could go to my place if you like," said Michelle, which was enough to send James' pulse higher.

"You have your own place then," said James hoping she didn't sense any change in his voice.

"I share with two other girls, but I think they both went home for the weekend."

James was directed to her flat, which was located at the western end of the Beaches area, not too far from the restaurant, but too far for her to walk at this late hour. It was very quiet even for one o'clock in the morning. The normally thundering rumble of streetcars could not be heard because of the transit strike.

"Beer okay?" Michelle said from the kitchen.

"Yeah, anything," said James as he chose to seat himself on the couch rather than the chair.

"I really did want to buy you a drink," said James as Michelle returned with two beers still in the stubby bottles.

"Maybe next time," she said and much to James' delight sat down next to him on the couch, stretching her lithe legs on to the coffee table.

They sat and talked, listened to soft, moody music, occasionally finding an excuse to touch one another to accentuate a point, and James had a second drink and then a third. Michelle was fascinated with James' accent and he demonstrated interest in her university studies and dancing, telling her of his plans to advance his education, and when the discussion came around to age he reluctantly admitted he was nineteen, and just as James had suspected she was already twenty-one. But to James' great joy she had not in the least been put off by his being younger than her, and that obstacle overcome he reached closer and planted a delicate, slow kiss on Michelle's full lips. As he pulled back he managed to accidentally on purpose have his left hand brush her breast and sought out her brown eyes for approval, but before he could focus she returned with a volley of her own, that in no way could have been misconstrued as a goodnight peck.

After much wrestling around removing various articles of clothing (the socks are always tricky), Michelle asked the poignant question that indicated to James that, indeed, yes, pending his ability to produce a little package from his wallet, sex was about to take place. From Michelle's standpoint she was about to make love in a beautiful and romantic, spontaneous moment of passion. But to James, he was about to get his beans waxed. He fumbled for the little packet, momentarily wondering if these things had a best before date, while Michelle rearranged the cushions on the couch and turned off the lamp. Condoms, what a fantastic invention thought James.

"I hope this thing is big enough," said James completing the installation and turning to face Michelle. But in the low light he could see that his line had not been as well received as he had hoped.

"The condom, I meant."

James decided to just dive in before Michelle lost the mood, making a mental note not to crack wise the next time he found himself in this situation. And so began that delicate balance between ecstasy and stamina.

James glanced over to check the clock on the wall. It was hard to make out in the dark, but to look directly at his wristwatch would have been a little obvious. He couldn't tell, but Michelle was cooing and moving into the cuddle mode, so he convinced himself that his performance had been at least adequate. He would have appreciated something a little more substantive from Michelle in terms of approval, but cooing was good he thought.

Chapter 21

"Tell me about your wife," said Ally as she leaned back, glass of wine in her right hand, and cigarette in her left.

"Could I have one of those please?" said James gesturing with his head at Ally's cigarette.

"Oh sure," she replied and fumbled around in a handbag that seemed too petite to have any trouble finding anything in there. James lit up, a little disappointed in himself, but he really had held out well, three days in fact, and he thought perhaps if he could stretch it out a little longer the next time, he would be well on his way to quitting for good.

"Karen. She's great. Don't know what she saw in me," James shrugged his shoulders and then enjoyed an exaggerated draw, being careful not to blow smoke in her face.

"Kids?"

"Three, all girls." He could have revelled in their accomplishments for an hour but sensed Ally's regrets on not having experienced the miracle of childbirth, and so he demurred in deference. James then remembered he kept their pictures in his wallet and he managed to extricate them for Ally to peruse.

"You're very lucky. Do you know that?"

"Yes, I know I am," said James thoughtfully and slowly, imbuing the phrase with a sense of deep meaning. But he was convinced of that.

"I've got an idea," said Ally, her eyes brightening to show their full size. "Let's get out of here and go watch the sunset."

"Sure," said James, rather taken aback. After taking care of the waiter, they left the restaurant. James followed Ally's instructions, ending up well south of the city in a secluded spot in the hills offering a fine vista to the west. They sat on the grass, still a little damp from the inclement weather of the day, but the skies had cleared, leaving the fading sun to set unhindered by clouds. Two magpies fluttered about by the path in their characteristically sporadic movements before another day was done and the sun sank slowly in the western horizon, late into a Scottish summer evening.

"Did you go and see that shit that passes for your uncle?"

"Yeah, yes I did. This afternoon," replied James as he moved into fifth gear on the deserted road heading back to the city.

"Hope you gave him a piece of your mind."

James chuckled at the thought.

"Ally, if you'd seen him. He's just a shell. It was hard to talk to him at all," said James pondering his own words and looking straight ahead.

"You mean his mind's gone. Alzheimer's. Ironic. Always said he was off his heid," she said unsympathetically.

"Elevator doesn't go all the way to the top floor," said James finally turning to Ally smiling. She returned the smile, but it was affected as her hackles had been stirred at the memory of Archie.

"Couple of beers short of a six-pack," said James attempting to soothe his companion, the tranquil experience of watching the sunset now lost.

"Do you ever wonder why you put up with it?" enquired Ally as they became engulfed in the orange lights of the city, that were like succulent ice-lollies hanging over the houses.

"Yes and no," said James. "I mean it's like how you sort of accept the shortcomings of youth."

Ally looked puzzled.

"What do you mean by that?"

"Well, back then it's what I knew. In those days it didn't occur to me I had any rights. It's not like today. You can't touch a kid or they'd sue you now. They know what their rights are, and maybe that's a good thing. But I don't know. Mabel must've known what her rights were but it didn't seem to matter. People like Archie; they have a power over you."

"Self esteem," said Ally.

"Mmm."

"People like Archie have power over people with low self esteem. They think they're worthless and deserve to be treated the way they are," said Ally.

"You a psychologist now, Ally?" said James trying to add a trailing laugh, but he couldn't quite pull it off so he cleared his throat as if that had been his intention all along.

"No, it's true."

"I suppose there's a lot of truth to that, but I've long since forgiven myself for not being more proactive. It's kind of like forgiving yourself for getting piss drunk at seventeen, or a one night stand. I mean it might come back to haunt you later, but it's done now and you can't beat yourself up forever. You make decisions that affect your life. You try to make the best decisions at the time, given the tools and maturity at your disposal. Sometimes they're not the best decision you could've made, so you learn and try and do better next time," said James, surprising himself with a speech.

"That your philosophy on life, James?"

"Pretty much."

"So why do you still smoke?" said Ally attempting to catch James out.

"Yeah, well, I'm working on that one, because that's definitely one that's likely to come back and bite me in the ass," replied James.

"Have you ever gone to see someone to talk about all this?"

"What, a shrink?" said James horrified.

"Well, yes," said Ally adamantly, stretching out the yes for punctuation.

"Well, I couldn't. I mean it's sort of become Karen's hobby. I mean what would she do with herself if she didn't have me to reform?"

"You're not taking me seriously," protested Ally.

James found a parking spot reasonably near Ally's apartment and before they got out he turned to her and said: "I take you very seriously and I appreciate your concern."

"Especially since you took off to Canada and left me alone," she interjected. She was kidding, but James sensed an element of meaning in the statement.

"The truth is I may be damaged, but it manifests itself in ways that aren't particularly unhealthy," said James.

Ally laughed audibly, throwing her hand toward her mouth in an attempt to muffle her outburst. "I'd like to talk to your wife about that some day."

"Yeah, well, we'll see," said James somewhat crushed because he really did believe his assertion, even although Ally seemed to be having trouble with it.

"I'll be up in a minute. I'm just going to the phone box to call home," said James.

"Why don't you call from my place?"

"It's just easier from the call box. I'll only be a couple of minutes," said James who didn't really feel like explaining to Karen why he was phoning from a private residence at eleven thirty at night, should the caller ID kick in.

They enjoyed the remainder of the evening. A little wine, some Steely Dan on the stereo, and free of the encumbrances of sexual expectation. After a while Ally retired to her room giving James a kiss on the cheek in passing. This time the scent of her perfume made him think of Karen who had been pleased with the news that he had met with his uncle. James had been short on specifics, but he had, he felt, succeeded in conveying a sense of having accomplished what he had set out to do. Karen seemed satisfied.

She was big on catharsis, and asked James if he was having a cathartic experience, using the word again and again as if it was an exhilarating experience just to articulate the word in her mouth. James had agreed he supposed it probably was, but he needed some time to digest things. He was happy with that because it was so open ended, yet it allowed Karen to be pleased with herself, that the trip, as he was sure she would tell her colleagues, had been a cathartic experience for her husband. It was not a topic for a transatlantic telephone conversation with a background that seemed to be ominously dominated by the antics of a puppy and three teenage girls buffeting about the kitchen at dinner time, so James had left it at that with the promise he would be home in a couple of days.

James arose and had breakfast with Ally and they said their goodbyes. There were vague promises of future meetings, but their parting had an eerie air of finality to it, as if one were suffering from a terminal illness. But Ally was a kindred spirit with a policy of non-committal. She had accepted James' invasion into her life like a Christmas present from an anonymous benefactor. Totally unexpected, with elements of mystery and possibility, and ultimately companionship in a fast moving world. It was as if there had been a seam opened in the time continuum, like an aside from a science fiction plot. But now she would go back to her normal friends, her normal job, and her normal world. It had been a welcome respite from tedium, to be regurgitated and relived when prompted by cues like the ending of Casablanca, or watching the sunset in the long days of June, or whenever she found herself walking past the fish and chip shop on Morningside Road.

James called Ronnie from the same box he had called his wife the night before, and woke him. Evidently Ronnie was not one to allow the possibility of gainful employment get in the way of a good night's sleep. James only wanted to confirm that indeed Ronnie would be at the address, and though surprised that James was already in the city, he gave the impression he would receive James like an old friend.

James found the address with little difficulty, and with some trepidation he left his rental car unattended and made his way up to the second floor flat. Pilton was one of those neighbourhood schemes that someone at some time must have thought was a good idea. It was hard to imagine how that was possible. Even on a bright and sunny June morning it was as if this part of the city was in black and white. Pilton did not need November to appear bleak.

As he climbed the stairs his shoes made the sound of sandpaper rubbing on wood, even though the steps were stone. There was a smell of stale food, refuse, and urine permeating the darkened stairway, so James avoided touching anything unless it was absolutely necessary.

Ronnie had apparently heard him coming, as the door was ajar.

"C'moan in," he shouted and James closed the door behind him. Ronnie emerged from the kitchen clothed only in a white vest that was too tight for a man of his girth, and a pair of well worn casual trousers badly in need of a wash. He wasn't so much fat as just wallowing in his clothes. He had that given up look that tends to afflict men by the age of forty, as if flabbiness was a rite of passage into middle age. The face looked used and hard, but it was framed by a still-black shock of hair that fell haphazardly over his forehead. There was, of course, the obligatory unshaven face that accompanies men who walk around in vests, and a kind of permanent tightening of the skin on his brow, the result of affecting a hard look for going on four decades.

There was no handshake offered by either man, James neither wanted to, nor did he feel it suitable, whereas it just probably didn't occur to Ronnie, who was otherwise quite convivial.

"Ah wis jist makin a cup i tea," said Ronnie, motioning with his head to the kitchen, causing the hair dangling on his brow to bounce wildly. James cleared some old newspapers off one of the two chairs, finally tossing them down next to the door after deciding there was not a better place for them. Ronnie hoisted two mismatched cups onto the table, having to clear a space amongst the array of condiments, coins, unpaid bills, and most disturbing, a pair of socks which judging from the smell were not clean.

"I saw your Dad," said James.

"How wis he?"

"He didn't really know who I was. It was a bit of a waste of time," said James curtly.

"Aye, well, he's in an oot, ken," said Ronnie as he slurped back some tea that had a very dark hue, such that James didn't want to risk trying.

"Yeah, well he was mostly out when I was there."

"Tell me aboot yer family then," said Ronnie, attempting to change the subject.

"Wife and three kids," responded James, who was by now cursing his curiosity for bothering to see his cousin.

"No married masel," said Ronnie, who seemed puzzled at James' taciturn and contemptuous ways.

"Seein someone oaf an oan like," he continued.

She must be a real prize, thought James. Were people so desperately lonely as that?

"That right?" was all James responded, not wanting to hear any more than he had to.

"Look, mibbee we could go roon tae the pub," said Ronnie, getting up from his seat.

"I don't think so," responded James, placing his still full cup of tea in the sink. "I think maybe I'll just go now."

"Ye jist goat here. What's the matter wi ye?"

"Look, I suppose I was just curious to see what a forty something delinquent looks like, and I've seen it so …" James started to make for the door.

"Ye turned oot tae be a right toff. Hud tae share ma room wi ye, stayed at oor house, an that's the thanks Ah get. Dinnae hear fi ye fir twenty years …"

"Is that really what you think, Ronnie?"

"Well, it's true enough. Wisnae luxury or nuthin but –"

"It was a hell hole, you idiot."

"Who are ye callin an eejit?" said Ronnie, pushing James out of the door.

James surprised himself by pushing back, and just as he felt that it was all rather childish, he had to move quickly to his left to dodge a right hook from Ronnie, who failing to land one, had his momentum carry him through the doorway. James just stood there waiting to see what he would do next. As Ronnie recovered his balance he ran at James from a crouched position ramming him against the wall, dangerously close to the stairs. Then they were both swinging, James the more agile, but Ronnie the more powerful. As James felt a stinging blow connect with his mouth, a rage began to engulf him. He let loose with a flurry of strong body blows. Ronnie folded. James continued with some shots to the head. There was one for his dog, one for Ronnie's frequent assaults on the smaller, younger Jimmy, and a thunderous jolt to the face because he had been unable to deliver it to his father. As Ronnie hit the floor, James caught himself and relented; the full impact of his actions reflected in the bloodied face of his cousin, who had covered his face with his hands, cowering against the possibility of more blows.

A door opened slightly across the landing, and an old man's head curled around to see what all the noise was about.

"Nae bother," said Ronnie, still out of breath, "nae bother, we're jist muckin aboot."

Ronnie started to get up and was helped by the now contrite James. The door across the landing closed quietly. James hoped that the old man wouldn't call the police, but he suspected that such incidents were probably not rare, and it was unlikely that the police would have been alerted.

James helped Ronnie clean up his face, and then tended to his own badly cut lip.

"Where the hell did that come fi, Jimmy?"

"I'm sorry. I think I'm still pissed at Archie."

"Aye, well, Ah'm no Archie," replied Ronnie who was now standing up applying a cold compress to his right eye.

"I know, but I never liked you either."

"Well then, Ah suppose that's that."

"How about I buy you some lunch and a pint," offered James, who now felt that he couldn't leave things the way they were.

Ronnie thought about it for a moment then acquiesced.

"Okay, but no around here. D'ye huv a car?"

"Yeah, I've got a car outside."

So in deference to Ronnie's pride James drove up to Ferry Road and east towards Leith, finding a pub where two men in their condition was not enough to cause a head to turn.

"Ah ken he's an old bastard, but he's ma Da, an Ah cannae change that. Ah've made a bit i a mess i ma life, Ah ken that too, but Ah didnae ken ony different really."

James listened, unwilling to interrupt or offer encouragement to Ronnie's unlikely offerings.

"Onywye, Ah suppose ye did the best thing by movin away.

Ah sometimes wonder if mibbee Ah should huv moved away. Gone tae London or somethin. Mibbee Canada."

Perish the thought, mused James, who was wondering if this was genuine or if he was about to be hit up for a sizeable amount of cash.

"Where's all this coming from, Ronnie? I mean are you just starting to think about these things now?"

"Ah did some time a few years ago an there wis this counsellor bloke who goat me thinkin aboot stuff."

"And …" prompted James.

"It's ower late fir me tae make onythin i masel, but he kept sayin that it wisnae, an that Ah hud tae start by sortin oot in ma ain heid why Ah did things, an why ma life wis like it wis."

"And why is it the way it is?"

"He said that Ah hud tae take responsibility fir ma actions an that Ah couldnae keep sayin that Ah wis the product i a bad home life."

"And what do you think about that, mmh?"

"Aw he's probably right, but Ah didnae get the best start in life."

"Nobody would dispute that Ronnie. Me least of all. But life's not a level playing field, is it?"

Ronnie was about to answer, but James continued his discourse as he had intended the question as rhetorical.

"If you take your situation. Some would have got an education, a good job, and maybe a nice family. Others, probably the vast majority, would lead average lives, bounce from job to job, maybe a wife, maybe a divorce, play the pools every week and never win. But some like you Ronnie can use it as an excuse to lead a life of crime."

"It's no like Ah'm Jack the Ripper," protested Ronnie, who struggled to sip back his beer, which flowed over a lip that stubbornly refused to cease trickling blood.

There was a time when James would have taken issue with that, but as he sat across from his estranged cousin he would have to concede he was no psychopath. There was something inside that offered some hope.

"I don't know what you've been up to in the last twenty years and I don't really care to," said James who leaned back in his chair and sighed dramatically as he wondered where to take the conversation.

Ronnie wasn't about to regurgitate his record, but it was evident he hadn't finished his explanation despite the distraction of the arrival of a greasy lunch plate.

"Ah've nivir hud bairns i ma ain," he said, as he plunged his fork into the doughy pie. He cast a fleeting glance at James as he said it.

"Why not?" asked James, but he hoped he already knew the answer.

"Didnae want tae risk it, ken."

"Yes, Ah dae ken," said James. "Yes, I do. You know there was a time I wondered about that myself."

"You did?" exclaimed Ronnie sincerely surprised.

"Yeah, but then I think you can go either way with that. I mean you can fall into the same pattern, or make a conscious effort to be the model father. But I wondered when our first was born. Even gave up the booze for a while as insurance."

"Worked out awright fir ye but ..." supplied Ronnie.

"Oh yeah, it's fine. Great actually. Three nice girls."

"Yer awfie lucky."

"I know that," said James, and he did.

Chapter 22

When most of James' fellow students at the university were toiling away at part time jobs, attempting to pile up as many eight or nine dollar, sixty minute increments as their schedule would permit, James was regularly walking out of the restaurant with in excess of one hundred dollars a night in tips. That certainly was not the case for the other waiters, who as a rule did not devote as much industry or charm to the task, as did James. He became thoroughly acquainted with the wine menu, able to direct the discerning customer toward the most appropriate selection that related to the meal. His ability to remember the cocktail of choice for customers who might only appear every couple of months won him a sort of celebrity status amongst waiters. Customers would often insist on being seated in his section, ready to see if he could remember that the last time they were there they had ordered a Sloe Gin Fizz and a Whiskey Sour. As a result, James was able to work toward his Bachelor of Commerce degree without sacrificing the benefits of a full time income.

James' finesse and charm that he would admit bordered on smarminess, endeared him to some of the regular business customers and he became privy to their financial discussions and projections. There were stock tips bandied about on a regular basis, but James was reluctant to invest his inheritance on unsubstantiated tips overheard at a Middle Eastern restaurant at lunchtime on Fridays. He had been quite content to invest in some five year bonds beginning in nineteen seventy-nine and the following year offering rates from thirteen percent to a staggering nineteen and a half percent guaranteed. Some had warned him that rates could go even higher, but as it turned out his instincts proved correct, as he was able to invest at the peak. He had made a commitment to himself when he decided to pursue a university education that he would live off his earnings and invest his inheritance toward a future business venture. He was quite sure his future lay in business, but he was as yet unsure as to what type of business it would be.

Comfortably invested as he was, his interest in the stock market was piqued by the incessant talk around the businessmen's tables regarding the demise of Chrysler. There were those, in the majority, who felt that Chrysler was inevitably tumbling toward bankruptcy. However, there were a few who argued that the government would never allow such a huge component of the US auto industry to fold. Perhaps it was a consequence of his British and more socialist background, but James found himself subscribing to the latter position, and though it initially caused him some sleepless nights, he decided to invest a significant portion of his savings in Chrysler stock.

James had originally bought in at six dollars and change in 1980, and then a later more sizeable investment at around the ten-dollar mark. By 1986 the stock reached giddy heights and was trading at forty-seven dollars a share at one point after a split, and although James did not stay invested till the peak, he did realise a huge return on his investment. Curiously he never believed himself to have acquired the Midas touch and with the exception of some minor investments in gold mine stocks, he was reluctant to embrace the unpredictability of the markets. As a result, between his market returns and his bond investments, which were originally the lion's share of the money, but were ultimately dwarfed by the Chrysler stock, he managed to accumulate a tidy sum of money.

Between working at the restaurant and attending university, James did not have a lot of free time to devote to relationships. There had been liaisons, dalliances with girls like Michelle, but no one special until a spring day in 1982. James had just completed his studies and was not working that night at the restaurant, but had no particular plans. Perhaps later in the evening he would venture out to a club, but for the present he was content to wash his car. Recently he had disposed of the oversize Fury in favour of a Volkswagen Rabbit. It was an abhorrent shade of orange; a refugee from the seventies, but it was infinitely better on gas and small enough to park in the driveway. It wasn't exactly a chick magnet but it was a definite step up from the Fury, which now that it was gone had seemed all the more absurd to James.

Fiona Galbraith came out on to the porch of the house, and with her hands holding each other primly behind her back she smiled at James with the type of look that plain women have when they are about to prevail upon you for something. James smiled in return. They had got along very well in a tenant-landlord relationship and occasionally Fiona would take pity on James and invite him to Sunday dinner. James politely obliged, but it was strictly out of courtesy, as he would have much rather avoided the perils of dining with a young family. Christmas was different, as James felt privileged to be included, and brought presents for the three children. But in general they respected each other's privacy, rarely coming into contact. On this day, Fiona was a mother snowed under; her husband the victim of shift work and overtime. And so after profusely apologising for her effrontery to even impose, she asked James if he would mind driving her daughter to a birthday party at six o'clock, a mere twenty minutes hence.

James was happy to help out, convinced as he was that Fiona wasn't the type to make a habit of such requests, and after cleaning up he found himself driving an excited girl to a birthday party. After making sure they were at the right house and reassuring the mother that he was not in fact the father, he was about to leave when a striking young woman about the same age as James appeared at the door dropping off her charge. The mother, perhaps doubting the rate at which she was ageing, felt it necessary to make sure this young woman was not a parent too. When the enchanting young woman had reassured her, the mother broke into cackles of laughter as middle-class women sometimes feel the need to do, but James couldn't even grant her a supporting smile, his attention now devoted to the lithe beauty at the doorway.

"I'm James, James McPherson," he said confidently as he walked down the path.

"Karen. Nice to meet you, James McPherson."

"So what's a nice girl like you doing in a suburban domestic scene like this?" said James.

"She's my little sister. I'm just dropping her off and I'll pick her up at eight," replied Karen, who was now leaning against her car, her golden arms folded, her blue eyes squinting to avoid the angle of the late afternoon sun.

"Big age gap there," said James who, not particularly put off by the arms folded, was anxious to keep the conversation alive any way he could.

"Oh, not that kind of sister. I'm with Big Sisters of Canada."

"Oh, I see," said James vaguely, but Karen's perception indicated that he did not understand.

"It's an organisation that hooks up volunteers with girls that don't have a mother, so they can have a positive female influence in their life," she explained as she unlocked her arms and rested them against the hood of the car.

"Well I'm not a girl, but I'm sure that you could be a positive influence in my life," said James.

"Well it's been nice meeting you, James McPherson," said Karen and she started to climb into her car.

Momentarily baffled by this angel who did not seem vulnerable to James' bullshit, he quickly recovered and crouched down so that she could see for herself how sincere he could appear.

"Look, I'm sorry. It's not every day I meet someone as beautiful as you and I think you've made me nervous. I would really like you to join me for some dinner and perhaps we could get to know each other."

Karen listened to James' speech and then tortured him with five seconds of silence before acquiescing.

It had not been anything elaborate; one of the better pizza and spaghetti establishments in the area, filled with staff who had apparently just completed a crash course on phoney conviviality. But the conversation had been flowing, free from awkward pauses, and when the clock neared the hour of eight it almost seemed inconceivable that time could have passed so quickly.

Karen had recently completed her schooling and was about to embark on a career in advertising, and James revelled in her enthusiasm and optimism, listening to her talk while she drove back to the birthday party with James. As he sat in the passenger seat he took advantage of the driver's need to focus on the road to examine Karen in her full beauty. As she talked, James was mesmerised by her glossy lips, the perfection of her white teeth that radiated from her unblemished, tanned face, and the lustre of her pert, blonde hair. The partially opened window wafted her scent across to James' nostrils where he drank it in. It was just a teasing suggestion of perfume. Unlike so many other young women, Karen had not marinated in cologne. James thought about putting his sunglasses on but the light was starting to fade and it would have been a little obvious. Instead he relied on that innate male ability to study the breasts while appearing to focus on the eyes, and he luxuriated in every breath Karen took.

The car was standard transmission, which offered James a special treat. There was something sensual, almost erotic about watching a beautiful woman manipulate her legs driving. The way the dress rode up ever so slightly when she pushed on the clutch; the subtle thrust of the pelvis associated with acceleration, the necessary parting of the legs from time to time. It had the power to transport the most prudish of strait-laced women into a state of almost carnal appeal.

This was information that James was not inclined to share with Karen, and he was almost angry with himself for his indulgence. For the remainder of the journey he decided to wholly concentrate on making eye contact, not wanting to risk her disapproval, and thereby improve the possibility of a future meeting.

Shortly before Christmas they were married. There had been no reason to get married; especially so quickly, but there had been no reason not to get married. The wedding was reasonably elaborate in deference to Karen's parents. James grudgingly obliged, not wanting to offend his in-laws, who were still a little unsure of James. There had been mutterings from time to time. At one point, Karen's Aunt Matilda was convinced that James must have been in the witness protection programme, but then she also lived alone with five cats and wore white gloves all year round, so her credibility was suspect.

The wedding itself went off rather well despite the presence of some of James' Egyptian friends from the restaurant. Hopelessly outnumbered, they had sat quietly at one table looking for all the world like bacon sandwiches at a Jewish wedding. With James' black hair and the artificial light of the ballroom, there were those who persisted in questioning his identity. The Galbraiths had been invited and they managed to set some people straight, vouching for his Scottish heritage and generally reassuring people that he was not in fact a clandestine member of Black September. James had made a speech which he managed to get some mileage out of, and by the time he was through he felt that arses had been sufficiently kissed, to the point that by the end of the reception he felt accepted.

The transition to married life was an easy one for Karen. James had merely officially moved into her apartment on a full time basis. He had spent most of his time there anyway so it was not so much a sudden event, rather an evolutionary process. It was a little more difficult for James, who had rather enjoyed having his own space. But with time, he fell into a pattern that made marriage all feel normal. The real change came when Lisa was born shy of their second anniversary. The pregnancy had come as a shock to both of them as they hadn't even discussed having children. It was sort of understood that some day, way in the distant future, children would be inevitable, just as thinning hair and retirement were inevitable. But Lisa had arrived, a testament to the unreliability of the rhythm method, and their lives changed overnight. After the dust had settled they developed a kind of in for a penny, in for a pound mentality, and so they begat Sarah and Valerie in quick succession.

Karen put her career on hold, and James, realising there would never be an appropriate time now, decided to pull the trigger and open his own restaurant. And so shortly before December, in the year of our Lord nineteen hundred and eighty-five, The Pentland Gardens was opened. James had hoped to finance the project in the traditional manner, with a sizeable influx of his own capital and the rest, a mortgage from the bank. It quickly became apparent however that the bank's definition of a sizeable down payment and James' definition were not at all compatible. As a result James had to risk more than he had wanted to and when the restaurant got off to a slow start he was a troubled man. But gradually business improved. A series of favourable reviews had begun to cultivate a loyal clientele and by the end of the decadent decade James started to realise the type of return that he had originally envisaged.

Confident of future prosperity James and Karen moved out of the city to a more rural setting to the north. James as usual had mixed feelings. On the one hand he shared Karen's aspirations of making a home of comfort and contentment away from the bustle of the city. However, there was a part of James that loathed the prospect of entering into more debt to build the house. Ultimately James deferred to Karen's wisdom on the matter as he was inclined to do, inexperienced as he was in the ways of a family. But in his mind, when lying in bed unable to sleep, or when he was driving, or when he was supposed to be watching one of his daughters play a jellyfish in the local skating production of the Little Mermaid, James would mull over worst case financial scenarios in his head. He did not enjoy the task, and indeed wished that he could refrain from such futile worries, but the fact was that try as he may, he bound himself with the chains of financial concern. He kept little charts on the inside of the closet door of his office, and each month he would write a line, a neatly ruled line with an HB pencil through each payment. And with each passing year, James felt, he was one step closer to the security he craved.

Chapter 23

James was almost ready to go home. He had come to Scotland ostensibly to see a dying man who had been asking for him, but the course of events that led to his decision to come now seemed like a long time ago. He had said goodbye to Ally, fought with his cousin, rediscovered a beautiful city, and discovered a few things about himself. He wasn't sure what he felt he had learned, but he would be sure to tell his wife he had had a cathartic experience. James was still unsure what that meant, but Karen would definitely be pleased if he said it.

And so James drove almost trance-like towards the sea, smoking deliberately, almost in slow motion, obeying every traffic rule, welcoming each red light as he gradually meandered to the cemetery. From memory James walked east along the broad, stone path, past the ostentatious edifices of the wealthy that in concert with the trees blocked out the light. Just as he remembered, it opened up to a wider, greener section that overlooked the valley to the south, but the more intricate details were harder to establish as the passage of time had brought with it changes in the vegetation, ageing of the stones, and additional remembrances for those who had more recently been laid to rest. Attempting to orientate himself he recalled that the grave was only paces from the large grey stone that marked the unfortunate twenty-two year old airman who "fell" in the last days of the war. As a boy it had stood out because the top of the stone was shaped in the wings of the RAF. James walked due east toward the sea, and before he felt he had walked far enough he was upon the grave.

It had held up well. Mr McCrae had helped make the arrangements; gold lettering on the black stone would always stand out he said, and the finish they could achieve with that kind of stone would mean it wouldn't suffer from the ravages of the elements. James stood and stared for a moment as if attempting to create an image of the lettering on his forehead. The dew was still heavy and it began to soak into his light canvas shoes and that seemed to break him from his trance. His mother, his father, his brother, his sister were still dead. No catharsis could change that. There was no closure, there never is, he thought as emotions of anger, and melancholy both filled him.

He placed the flowers he'd brought in the vase affixed to the stone, took four steps backward and, making sure his finger was not covering the lens, snapped a picture. His siblings would have been in their thirties by now, and his parents would still have been very much alive, all things being equal. It was hard to imagine what it would be like, but James decided to stop trying. It was never a good idea to do that he reminded himself.

He stayed a while and then walked leisurely back toward the car. He read the stones as he went; always interested to see how long the people had lived. There was the occasional one who had neared their one hundredth birthday, but they were rare. It always made James think of the Albert Camus story of Merseault. In the big picture of things it didn't matter when you died really, or how long you lived. The frail centenarian with the paper-thin skin was really no more significant than the life of the twenty-two year old airman. *Given that you've got to die, it obviously doesn't matter exactly how or when*, that was how it went, he was sure, when Merseault knew he was going to be executed.

Some stones had the acronym RIP, and James remembered how as a youngster he had always wondered why people had put that on a headstone. The intention of Rest In Peace had in James' mind always been overshadowed by the word Rip, which had seemed entirely inappropriate for the dearly departed. Even now, that was his first impression when he saw the letters boldly set in the stone. Rip! There goes another one. Rip! There he would go one day, and so would everyone else for that matter. As he passed by a waste container, James banished the remainder of his cigarettes. They sat defiantly on top of a pile of decayed flowers as if appealing for a second chance, but James felt this would be a good time to kick the habit and he didn't look back, determined to delay man's curse as long as he could.

He had only been killing time, driving on down to Cramond, when it occurred to him that Mr McCrae wouldn't have been that old really. Probably in his early seventies if his calculations were correct. And so he drove to the house where he himself had stayed for a short time in the hope that perhaps they still lived there.

Before exiting the car, James checked his face in the rear view mirror and was relatively pleased with the way his wounds were healing. They didn't scream out *fight* anymore and could have passed for banging into a door.

An old lady straightened herself, getting off her gardening cushion where she had been attempting to reign in stray peonies that were encroaching on the path. She smoothed her apron with one hand while clutching a straw hat with the other, lest the breeze would cause it to fly away.

James strolled up the path being careful not to step on any flowers, hoping that his careful manner would allay the old woman's fears.

"Hello, I'm looking for the McCrae residence," he said.

"I'm Mrs McCrae," she said dubiously, expecting to be fodder for a sales pitch at any minute.

"I'm not sure if you'll remember me, but I'm James McPherson, I knew …"

"Oh for Heaven's sakes," said Mrs McCrae, risking losing her hat to the wind as she used her hand to dab her bottom lip in an effort to soak up the words that had left her mouth.

"Jimmy McPherson," she continued. "You're all grown up. Well of course you are, that was a long time ago."

"I just wanted to say hello, you know and …" but James really didn't know what he wanted to say. Probably nothing, but he had wanted to see them. People like the McCraes should get to see that their efforts and kindness were repaid in some small way, even if it simply meant revealing to them that yes, things had turned out alright for him and they had played a part in that. However, as he stood on the garden path exchanging pleasantries, he wished he had at least thought to bring some flowers. He missed Karen at moments like this. She would have armed him with the right kind, and maybe a box of chocolates, or a photograph of his family. Yes that would have been the thing; a photograph. Oh well, too late now.

As they made their way into the house for a spot of tea, a car roared into the driveway, coming to an abrupt halt just when it seemed it would plough through the garage door. To James' great delight, out popped Mr McCrae, still spry for a man of his age. James had taken Mrs McCrae's lack of reference to her husband as a sign that he was deceased, but there he was very much alive. He scurried along the path, ducking to avoid the climbing roses, anxious to see who the visitor was, but before he had the chance to guess, Mrs McCrae excitedly enlightened him.

"My word," exclaimed Mr McCrae and he shook James' hand vigorously, patting him generously on the back with the other.

"What a splendid surprise, come inside, come inside."

James was ushered into the sitting room with Mr McCrae while Mrs McCrae went to make the tea, as if it were not possible to make do without it. The room had the unsullied quality that suggested children never entered. Little china ornaments that must have required hours of dusting were in bountiful supply around the room, balancing on ornately carved pieces of furniture appearing to weigh about three tonnes each. The curtains were heavy and overbearing with an autumnal theme that seemed unfortunate for such a bright summer's day, but they were sufficiently opened to allow ample light to filter through. There was a large picture above the gas fireplace that sported a hooded light above, so that the image could be illuminated at night. But James wondered why anyone would want to draw attention to such a piece, with the absurdly large mountain and the obligatory deer in the foreground. Although he was no expert, it appeared to him to be a starving artist special as advertised on late night television. As a concession to visual health the world over it would have been much better to let this artist starve, thought James, along with all the others who created velvet images of Elvis Presley and dogs playing poker.

"I can't get over it, James. You here in our living room," gushed Mr McCrae, who was reluctant to sit all the way back in his chair.

"Yes, well it has been a long time, hasn't it," said James.

"So tell me about yourself."

"Well I have a family. Wife and three girls, and apparently we've acquired a dog in my absence."

"That's wonderful, and you're still in Canada, I presume."

"Oh yes, I'm very happy there. Actually I own a restaurant now," said James who always felt rather apologetic for his success, so he accompanied the statement with an upturned palm gesture that seemed to say he didn't know how that had happened.

"A restaurant, well, that's excellent," effused Mr McCrae, well pleased.

"And is your family with you?"

"Oh no, not this time. Actually I came back because, well, my cousin contacted me. His dad, Archie, wanted to see me," faltered James, who really had had no intention of sharing this.

"Oh, really?" Mr McCrae seemed somewhat surprised. "And how did that go?" he said, finally working his way all the way into the armchair.

"Oh his mind's gone. He's in a home out Corstorphine way. He thought I was my dad most of the time." James smiled capriciously at Mr McCrae attempting to display that it hadn't mattered to him. Mr McCrae however, armed as he was with years of experience, had by now transformed into his counselling mantle and wore a pensive look enhanced by the act of squeezing his palms together just above his lap.

"That was very good of you to do that, James, given what the man was like."

"Well, I don't know that it accomplished anything really. I mean he really was out of it you know."

"Still, it shows an attitude of forgiveness on your part, and that's admirable."

James was about to correct Mr McCrae. Whatever the reason he had embarked on this pilgrimage he was reasonably sure that it was not in a spirit of forgiveness. But before he had the chance, Mrs McCrae came through the open doorway armed with a tray full of tea and biscuits.

"Would you like a biscuit James?"

"Perhaps just one," he said reaching for a Rich Tea. "Actually I had hoped you would be able to join me for lunch. It's a small gesture I know, but I'd like to make some effort to repay the kindness you showed me." Karen would have approved of that, James thought, rather pleased with himself.

"Oh no, that's not at all necessary," they responded almost in unison.

"No really, I insist," countered James, putting the biscuit back, the idea having soared in his mind. "There's a nice hotel not too far away …"

"Oh we couldn't possibly," protested Mrs McCrae, but her husband had by now sensed that it was important to James, so he accepted on their behalf with the concession that they be allowed to choose the place.

James was directed to a cottage that had been transformed into a genteel tea-room, complete with delicate finger sandwiches, scones and intricately designed little cakes, that were comforted with a background of classical music. It was probably how saintly old women visualise heaven, and you could be well assured you would not be likely to encounter any flatulent, belching lorry drivers at the adjoining table. James felt a little underdressed and a lot underage, but the McCraes appeared to be basking in viewing the fruits of their ancient labour and James was very accommodating, even remembering to extricate the photos of his daughters from his wallet.

"And do you attend church in Canada?" enquired Mrs McCrae, who seemed to assume that James and his family would, and was only interested in discovering what it was like. James thought about lying if only to avoid spoiling their euphoria, but found he couldn't.

"Well, Christmas and Easter. That sort of thing, you know," he said awkwardly.

"Oh," said Mrs McCrae, not quite sure where to look, and James questioned whether it would have been wiser to have fabricated a different scenario, maybe even involving some charity work.

"Never turn your back on the Lord," said Mr McCrae slowly and solemnly.

"No, no, of course not," said James, but if he had been honest he would have admitted to worshipping at the god of self-sufficiency. When it came right down to it, James was the only one he could really trust in, but he wasn't about to share that with the two elderly stalwarts of the faith.

"In fact, I've been thinking lately that it would be good to get back into the church thing," James continued, hoping to appease them, but it had sounded a little weak.

"Well …" started Mr McCrae. He stretched it out so that James knew a little sermon was on the way, and he squirmed in his seat wishing that instead of tea he was sipping on a pint and chasing it with some scotch.

"Weeeell, it's not so much church you should get back into, Jimmy, but God."

"Oh yes," interjected James but Mr McCrae had not finished. He was merely pausing for effect. Mrs McCrae nodded and smiled munificently in support.

"You see," he said, the tips of his fingers touching their counterparts in a prayerful pose, hands slightly undulating, "if you put faith in man, any man, they will let you down eventually. But God will not, Jimmy. Yes, you should seek out a church and that will help you to focus on God. But remember that churches are run by people."

He sat back and took a long sip from his tea cup, and when James was sure he was quite finished he first nodded and then verbalised his agreement.

Thankfully for James the preaching ceased after that and the conversation moved on to the more trivial, and when James had told them all he could possibly tell about his three girls, they took their leave. James promised to come back and see them when he brought the family back on holiday at an as yet undetermined time and as he pulled away they waved frenetically from their garden until they were sure he was out of sight. That night they would go to bed with the kind of contentment that cannot be achieved with wealth or fame, and that made James glad when he reflected upon it.

The little sermon was something that had to be endured at the time, but lingered in James' mind as he drove. Mr McCrae was probably right about all that, but one catharsis at a time, he thought, and attempted to push it to the back of his brain by concentrating on a spirited debate concerning beef exports that was being spewed from the radio.

Chapter 24

While James waited to clear customs he was able to borrow a cell phone and alert Karen as to his arrival. It was a system they had devised wholly designed to relieve the tedium of hanging around airport arrival gates. In this case Karen was working on her laptop at a nearby coffee shop awaiting James' call, or, failing that a page with a pre-arranged code number. Upon getting the call she would drive through the pick-up concourse and meet James, who barring an unforeseen delay, would be waiting. On this day it worked flawlessly which always pleased James more than Karen, who would have been quite prepared to mill around inside with the sweaty hordes. Besides, with the money he saved by not parking at the airport, James calculated he could probably finance the children's education.

"I think I had a cathartic experience," declared James, reasonably pleased with the way it sounded.

"A cathartic experience," repeated Karen rather dubiously. "And knowing you that'll be the extent of your synopsis of the trip."

He was barely in the car and he was busted. He had thought telling her that was what she would have wanted to hear, but upon reflection he admitted to himself that would have been too easy. He had been away from the house of estrogen for too long, and with a thud he realised that he was just a man, not capable of understanding women. Best wait for a question to answer he thought.

"Okaaay, so did you answer some questions?"

Was this a trick, he wondered.

"I can't believe you," said Karen in an exasperated tone. "You go away for a week to rediscover your past and I have to squeeze you for information."

Rediscover my past, thought James, wishing he had thought of that first. Now that he thought about it, it would have sounded much better than that bit about a cathartic experience.

"I think you want that lane," said James, waving his arm to the right.

"I know how to drive," said Karen, as she careened across three lanes of traffic.

"So what did your uncle have to say?" she enquired, adopting a more direct tact.

"Oh, he didn't have much to say at all really."

Karen directed an at once incredulous and threatening look at James, who would have much preferred if she would have given her full attention to driving.

"No, I don't mean like that," faltered James. "He's not all there. His mind's gone you know."

"Oh I see. And how did you feel about that?" asked Karen, returning to her calmer, caring self.

"I felt like he didn't understand a blind word I said."

"Were you disappointed was what I meant!"

Then why didn't she just ask me if I was disappointed, wondered a confused James.

"Well, I suppose so," he said with little conviction, then recovering he added: "I mean I would have liked to know why he wanted to talk to me. I mean maybe he wanted to apologise or something."

"I guess you'll never know," said Karen, her voice tailing off, saddened by the realisation.

"It wasn't really that important Karen," said James. "I mean I know that's why I went, but as it turned out I'm glad I went for a host of other reasons."

"And what were they?" enquired Karen enthusiastically.

James thought for a moment.

"Magpies and sunsets," he said, smiling to himself.

"Excuse me?"

"It's just all the things I'd forgotten about. I mean I've been carrying around all these bad memories and they sort of drowned out the good."

"Like?"

"Do you realise how late the June sun sets in Scotland? If you look on the globe, it's almost the same latitude as Churchill, Manitoba. Did you know that? And the hills. Edinburgh itself, I mean there's a huge castle smack dab in the middle of the place."

"Magpies, what about magpies?" asked Karen, thrilled that her husband was finally revealing some passion about something.

"Oh well, it's no big deal really. It's just that I'd forgotten about them that's all."

James unlocked the front door of the house expecting his three daughters to welcome him, but he was confronted at first by a boisterous puppy intent on licking his face. James dropped his bag and allowed the little dog to welcome him.

"Hi Dad!"

Val emerged wondering where her puppy had gone.

"Hey Val. Give me a big kiss," said James as he threw his arms around his youngest daughter.

"Like alright, Dad. You were only gone like a week," said Val.

"Val. Your Dad's just happy to see you," said Karen as she entered, laptop and briefcase in tow.

"So this is the dog formerly known as Prince," said James.

"It's Princess," declared Val, full of pride.

"Well, that'll work," said James approvingly.

At dinner James dispensed T-shirts and souvenirs to the girls. Lisa reminded him about wanting to work at the restaurant, and Sarah told him she'd started a new band called the Sturdy Beggars. Val talked intermittently on the phone, the dog peed on the carpet, and James basked in his domestic bliss.

Later that night as James and Karen lay in bed, Karen couldn't resist pursuing her psychological queries.

"So was it really a cathartic experience?" she said, which almost sounded as if she was asking him if he'd faked an orgasm, but James, concerned about breaking the mood, refrained from cracking wise.

"Cathartic experience, closure. I don't know about all that. There's just a lot of time gone by. That's the main thing. A lot of time."

The End

Also Available from BeWrite Books

Crime

The Knotted Cord	Alistair Kinnon
Marks	Sam Smith
Porlock Counterpoint	Sam Smith

Crime/Humour

Sweet Molly Maguire	Terry Houston

Horror

Chill	Terri Pine, Peter Lee, Andrew Müller

Fantasy/Humour

Zolin A Rockin' Good Wizard	Barry Ireland
The Hundredfold Problem	John Grant
Earthdoom!	David Langford & John Grant

Fantasy

The Far-Enough Window	John Grant
A Season of Strange Dreams	C. S. Thompson

Collections/ Short Stories

Odie Dodie	Lad Moore
The Miller Moth	Mike Broemmel
Tailwind	Lad Moore

Thriller

Deep Ice	Karl Kofoed
Blood Money	Azam Gill
Evil Angel	RD Larson
Disremembering Eddie	Anne Morgellyn
Flight to Pakistan	Azam Gill
Matabele Gold	Michael J Hunt

Historical Fiction
Ring of Stone	Hugh McCracken
Jahred and The Magi	Wilma Clark

Contemporary
The Care Vortex	Sam Smith
Someplace Like Home	Terrence Moore
Sick Ape	Sam Smith

Young Adult
Rules of the Hunt	Hugh McCracken
The Time Drum	Hugh McCracken
Kitchen Sink Concert	Ishbel Moore
The Fat Moon Dance	Elizabeth Taylor
Grandfather and The Ghost	Hugh McCracken
Return from the Hunt	Hugh McCracken

Children's
The Secret Portal	Reno Charlton
The Vampire Returns	Reno Charlton

General
The Wounded Stone	Terry Houston

Autobiography/Biography
A Stranger and Afraid	Arthur Allwright
Vera & Eddy's War	Sam Smith

Poetry
A Moment for Me	Heather Grace
Shaken & Stirred	Various
Letters from Portugal	Jan Oskar Hansen

Romance
A Different Kind of Love	Jay Mandal
The Dandelion Clock	Jay Mandal
365 Days of Lara Branson	Kit Tunstall

Coming Soon

Kaleidoscope	Various
As the Crow Flies	Dave Hutchinson
Loss of Innocence	Jay Mandal
Scent of Crime	Linda Stone
Redemption of Quapaw Mountain	Bertha Sutliff
Masters of the Hunt	Hugh McCracken

All the above titles are available from

www.bewrite.net

Printed in the United States
36335LVS00001B/52-60